WEB OF LIES

By Barbara Nadel

a&b

WEB OF LIES

BARBARA NADEL

Allison & Busby Limited
11 Wardour Mews
London W1F 8AN
allisonandbusby.com

First published in Great Britain by Allison & Busby in 2022

A CIP catalogue record for this book is available from
the British Library.

First Edition

ISBN 978-0-7490-2748-3

Typeset in 11.5/17 pt Sabon LT Pro by
Typo•glyphix, Burton-on-Trent, DE14 3HE

The paper used for this Allison & Busby publication
has been produced from trees that have been legally sourced
from well-managed and credibly certified forests.

FSC
www.fsc.org
MIX
Paper from
responsible sources
FSC® C171272

Printed and bound by
CPI Group (UK) Ltd, Croydon, CR0 4YY

To my father – a London wizard.

PROLOGUE

There is a myth that children, particularly teenagers, do not listen to their parents. It's as if a hidden switch trips at the age of thirteen barring all words emanating from parents, teachers and any other responsible adult. But this contention can be flawed.

Listening children exist. Those who only appear not to hear. Those who do hear, and store up what has been said for future reference and use.

Those who have an agenda . . . Those who have problems in need of solutions.

Mumtaz Hakim had grown up with boys like Habib Farooqi. Small, owlish behind his thick glasses, clever. He was fifteen, she'd been told, and wanted to go to medical school. Lee, when she'd informed him about the kid, had given her a look which had seemed to say 'Asian boy wants to go to medical school – so far, so clichéd.' But Habib's parents were Mumtaz's parents' neighbours and her dad, in particular, would not have been denied.

He'd told her, 'The boy is good. I don't know exactly what he's done, but he and his friend say they will only speak to you. It could be something and nothing.'

Had the private investigation organisation for which Mumtaz worked, The Arnold Agency, not been hard up for work, she would have told her baba that she didn't have time. But, after a summer of too much work, they'd now hit a fallow period.

Lee Arnold, her boss as well as her romantic partner, had said, 'But we can't charge a fifteen-year-old kid! Where's the money in it?'

There was none. But with a caseload that contained nothing but process serving – delivering court documents to defendants – for the foreseeable future, Mumtaz was bored.

As she looked at Habib and his friend Lawrence, she couldn't actually see a crime of the century situation developing, but she was prepared to hear the kids out.

She said, 'Start at the beginning. Tell me everything. If you don't, I won't be able to help you. Let's start with the cream. Why did you make it? Was it to make money for something specific?'

The boys, one small for his age, blinking behind his specs, the other a lanky white kid with spots, looked at each other. Then the white boy said, 'It's all my fault. Habib was just trying to help me out because I'm a fuck-up and he's a mensch.'

8

Before her parents had emigrated to Spitalfields from what in the 1960s was then East Pakistan (now Bangladesh), Brick Lane and its environs had been a Jewish area for decades. People usually spoke Yiddish back then. In fact, it had seeped its way into the language of the local population who lived alongside the Jews. Had Lawrence Williams' family been one of those or had they been, at one time, Jews themselves? Whatever, it was unusual to hear the word 'mensch', meaning good friend, on the lips of one so young.

'Tell me about it anyway,' Mumtaz said. 'I won't tell anyone unless you give me permission.'

'You won't tell his dad,' Lawrence or 'Loz' said, nodding his head towards Habib.

'No.'

Ali Riza Farooqi was a respected local pharmacist. Not known for anything like bad temper or rudeness, as far as Mumtaz knew he was a devoted husband and doting father to his children Iqra and Habib. Her baba was always going on about how those kids were spoilt.

She saw Loz gulp and then he said, 'Kym told me she was on the Pill, but she weren't.'

Mumtaz didn't know what she'd expected the boys to say about why they'd suddenly taken to what had been basically snake oil salesmanship, but this had not been amongst the options she'd considered.

'Kym?'

'Fam with benefits, weren't it,' he said.

Habib translated. 'Loz was going out with Kym. She's a girl at our school.'

'OK, and . . .'

'She says she's pregnant,' Loz said. 'She's sixteen but she says it's mine and she wants this phone and . . .'

Habib said, 'She told him if he doesn't get her the new Samsun' Galaxy, she'll tell her dad.'

Mumtaz, at thirty-seven and with one marriage already behind her, wasn't easily shocked, but she hadn't been expecting something like this. The boys had apparently been selling a home-made pain control cream called capsaicin. Used by a lot of elderly people to counteract arthritic pain, it had been in short supply since September. Habib's father had apparently sounded off to all his customers about it. He was very sorry, but there was a supply issue and he just could not get hold of it. Habib had listened to this for some time before he'd actively sought out the recipe for a home-made version of the cream online. It had taken Loz's 'problem' to spur him into action.

'Kym's dad's a cage fighter,' Loz explained.

The only thing Mumtaz knew about cage fighters was that they fought, bare knuckle, in cages and that one of media star Katie Price's many husbands had been one. Loz was probably right to be scared. If indeed Kym was pregnant.

Remembering the little her father had told her about the boys, Mumtaz said, 'This capsaicin cream, you sold it locally? Door to door? On the market . . .'

'Door to door,' Habib said. 'But not locally. In the City.'

'Lot of old people round here,' Mumtaz began.

'Who all know my dad!'

This was true.

'We only charged a pound for it,' Habib continued. 'And I told them if they didn't put it in the fridge it would go off.'

'You told my baba you mixed cayenne pepper with ghee,' Mumtaz said.

'Yeah.' Habib dropped his head.

'Yeah.' Loz followed suit.

'So, OK . . .' Mumtaz flicked the loose end of her headscarf away from her face and said, 'And this you sold in the City, as in the Square Mile. Why? Very few people live there, it's all offices.'

'No it ain't,' Loz said. 'Not where that kid lives.'

'This is the boy . . .'

'Covered in blood, yeah,' Habib replied. 'From his mouth I think, maybe. Certainly all down his front.'

ONE

'Carter Court,' Lee Arnold said, 'looks like somewhere merchant bankers might live.'

Mumtaz, who was accustomed to Lee's Cockney rhyming slang, said, 'So, low opinion of the wealthy . . .'

'Maybe, maybe not,' he said. 'I'll give you not all wankers are merchant bankers, although a lot probably are.'

'But all merchant bankers are?' she asked.

He smiled. Swearing still sounded weird coming out of Mumtaz's mouth. When he'd first employed her she'd been a timid, covered Asian widow lady with a psychology degree. Now, although the headscarf and the degree remained, she was a confident, sassy woman with a sharp sense of humour. He was also in love with her.

Lee was looking at Street View on his computer screen.

13

'Just up Ludgate Hill from St Paul's,' Lee said. 'Flats mainly.'

'The boys said this kid was in a house. An old one.'

Lee frowned. 'Most of the old places round there were flattened by bombs during the war,' he said. 'Must be one of the few that survived.' He pointed to the screen. 'Maybe that place beside that pub.'

Mumtaz peered at the screen. There was a tall, thin building next to a Victorian pub.

'Mmm.'

Lee turned his chair round to face her. 'So what happened?' he said.

'The boys say they had been to some of the flats and were surprised to find that most people were out,' Mumtaz said.

'You'd think they'd know . . .'

'They're both a bit other-worldly,' Mumtaz interjected. 'Even Loz. I think we imagine that kids living so close to the financial centre are clued in about it, but loads of them aren't. I grew up there myself. The Square Mile might just as well have been on Mars.'

'OK.'

'They approached what they called an "old" blue door.'

Lee looked back at his screen again. The doorway to the house next to the pub was painted the shade of blue that always reminded him of launderettes. Watery and faded.

'And then . . .'

'And then,' she said, 'before they could actually knock, they heard someone running.'

14

'OK, running where?'

'Towards the front door. He, as it turned out, opened the door, breathless and bleeding. Blond, so the boys said, sixteen-ish.'

'Where was he bleeding from?' Lee asked.

'Not sure, but Loz reckoned he had a cut lip. There was blood on the jumper he was wearing.'

'Kid with a nosebleed?'

'I put that to them,' Mumtaz said, 'but the boys told me they didn't think that was the case. This youngster, according to them, looked scared, he had bruises on his face and he said "help me". There was an elderly man watching him from the other end of the hallway.'

'Meaning what?'

'Meaning, they thought at the time, that the man was preventing the boy from leaving. As they had approached the front door, he, the boy, was clearly on his way out. He saw Habib and Loz, it shocked him, and so he stopped.'

'He didn't push past them to get out?'

'No, just stood, looking at them, asking for help.'

'With this older bloke at the end of the corridor?' Lee said.

'Yes. Looking at them apparently. Then, according to the kids, the boy shut the front door in their faces, but he was shaking when he did it. And that was that.'

His granddad had laughed when Jordan had said his ambition was to join the City of London Police. He'd seen them at the Lord Mayor's show when he was five and had wanted to be one until he actually joined in 2014.

His granddad had continued to laugh at him then and continued to laugh at him now.

'Taller'n other coppers, the City Police always was, back in the old days,' the old man said whenever he saw Jordan in his uniform. And Constable Jordan Whittington wasn't tall. Not that his height was the point. What really worried his granddad was that his grandson was a black copper in a predominantly white city. Granddad Bert didn't really 'do' the police and couldn't understand why Jordan had wanted to become a copper. The boy's parents, Bert's son Derek and his girlfriend Gina, had been junkies and had subsequently been arrested by the police on numerous occasions. They had not been treated well, especially Gina, Jordan's Afro-Caribbean mother. Just sick kids the both of them, Bert often felt. Poor kids.

A few months after Jordan's birth, when they could no longer look after their child and feed their habits, Derek and Gina had put the child in his Moses basket on Granddad Bert's doorstep in Bethnal Green. Then they'd run away, leaving their newborn with a pensioner with a dodgy leg.

Derek had been a junkie since he was in his twenties, and by the time Jordan was born, Gina was too. The old man had heard on the grapevine that his son had died by 1999, and none of Gina's God-fearing West Indian relatives had heard from her in decades. For just shy of twenty-six years, it had been the old man and Jordan against the world. And Jordan wished that his crusty, arthritic old granddad was with him now.

Long, long ago, back in the mists of time, what was now

the City of London Police had been divided into 'watches' – the 'Day Watch' and the 'Night Watch'. Patrolling either in the day or at night, the Watches sought to protect both the residents of the Square Mile and the financial institutions and legal Temples within its boundaries. They were not and had never been part of the Metropolitan Police and, as well as encompassing almost untold wealth within their patch, the City Police were also responsible for some key national monuments – like St Paul's Cathedral.

That old copper's friend, the Observant Drunk, had tipped them off in the early hours of that morning. On his unsteady way from his office Christmas Party in Hatton Garden to an assignation with a pole dancer called Minx at the Polo Bar on Bishopsgate, Ryan Faulks had noticed someone doing some late-night gardening in St Paul's Churchyard. And because there was a police station just down Bishopsgate from the Polo Bar, Ryan had done his civic duty and reported it just before he met up with and paid for Minx to have a Harvey Wallbanger and a Full English. Two hours later, Jordan and an almost unconscious Ryan had been sent over to St Paul's Churchyard to check it out. It was four in the morning by that time and Ryan wasn't happy.

What they'd found had been grim beyond either of their imaginings.

'So tell the coppers,' Lee said.

They were both sitting on the steps of the iron staircase outside their office on Green Street, Upton Park so that Lee could have a fag.

'The kids were trying to sell hooky arthritis cream,' Mumtaz said.

Lee sighed. Then he said, 'And this was the day before yesterday?'

'Yes.'

'So what can we do about it?'

'Have a look,' she said. 'Find out who lives there and what they do. Find the boy and see whether he's OK.'

Lee puffed. 'What do the kids think was going on?'

'They're afraid the boy is being held against his will,' she said.

'What, in a sort of paedo kind of a way?'

She shrugged. 'I don't know. But Lee, if someone is brutalising this boy then it has to stop.'

'Agreed, but we can't just go stomping in there like the US Cavalry.' He stood up. 'Anyway, I have to get out to Romford.'

Process serving. Mumtaz had two herself; one in Barking and another just up the road from their office.

Before he left to go to Romford, Lee said, 'I'll have a think about those two kids of yours. See you back at the flat?'

She said that she would. Whether or not she'd stay the night, Mumtaz didn't know. But if she stayed with Lee he always did the cooking, which was fine by her. Now that her stepdaughter Shazia was either at university or, when in London, staying with her boyfriend, Mumtaz rarely had either the need or the inclination to cook herself. Her own mother, a traditional Bangladeshi amma, was quite bewildered by the whole situation.

18

But then so, in many ways, was Mumtaz. Falling in love with Lee had come as a shock and she was still working out how that might or might not pan out in the future. For the moment things were on an even keel. They led fairly separate lives for much of the time, while her mother chose to believe that her daughter and her white boyfriend had an entirely platonic relationship. It wasn't ideal but it was way better than the abusive marriage she'd had before. Shazia's father, Ahmet Hakim, had been a violent drinker addicted to gambling and the company of gangsters. Now he was dead.

Mumtaz put Ahmet from her mind and got on with her day. What, she wondered, did Lee have in mind with regard to the two young boys from Spitalfields?

He'd seen that SOCO tent erected over outdoor crime scenes a few times during the course of his career, but Constable Jordan Whittington always felt cold whenever he saw one. There was usually a dead body underneath it and in this case, that was a certainty.

Ryan Faulks, the thirty-five-year-old Observant Drunk who had led Jordan to the scene in the early hours, had thrown up what must have been several pints of wine and at least half a bottle of vodka when Jordan had moved the pile of earth to one side and seen that hand. At first he had thought that it belonged to a doll.

But dolls were not pliant like that. Dolls didn't have bruised faces.

Dolls, unlike babies, never die.

* * *

19

'The house where you saw the boy,' Mumtaz asked, 'was it next door to a pub called The Hobgoblin?'

Mumtaz had calculated it had to be lunchtime when she called Habib Farooqi on his mobile. He'd answered almost immediately.

Habib had thought for a moment when she'd mentioned the pub. Yes, he'd seen a pub, but what it had been called was another matter.

'Was the front door of this house blue?' she continued.

Another pause and then he said, 'Yes. Are you going to look into it then, Mrs Hakim?'

She was. She knew she was. But would Lee be on board with her? And if he wasn't, what then?

Eventually she said, 'I'm not sure at the moment, Habib.'

'Oh.'

'But I'll call you tomorrow morning and let you know without fail. Habib, do you know whether Loz's girlfriend is really pregnant?'

'She says she is,' he said. 'Why would she say that if she wasn't?'

Mumtaz sighed. There had been a girl at her school who had told everyone she was pregnant when she hadn't been. Diane something or other. She'd been going out with a boy called Jayden who had a stall in Spitalfields Market with his brother. They sold handbags, which had been part of the appeal. Nothing had ever come of Diane and Jayden's brief affair, and word at the time had been that Diane hadn't even got a fake Prada bag out of it. Mumtaz changed the subject.

'Look, can you email me a list of things you remember about that boy and where he lived?' she said.

'Can't we do it on WhatsApp?' he asked. 'I mean then I can, like, write things down when I think of them?'

He had a point, even though Mumtaz was loath to admit it. Shazia communicated almost exclusively via apps these days; Mumtaz wasn't a fan. She decided to stick to her guns.

'You've got my card so I'd prefer it if you emailed me,' she said. 'Just sit down for a few minutes and try to remember what you saw. Even better, do that with Loz – he may remember things that you don't and vice versa.'

'OK.'

But he didn't sound pleased about it.

Tough.

TWO

The six o'clock news was on and so Chronus, Lee Arnold's mynah bird, had turned his back on the TV. He'd always been a bird with good taste. Over the years since his old friend and colleague Detective Inspector Vi Collins had given the bird to him, Lee had taught him to squawk 'I'm Forever Blowing Bubbles' as well as a whole list of West Ham United team line-ups from the 1980s and 90s. He could also swear.

'Fuck.'

Chronus repeated Lee's expletive as his master sat down in front of the television.

Often stories about babies – usually newborns, found dead in parks, in the street or in rivers – passed him by. Behind these tragedies were usually fearful or ashamed young women, giving birth in secret and then abandoning their infants out of fear. Rarely was infanticide involved. But in this case there appeared to Lee to be an implication. He'd been a copper, he knew how they put things. It didn't always mean that foul play was involved when cause of death was 'unknown', but it could do.

The child's body had been found in the churchyard of St Paul's Cathedral, sometime in the early hours of that morning. Police had been alerted by a member of the public who had seen someone digging in the churchyard in the middle of the night. Who that had been and why he or she had been doing it could be entirely unconnected to the discovery of the child's body. But it seemed to Lee that the idea of digging in the night and concealment of a body went rather well together. It was also in a part of London he was currently thinking about.

Mumtaz, like him were he honest, bored easily and all the process serving with the occasional foray into observing potentially unfaithful husbands was doing her head in. Habib and Loz's bloodied boy was probably, sadly, a case of domestic abuse, but he knew that Mumtaz was dead set on doing it even though there was no money in it at all. That went against every cell in Lee's body, but . . .

His dad had knocked them all about when Lee had been a kid. Him, his brother, their mum. A violent drunk, he'd made their mum fearful; Roy his brother had copied their old man while Lee had got out as quickly as he could by joining the army and then the police. Kids being brutalised by their parents was something that was still overlooked in spite of social service reforms, in spite of campaigns against it by celebrities. Did Lee feel more angry about that than he did about losing a bit of money?

He knew the answer to that and picked up his phone.

'Was it a win?'

Bert Whittington put the kettle on the stove and turned to face his grandson. Jordan and the old man had a running joke between them that every day the young man wasn't called a 'cunt' by someone or other, public or fellow copper, it was a 'win'.

Jordan flopped into a chair at the kitchen table and said, 'It was a win. If you can call a day when you find a baby murdered a "win".'

The old man sat down opposite. Jordan had called home at ten that morning to let Bert know that he'd not be coming home for some hours. He'd explained why, but briefly.

'You sure the kiddie was murdered?' Bert asked.

On the stove, the kettle began to 'sing' a little as the gas flames licked up its ancient, battered sides. Bert didn't 'believe' in electric kettles, just like he didn't 'believe' in the Internet or mobile phones.

'Yes.'

'Tell me about it?'

'I can't,' Jordan said. 'You know that.'

The old man shrugged. In reality Jordan would have liked to tell Granddad Bert to get it off his chest, but he knew he couldn't. The details of the case were under wraps for the time being, and quite rightly so. It had been horrific. A newborn the doctor had reckoned, stabbed. Not just once, five times. A girl, it was mixed race, like

25

Jordan himself. To do that to any living creature was an abomination but with racism on the rise, he couldn't shake off the possibility that had been at least part of the motivation.

Bert changed the subject. He said, 'Your Nana Willi called to speak to you. I think she'd like you to go over there.'

The mother of Jordan's mother, Wilhelmina Banks, or Nana Willi, called often and usually about the same thing.

'She wants me to go to church,' Jordan said.

'So go with her,' Bert said. 'She's a little old lady as wants to parade her eldest, handsomest grandson to her mates.'

'She wants me to be "saved",' Jordan said.

Nana Willi and her family were all born-again Christians who attended a huge, mainly West Indian, church in Brixton. Jordan's cousins were all very involved in the church and, as a family, they did a lot for the local community. That bit of it, Jordan could get and he was very proud of them. It was just the religion side of things he couldn't come to terms with. What he saw almost every day, and especially in light of this baby killing, seemed to Jordan to mitigate against the possibility of a caring, loving God. Also, with Granddad Bert as his guardian, he'd not exactly been brought up with any real concept of an Almighty.

The old man sighed. 'So go to make the old girl happy,' he said. 'You don't have to go full-on happy-clappy Praise-the-Lord.'

'I do,' he said. 'They expect it.'

'So what does it hurt to do it for their sake for once?' Bert said.

'It doesn't, but . . .'

'But what?'

The kettle boiled and Bert poured the hot water into a teapot. He still used tea leaves as well as a non-electric kettle. Jordan sometimes thought that the way he clung to the past was probably something to do with wanting his son back as he'd used to be when he was a kid, before smack.

'She tries to hide it, but I know Nana Willi blames my dad for my mum's addiction,' Jordan said.

'And she's right,' Bert replied. 'Our Derek did get her into it.' He looked choked up for a moment. 'Used to take Gina with him when he went to score.'

'She could've said no . . .'

'Nah.' The old man shook his head. 'You never knew your dad. People never said no to Derek. Charm the fucking birds out the trees. And she loved him – up until they both got heavy into heroin, then she only loved that.'

They sat in silence for a little while then, until Jordan changed the subject. After that he drank his tea and went up to lay down for a while. Alone in his bedroom he tried but failed to get the little girl's face out of his mind. Then he cried.

Mumtaz took the Tube to St Paul's and then she went for a walk. Elated by the news that Lee was going to take the two boys' case, she was going to have a look at the lie of the local land. It was dark and it was cold but, when she got out at St Paul's, the Square Mile was still buzzing with activity. Not everyone wanted to just get home after a day at the office, and all the bars and pubs she passed on Ludgate

Hill were full. There were also a lot of police in evidence. A dead baby had apparently been found in the churchyard. Mumtaz shuddered at the thought. Looking to her left, she walked past the entrance to the cathedral as well as the far from flattering statue of Queen Anne on her right, until she came to Creed Lane. This, if her GPS was correct, would then lead her on to Carter Lane which in turn, if rather hazily, would then lead into Carter Court.

As soon as she turned off Ludgate Hill, Mumtaz felt, and heard, the change. Not only was Creed Lane narrow, it was also silent. Tall buildings – some four storeys high, some five – lined a thoroughfare of thin pavements and a cobbled road. Some of the buildings were clearly old, others of indeterminate age. Lee had told her that this part of London had been heavily bombed during World War II as the Nazi war machine attempted to destroy the cathedral. But some buildings had survived; she could see what looked like an Edwardian pub at the end of Creed Lane.

As she moved forwards, Mumtaz experienced what she interpreted as a chill coming from these buildings. They were dark and apparently empty, and a thin mist had begun to cover some of their roofs, obscuring any High Victorian embellishments that may have been apparent during the hours of daylight. She recalled the famous wartime photograph of St Paul's Cathedral rising up out of the smoke caused by incendiary bombs, and pulled her coat tightly around her body. Hundreds, maybe thousands of people had died in this area, not just in World War II but over the many centuries this part of London had been the centre of both faith and commerce. Of course the narrowness of the street, allied with the incoming mist and the darkness, contributed to her feeling of disconnection to the world. But she also experienced a haunting sensation, and when a man came towards her out of the mist she wondered whether he was real. Wearing a long brown overcoat and a flat cap, he looked like a character from a Dickens novel.

At the end of Creed Lane was Carter Lane which stretched to both her left and right. It seemed, according to the GPS, that she should go right and so she did. There was a pub on the corner, but it wasn't called The Hobgoblin. Looking in the windows she saw a lot of people inside drinking and apparently chatting, but there was almost no noise. When she'd lived back at home in Spitalfields some of the old white people she knew had reckoned that the area around Christ Church was haunted. Her amma had a friend called Betty who told her that back in the old days there had been something called a charnel house in Christ Church's cemetery. Harking back to a time in the late eighteenth century when London's population was exploding, a charnel house was a place where the bones of the long dead were stored after they had been dug up to make way for more recent corpses. It was long gone now, but Betty reckoned that ghosts still remained. She said that every time she walked past the church when she had her son Tom in his pram, the kid would scream and cry in fear.

As the mist thickened, Mumtaz walked on. But then she stopped. Not because she couldn't go any further, but because the hairs on the back of her neck were standing up. Someone was following her.

*　*　*

People didn't chat in The Wren. Not on the stairs, not in the lift, not in the corridors. Putting the recycling out round the back of the block would only spark the odd smile if you were lucky. Most of the time those putting out their recycling combined it with jogging or cycling or 'breathing'. One thing that was always involved, however, was a huge mug of some posh coffee or other.

Danielle actually liked coffee. But not like that. Not clasped in some weird leather mitt by some grey-faced, Lycra-covered bloke on a push-bike that cost more than her dad's car. Whether or not they were actually judging you, they and their floral-print women always looked as if they were. A lot of how they were was to do with wanting to have the bare minimum, or so Henry said.

'It's all about being greener and more socially responsible,' he'd said when she'd asked him about these cycle-helmeted warriors who frequently pushed her aside in Tesco Metro as they attempted to reach the oat milk. 'They're lovely people.'

And of course he would say that, because he was one of them. That had become very apparent the first and only time Danielle had invited their immediate neighbours for 'supper and drinks' a month after she'd moved into The Wren. Zander and Pippa, the neighbours had been called. He'd rocked up sweaty and encased in Lycra while she wore the regulation flowery dress and hand-made espadrilles.

Henry had cooked. Some vegan thing that had been very nice in spite of the tofu. Their guests had kept going on about it, she remembered, about how you could have it smoked now. In fact, provided you had the right equipment, you could smoke it yourself. Who knew? All Danielle could really recall about that evening was the way that Pippa kept on looking at her.

Would she and Henry be together were she not pregnant? Probably not. She'd been his PA for two years before their affair. Tragically they'd got together first at the Christmas party, then he'd cooled, then after one drunken evening in El Vino's they'd had sex al fresco in the Inner Temple and that was when she'd got pregnant. Of course he'd asked her to get rid of it, but she wouldn't. Then, after a period of reflection at his parents' villa in Greece, he'd asked her to move in. Her mum had told her she was mad. But this wasn't yet a permanent arrangement – more a trial period to see whether they could become a couple.

Looking out of the front window into the darkening street below, Danielle thought about this. Of course she'd had to leave her job. Henry was a partner at Blizzard Solicitors LLP – along with his father and a cousin. Once the baby was born, Henry said, she might be able to go back. Danielle hoped so. She'd enjoyed her job; she'd liked the people she'd worked with and her position of 'smart common girl done good'. But, although she'd never in a million years thought she'd feel like this, she missed being at home in Dagenham with her parents and her sisters. Though not stylish like Henry's apartment, her old house had been full of life. This was like living in a tomb.

It was then that she saw a figure running down the street. Not in the usual way the joggers ran, but full pelt as if he or she was running away from something or someone.

31

She couldn't see anyone behind the running figure. But then it was foggy. Fog tended to gather in these narrow, steep-sided streets. The figure looked up and behind itself and through a fleeting glimpse of its face, she could see that it was a woman.

'Where are you?' Lee asked.

'Blackfriars Tube,' she said.

How she'd ended up there, Mumtaz didn't really know. Running down narrow streets, choked with mist, guided by the odd street lamp, she'd arrived at Blackfriars Tube Station, slathered in a weird, cold sweat.

'Did you see anyone?' Lee continued.

'No. It's foggy here. But I heard footsteps behind me.'

'Could've been the echo of your own footsteps. See people about?'

'No,' she said. 'I'm not an idiot. I think I'd know the difference between an echo and footsteps behind me. I'm telling you, someone was there.'

'That's a really old and spooky bit of the City,' Lee said. 'Everything's haunted up there.'

Mumtaz lost her temper. 'I don't believe in ghosts, as well you know,' she said. 'No, this was a person and he or she had ill intent.'

'How do you know that?'

She pulled a face at her phone. Sometimes he could be such a moron.

'Piloerection,' she said.

'You what?'

'When body hair stands up in response to cold or fear,'

she said. 'It's a hangover from our evolutionary past.'

'I thought you didn't believe in all that.'

'That's irrelevant!' she said. 'It's a fact, a thing, and it happened to me just now!'

Getting into where Islam stood on natural selection wasn't something she wanted to do. What she wanted from Lee was a bit of validation.

She said, 'I'm not saying I was so scared only the comfort of your voice can make me feel better.'

'I know. You're an independent—'

'I didn't dream it or make it up, Lee,' she said. 'I accept that at least some of what happened was mediated by my own consciousness, but not all of it. I'm telling you, I was scared and I don't get scared by nothing. For all its posh flats and quaint corners, I don't like the area around the cathedral, it's . . .'

'What?'

She shook her head and then she said, 'Maybe it's something to do with how old it is, how much time it has absorbed, how much blood . . .'

'Did you find the house in Carter Court?' he asked. Lee couldn't really manage too much esoterica.

'No,' she said.

'No?'

'I looked. Of course I did, but what with the mist and the footsteps . . . I kept either missing it or going round in circles. I need to come back in daylight.'

'We need to come back in daylight,' Lee interjected.

'I thought you didn't want to get involved,' she said.

'You know how I feel about this pro bono work, but

that don't mean I'm not interested,' he said. 'Anyway, look, you want me to meet you at Forest Gate?'

He meant the train station. She lived further away from it than he did and a walk back to her place at night could be a slightly unnerving affair. However, albeit in a very secondary way, he was angling for her to maybe come back and stay at his place. But before she could answer him, he realised this and said, 'No strings . . .'

Loz had only ever seen Kym Franks' dad twice before, and that had been enough. Now he thought he could hear him when Kym phoned him that night. Something or someone very loud was swearing and hitting stuff somewhere in the background. Loz cringed. If that old knuckle-dragger ever got hold of him in anger, he'd snap his head off like a ring-pull.

'It's the phone or I tell me dad,' Kym said. She sounded as if she was putting on lipstick. She probably was. Kym had made it clear to everyone at school that she was working on becoming a beauty influencer. Companies sent you lipsticks and mascaras and stuff to try and comment about online. Loz had once been into some games influencer kid about a year back, but Habib had told him that the kid didn't know what he was talking about. And Habib knew stuff.

Loz, who had to his credit said this before, kept his voice down so that his mum didn't hear. 'He'll have to find out in the end . . .'

'Not if I have an abortion,' Kym said. 'Which, by the way, you'll have to pay for too.'

Loz felt his face drain. 'How much?'

She paused for a moment and then said, 'A grand.'

'A grand!'

'Everything costs,' Kym said. 'You think I'm going down some rough old clinic down Bow or somethin'? You need to spend some drip on your woman, you get me?'

'Yeah, but the phone's a grand! I ain't got no drip, man!'

'You got a week,' Kym said.

'Yeah, but . . .'

'Your rents work, innit?'

Rents were parents, of which Loz had only one and all she got was minimum wage. Kym was the one with two working parents – her dad in the cages and her mum as a hairdresser in East Ham. It was also said that her dad did the odd 'job' for certain local 'faces'. Even kids like Loz knew that chucking weighted corpses into the Thames wasn't a service that came cheap.

'Kym!'

It was that terrible roaring voice again!

Loz heard Kym say, 'Yes, Dad?'

'Get off that fucking thing for five minutes, will ya? Over a ton you spent of my money on that fucking thing, last month!'

It sounded as if she moved to another room. She said, 'I gotta go or he'll lose his shit. One week you got. Say less?'

Say less? She was so into all the latest street talk. Really, she was a dick. Say less meant to understand, and he said that he did and then cut the connection.

Not only hadn't he been able to talk to her about whether she was really pregnant – of course she'd say she was, but Mrs Hakim had told him about hearing doubt in her voice. He thought he knew what she meant. But he hadn't managed to tell her about the house he and Habib had been to and the bleeding boy. She'd understand they had to do something about that before her phone or anything – wouldn't she?

Loz felt a shiver run up his back as he realised that Kym wouldn't give a shit.

THREE

More than anywhere else in London, the Square Mile was probably the best place to be if a person wanted to disappear. This was firstly because few people lived there and secondly because, in the twenty-first century, those that did live in the City had no notion of community. Many were young, professional types who had chosen to live near their places of work before migrating out to Surrey or Hampshire to become commuters, long-distance parents and owners of executive housing.

Mumtaz and Lee had waited until 10 a.m. to go to St Paul's the following morning. In spite of everything she'd told herself about how she could easily get herself home from Forest Gate Station in the dark, Mumtaz had been glad that Lee had come to meet her. Her experience the previous night had unnerved her and so she ended up staying over with Lee. Although they didn't make love, they both found sleeping in the same bed comforting and relaxing.

Carter Lane and its environs were totally comprehensible by day, and within minutes Lee had guided them to Carter Court. The place was accessed down a narrow alleyway, and Mumtaz could both see and not see how she had missed it. Exactly where the GPS had indicated, it was nevertheless a place easily overlooked, especially in the mist.

On two sides, Carter Court consisted of characterless, some would say discreet, low-rise apartment buildings. A third side – the entrance to the court – was what remained of what appeared to be an old agricultural building – that or the remnants of a coaching inn. The fourth side, and what came into view first when one entered the space, was an ornate Victorian pub called The Hobgoblin and an old house next to it which had a blue front door.

Lee looked into the court, looked at Mumtaz and then said, 'Easy when you know how.'

She elbowed him in the ribs and said, 'Sod.'

He took her hand and they entered Carter Court. Just briefly, Mumtaz saw a face at one of the top windows of the house, but then it disappeared. It was such a cliché she wondered whether her brain had simply created it for her own amusement.

The pub, which had long ago been painted a dirty cream colour, had mouldings of what looked like bunches of grapes and horns of plenty picked out in black. There were sconces above the large, partially obscured windows used to hold gas jet flames or even perhaps flaming torches.

Lee went up close to look through the windows. Mumtaz said, 'What's it like?'

'Reminds me of the old Ferndale in Cyprus,' he said.

Mumtaz said, 'What the hell are you talking about?'

'You know Cyprus?' Lee said.

'Country in the Mediterranean, yes.'

'No, Cyprus in Newham,' he said. 'Down Beckton, you know!'

She didn't, but then the southern part of the London Borough of Newham was a bit of a mystery to a lot of people, unless they actually came from the area. Lee, who had been born in nearby Custom House, knew it well. He said, 'It's on the DLR.'

Mumtaz vaguely remembered seeing a station called Cyprus on a map.

Lee continued. 'Cyprus was an area built for dock workers,' he said. 'There was a pub there called The Ferndale. Flats now, I think. Anyway, back in the eighties it was still a pub. My old man used to go down there, it was his sort of place. Lot of old boozers, sticky carpet, Union Jacks.'

'And it looks like that in there?' Mumtaz asked.

'Yeah.'

'Seems a bit weird in an area like this?' Mumtaz said. 'Do you think it's sort of ironic?'

Lee laughed, a weird burst of sound in an otherwise silent place.

CID were on the dead baby case now. In charge was DI Scott Brown. Jordan knew him. Didn't like him. Fancied himself as some sort of British version of an FBI G-man – all sharp suits, casual sex and the St George's flag up his arse. Everything Jordan wasn't.

Granddad Bert was still in bed when Jordan got up, and so he took the old man a cup of tea. It was his day off and he didn't have to rush about getting ready for work.

'What you up to today?' the old man asked him.

'Dunno,' Jordan said.

Although he did. During the course of the previous day one of the officers who had turned up in St Paul's Churchyard had been Sergeant Wilkinson. A tall, uniformed officer, Colin Wilkinson seemed to have been around for ever. Jordan had once asked a colleague whether 'Wilko' was ever going to retire. He'd received the answer, 'No.'

Wilkinson, also on leave that day, had told Jordan he was going back to the crime scene to have a 'bit of a think'. And while Jordan hadn't taken that as an invitation to join the older man, he knew that Wilko, at the very least, wouldn't tell him to fuck off.

'You wanna go down Brixton,' Bert continued, as he poured his tea from his cup into his saucer and slurped it into his mouth. 'Your grandma'll—'

'Oh give it a rest, Granddad!' Jordan said.

Bert, who knew Jordan almost as well as he knew himself, said, 'Heard you crying last night.'

'Yeah, well . . .'

'Say what you like about Willi and her family but they're a force of nature, the lot of them,' he said. 'Willi'll stuff you full of food, you've got your cousin Ann dancing through life and Gabriel, if he's got a second to spare. They ain't all happy clappers.'

He was right. His cousin Ann was a student at the Royal Ballet School and her brother Gabriel was a solicitor. To be fair the rest of the family were, in one way or another, in 'ministry', but then that didn't make them bad – exactly. Just – incomprehensible.

'Anyway, I need to do some Christmas shopping,' Jordan said.

'Well don't bother getting nothing for me,' the old man said. 'What I ain't got I don't want or need.'

He always said that, every year. Jordan smiled and said, 'We'll see. Anyway, look, I'll be out for a few hours. Anything I can pick you up?'

Bert thought for a moment and then said, 'Skate. Middles if you can find 'em. I could do with a nice bit of skate.'

A man plus his bike broke the silence. On the thin side of slim, he wore an all-in-one cycling suit and a helmet with a camera on the top. He walked over to Lee and Mumtaz and said, 'Pub doesn't open until midday.'

'Oh, don't matter,' Lee said. 'We're just having a look round the area.'

The man swung his leg over the bike and prepared to mount. He was probably in his thirties although his face was rather heavily lined, gaunt almost.

'Looking to buy somewhere?' he asked.

Lee, for the sake of simplicity said, 'Maybe. What's it like?'

41

'Convenient for the City,' the man said. 'Quiet. Except for that place.'

'The pub?'

'Last outpost of the original residents,' the man said.

'What do you mean?'

He sniffed. Then he said, 'You'll see,' and cycled off.

Lee looked at Mumtaz and said, 'Charming.'

'What do you mean?'

'You clock him?' Lee said. 'Posh bike, all the gear, voice courtesy of the Home Counties. Christ, I expect a few old costers get together in the boozer of a Saturday night. Few roll-up dog-ends out by the bins, the odd brown ale empty on the cobbles. I know his type. Probably wants this pub shut down to make way for an artisan coffee shop or some posh baker's where they only sell sourdough.'

'Wow, but your working-class cred is up and running today!' Mumtaz said.

'Well . . .'

She took his arm and they began to walk out of the court.

'Anyway,' she said. 'Now we know the place exists, what do we do?'

'What do you do, you mean,' he said. 'I'm stuck with the process serving while you help those two lads of yours.'

'They're not mine!' she said. 'And anyway, if the boys are right then we have to get a move on. There could be a child in trouble right here, right now.'

'There could,' he said. 'But if they was that worried your lads would've called the police.'

'And expose Habib to the disappointment of his

father? You don't know Asian families at all, do you?'

He ignored her. 'I s'pose the house hunt thing isn't a bad idea.'

'No, but I don't see too many For Sale signs,' Mumtaz said.

They walked up Carter Lane and came out opposite the cathedral. All signs of police activity seemed to have disappeared.

'So who you gonna be then?' Lee asked her as they crossed the road and walked into the churchyard. 'The Avon lady?'

'No, I—'

'Wilko!'

Suddenly he'd unhooked his arm from hers and Lee was running.

'People lie,' Habib said.

'Yeah, but . . .'

'Loz, you've got to listen!'

The two boys were up in the Arnold Circus bandstand, at the top of Brick Lane, eating rainbow bagels stuffed with salt beef, mustard and pickles.

'If Kym really is pregnant and she really does need money for an abortion then she'd ask you for that first, not a phone,' Habib said. 'And anyway, she doesn't need money for an abortion. We have the NHS!'

'She wants to go to some clinic,' Loz said miserably.

'So she can bloody do one, then, can't she!' Habib shook his head. 'Loz, I know you said you . . . with Kym, but . . .'

'I shagged her!' Loz said. 'Alright?'

While not being the boy least likely to induce a teenage pregnancy at their school, Loz also wasn't the most obvious candidate. He wanted to have sex – they all did – and he'd boasted about it when he'd supposedly done it. But he hadn't mentioned Kym. Not like some of the other lads they knew, who would go on to call their conquests 'slags' and 'hoes'.

'OK! OK!' Habib waved his bagel at his friend. 'But look, you've seen her dad. If you were a girl and you got pregnant, wouldn't you be more afraid of him finding out than anything?'

'He calls her his princess,' Loz said.

'Yes, but she won't stay one with a baby on the way, will she?'

'Dunno . . .' Loz chewed, then he said, 'But if she tells him, I'll get in trouble with the law.'

'No. No!' Loz was his best mate but he could be thick as mince sometimes. And this wasn't the first time Habib had told him. 'No, she'll get in trouble because you're fifteen and she's sixteen.'

'Yeah, but it was me what . . .'

'Doesn't matter!' Habib said. 'Listen, you know my cousin Nazrin, you know she's a lawyer, right? She says sixteen is when you're allowed to have sex. You're fifteen—'

'So I done wrong!'

'Yes, you did but . . . Look,' Habib said, 'it was wrong, but you're not in the wrong, do you understand? Kym's in the wrong because when you had sex, she was sixteen and so . . .'

'Oh . . .'

Habib wished he'd spoken to Nazrin before all this had started, but she was working and preparing for her wedding and so she had been difficult to catch. And he was her 'little' cousin and so she had really treated him a bit like a child. Then he'd had to explain to her that he hadn't got anybody pregnant, and then he'd had to swear to that.

Nazrin had said, 'Because if your parents thought that I knew and said nothing, there would be bloody hell to pay!'

'I wish we'd known all that before we made that cream,' Loz said, bringing his friend back into the present.

'Yeah, well . . .'

In reality, Habib had enjoyed making the cream. He'd felt like a real chemist for a bit. Then he thought of something else too.

'We'd never have found that boy if we'd not made the cream,' he said.

'Have you heard anything about that?' Loz asked.

'No,' Habib said. 'Just leaving it to Mrs Hakim.'

'Yeah,' Loz said as he continued to work his way through his bagel.

Habib nodded.

'Yeah, man.'

Lee was shaking hands with a tall, moustachioed man in his late fifties when Mumtaz caught up with him. Smiling, Lee said, 'Mumtaz, this is my old mate, Colin Wilkinson.'

The man, who was older than Lee, extended his hand. Mumtaz took it and said, 'Mumtaz Hakim. Are you old friends or . . . ?'

45

'Inasmuch as the City and the Met can be friends, yeah,' Colin Wilkinson said.

'Well, mate, if you do like guarding banks . . .' Lee began.

Wilko shook his head. 'You don't know the half of it!'

Mumtaz, confused, said, 'What are you talking about?'

'Col, Wilko here works for the City of London Police,' Lee said.

His friend expanded, 'Square Mile's our jurisdiction. So Met rats like your mate here josh us about protecting banks. Like we're a sort of glorified security service. You his business partner, Mumtaz?'

'Yes,' she said.

He said to Lee, 'Heard you had your own PI empire up your manor. Heard you had a very clever lady on board.'

Mumtaz didn't know how she felt about being described as a 'clever lady', but she took it. 'Wilko' seemed as if he was a rather old-fashioned soul, which was not always a bad thing.

'So what you doing up here, then?' Wilko asked.

The older man was a serving police officer, so Mumtaz knew that Lee wouldn't want to discuss what they were doing with him. Not necessarily, not unless he had to.

'What are you doing?' Lee countered.

Wilko offered Lee a fag, which he took, and both the men lit up.

'We've got a possible murder,' the older man said. 'No secret. Been on the news.'

'A baby? Yeah?'

'Yeah.' Wilko looked down at the ground. 'I've seen a lot but that . . .' He shook his head.

'Wouldn't have thought you'd've been involved,' Lee said.

'Nah, CID,' he said. 'But uniform found the body. Young lad.' He shook his head again. 'I'm here because . . .' He shrugged. 'Day off. What else can I do?'

Lee knew that Wilko's wife had left him a few years ago. Probably tired of waiting in for him all the time, tired of coming second to The Job.

Lee looked up at the cathedral. 'Not too many things like this happen here,' he said. 'More likely on my old patch.'

'Dead babies and poverty.' Wilko nodded. 'Common pairing, yeah,' he said. 'Not many babies born round here I don't suppose. But, what this place does have is history and not all of that's pretty.'

'Weren't the Gunpowder plotters executed in St Paul's Churchyard?' Mumtaz asked.

'Good London knowledge,' Wilko said. 'Yes, they were. But that's not what I'm talking about.'

Then suddenly a young black guy appeared at Wilko's side, and the older man put a hand on his shoulder and smiled.

She'd heard about this pub. People bad-mouthed it, said it was rough, that just men went there, that the landlady was a mad old hippy woman – as if that automatically made her a bad person. The Hobgoblin was probably like a lot of pubs back home in Dagenham. Not that Dagenham pubs only admitted men, but they could be said to be dominated by them. Danielle's uncles was like that. They enjoyed going down The Cherry Tree where they could watch football with their mates, play a game of pool and not be too bothered with women if they timed it right. Her uncles and their mates would talk about things you couldn't talk about any more, like immigration. Her dad never went out with them because he was different. A bit embarrassing sometimes, Danielle felt.

Danielle stood on her tiptoes and looked inside. It was dark in there – and proper old-fashioned. No soft seats, just wooden benches. Not a lot of light but enough to see that the bar was covered by St George's flag bunting. Seemed odd such a place was here. How did it make a profit?

'Looking for something?'

She'd not heard as much as a squeak, and so the appearance of a small, elderly man behind her made Danielle gasp.

'Fucking hell, you gave me a fright!' she said as she put a hand on her chest.

He smiled.

'You ain't from round here, are you?' he said.

Wearing a grey, drizzle-spattered raincoat, he was small, apple-cheeked and had a twinkle in his light blue eyes.

'No,' Danielle said. 'What do ya want?'

He shrugged. 'Saw you looking in the Hob,' he said. 'Don't open until midday.'

'Oh, I'm not going in . . .'

She looked down at her swollen belly. He followed her gaze.

'Nah.' Then he said, 'You visiting, are you?'

'No, I live here,' she said. Then she wondered whether she should have told him but then thought, *fuck it*. What was some little old geezer going to do to her?

He said, 'You don't sound like you come from round here.'

'What do you mean?'

She knew what he meant, but she wanted to hear him say it.

'You ain't posh,' the old man said.

'No,' she replied. 'Why do I need to be?'

The old man smiled again. She had the distinct feeling he was playing with her.

'Course,' he said. 'They're all bankers and briefs round here. Middle class. You married to one of 'em, are you?'

'Maybe. Why?'

'Don't get people like us round here,' he said.

'You're here,' Danielle answered.

'I am,' he said. 'Course I am. I've always been here, me.'

The young man was called Jordan and he was a constable in the City of London Police. It had been this young man who had found the body of the baby. Like Wilko, he had a day off and, as far as Mumtaz could tell, the two of them had met up to talk about it. It must've been a terrible thing for such a young man to experience. Mumtaz felt that she and Lee should really leave them alone. It wasn't, after all, as if they could share details about the incident with anyone outside the police.

But Wilko was now in full flow.

'Christopher Wren was a Freemason,' Wilko said. 'Well known. If you know where to look you can find all sorts of Masonic motifs all over the cathedral. The Square

49

Mile has always been the centre of this country's spiritual life, long before Christianity. Long before the Romans.'

Jordan, who Mumtaz felt wanted to talk to his colleague alone, said, 'Yeah, but not really the point at the moment . . .'

'Oh no,' the older man said. 'Sorry, I get a bit carried away with all the history. I'm that rare thing, Square Mile born and bred.'

'Oh,' Mumtaz said, 'where?'

People born in the City were few and far between and she was curious.

'Leadenhall Street,' he said. 'Mum and Dad was caretakers of an old office building. Long gone now. Full of insurance companies it was. Used to have to climb six flights of stairs to get to our old place. My old man had a roof garden long before all these roof terraces advertised with them posh flats you see for sale these days. Geraniums, my dad grew.'

'That's amazing,' Mumtaz said. 'You should write a book about it.'

Wilko shrugged. 'What, me? Who'd be interested in that?'

'Social history's really popular these days,' Mumtaz said.

Jordan poked his mate with his elbow. 'Told you,' he said. Then addressing Mumtaz, he continued, 'He's got loads of stories about the City in the sixties and seventies. It was like another world. And not that long ago, you know.'

'No.'

Wilko shuffled his feet. He wasn't comfortable with

this subject, even though it was he who had originally invoked it.

Lee, who knew him rather better than the other two, said, 'Well, we ought to leave you boys to your chat now.'

The older man said, 'Good to see you, mate.'

They shook hands again and Lee and Mumtaz began to walk away. Once out of earshot, Lee said, 'Sorry about that. Once Wilko gets going about the City, he can drone on for hours. We were lucky to get away before he started about the Temple of Mithras.'

Mumtaz frowned.

'Roman,' Lee said. 'We learnt about it at school. Can't remember much now except that Mithras was a Roman god worshipped by their soldiers. Back in the fifties a Mithras temple was discovered when they were digging out the foundations of a new building in the City. Wilko's dad used to go down there and watch, so he says.'

'Wilko seems to be quite the local historian,' Mumtaz said.

'Oh, he can bore for Britain.'

'You say that, and yet he has given me an idea,' she replied.

'What about?'

'About how to ingratiate myself with the residents of Carter Court.'

FOUR

Up above, in the world, it was sometimes dark and sometimes light. Down in the earth it was always black. Was that because in such overwhelming absence – an absence that could be tasted, heard, smelt – even seen, albeit only in the mind's eye – there was no day or night? No way to measure time except through the occasional outburst into the world?

Or was it because the darkness soaked up blood?

Arthur, the old man she'd met outside the Hobgoblin pub, had proved to be an intriguing bloke. Like a lot of people, Danielle had assumed that all the residents who lived in the area around the cathedral were young, new people. But there were, so Arthur had told her, more old residents than people might think. He claimed his own family had been in the area for centuries. He'd also told her that Charles Dickens had set his most famous murder scene – that of Nancy in *Oliver Twist* – at the end of London Bridge, beside the church of St Magnus the Martyr, just east along the River Thames. She'd been to see the church, for want of much else to do, and was now looking it up online when Henry came home.

Unlike her dad, her mum, her sisters and their partners, Henry didn't kiss Danielle when he came home from work. He just said 'Hey' and she said 'Hey' back, and then they talked about food.

'I fancy going out to eat tonight,' Henry said.

He stood in the middle of his great white living room, a tall, dark and handsome man in his late thirties. Soon he'd be going on about carpaccio or crushed something or other and Danielle would want to punch him. Why was it that posh men always felt the need to discuss ingredients now? Henry even photographed his dinners and talked about them online.

Not eliciting an answer from Danielle, Henry said, 'What are you looking up?'

'A church,' she said.

'What church?'

'St Magnus the Martyr. It's at this end of London Bridge.'

'Yes, I know,' he said. 'Why?'

'It's where Charles Dickens set the murder scene of Nancy in *Oliver Twist*,' Danielle said.

'Oh, learn that online, did you?'

'No, I met an old man in the street today,' she said. 'He told me. Lived round here his whole life, he said.'

'Really?' Henry frowned. 'Thought all these places were new.'

'He lives in Carter Court,' she said. 'He was right about the murder of Nancy and that church is really old too. Really dark . . .'

'So what about dinner?'

He wasn't interested.

'I was thinking The Harrow on Whitefriars Street,' he continued. 'Nice selection of healthy options . . .'

'Whatever.'

He walked into their bedroom to change for the evening. Danielle remembered the smell of incense from inside the church and the darkness of the images of its saints.

'This is going to be a lot of work,' Lee said.

Mumtaz rolled her eyes. 'No, it's not,' she said. 'There's loads of stuff about the history of that area.'

'So why'd anyone want to write a book about it, if it's all out there?'

'Because as I said to Wilko, there's still a lot of social history to be explored,' Mumtaz replied. 'And that young constable agreed with me.'

'Bit of a looker, him,' Lee said.

She punched him playfully on the shoulder. 'Oh shut up. People these days want to know how ordinary people lived. It's not all about kings and queens and great cathedrals.'

He sat down beside her at her computer.

'So what's gonna be your angle then?' he said.

'I'm looking for people who have lived experience,' she said. 'People who still live and work in the remaining old buildings. I'll start with the pub, The Hobgoblin.'

'You. In a pub.'

She couldn't decide whether he was being deliberately obtuse or just forgetful.

'I've done it before,' she said. 'And if you do happen to remember, I wasn't wearing my hijab and that was fine, and I was drinking orange juice and that was fine too.'

He raised his hands in surrender. They both knew their relationship was odd. Mumtaz was religious but she had very much her own relationship with Islam, which involved being an independent working woman who just happened to have a non-Muslim lover. Lee, on his part, adored the ground she stepped on. There was a lot of laughter in their relationship, but no talk of marriage which, since they'd been together for a number of years now, they both appreciated. They were comfortable where they were, even if others were not.

'There was a sign on the door that said "Food",' Mumtaz continued. 'And so I'll go tomorrow for lunch.'

Lee put a hand out towards her and said, 'Quid says it's mystery meat pie and chips.'

She shook his hand. 'Done. I think you're onto a winner. But I'll take one for the team.'

'You're a soldier.'

He kissed her.

Afterwards she said, 'I just hope we're able to get to the truth about this boy. There's part of me wants to break that blue door down and go in there and get him out. But until we can find out more . . .'

* * *

'Fuck off!'

DI Scott Brown wasn't the type of man who minced his words. If he didn't like an idea, he said so. Tall and thin, with enormous, sad brown eyes, he looked like a Byzantine saint. But not only did he swear like a sailor – he also had no patience, the morals of an alley cat and a rumoured addiction to cocaine. Any suggestions by anyone about his work were not welcomed, especially when they came from an old git in uniform. But Wilko ploughed on. He was used to Brown.

'I'm not saying we get him in to deliver the place . . .'

'Well, woop-di-doop!' Brown said. 'Thank fuck for that!'

'I'm just saying that how the kiddie was killed and where its body was found could, *could*, indicate some sort of ritual behaviour.'

'Could, but it might not and chances are, it doesn't,' Brown said. 'I'm investigating a murder, Wilko, not some bloody case of fucking possession!'

'I just think a historical—'

'Mate, this is happening now,' Brown said. 'Not in thirteen fucking ninety. Know what I think? I think this is County Lines.'

'What?'

'I think it's gangs. Some fucking seventeen-year-old godfather's got his thick as pigshit white girlfriend up the stick and killed the result,' he said. 'You know what these kids are like! Some muppet on some sink estate thinks he's a cross between *Boyz n the Hood* and fucking *Fast and Furious*. Whacked up on ketamine . . .'

'Father George knows the City and he knows his history.'

'So let him do an exorcism on the ghost of Robert Maxwell,' Brown said.

'He doesn't want to do an exorcism.'

'So what's he want to do then?'

'I want him to look at the site and I want to share some details about the offence with him,' Wilko said. 'DI Brown, you've seen the corpse. What was done to that kiddie was strange and unnecessary and . . .' He wanted to say 'evil' but managed to stop himself. 'Deliberate. That wasn't some desperate girl who found herself knocked up, getting rid of her kid out of desperation. I don't even believe it was some young blud off the estates. There's something altogether . . . It's weird, disturbing, and given what I know about the City . . .'

'Alright.' Brown waved a submissive hand as he sat down at his desk. 'Alright, have your bleedin' exorcist—'

'Deliverance minister.'

'Whatever. Have him look at the site, tell him about it and see what he thinks. But don't think for a moment I go along with all this mumbo jumbo. Me and my team'll pursue the bad bastards while you and Father Ted—'

'Father George.'

'Whatever. While you fiddle with your rosaries or whatever the fuck you people do.'

The old man had been down the chippy. Dinner was meat pie, chips with a saveloy on the side. There wasn't a vegetable to be seen.

Jordan sat down at the kitchen table and began eating.

Granddad Bert, who was drinking the gravy from the pie by tipping the plate into his mouth, swallowed and then said, 'Get your Christmas presents, did you?'

'Er . . .' He'd forgotten that was what he'd told the old man. Spending the day effectively in Wilko's head had pushed that out of his mind.

'It's alright,' Bert said, 'I know you, you done your own thing and I know that was probably to do with your work. I s'pose it could have been a young lady, but then why you'd start courting now . . .'

'Granddad!'

'Well, you never bring no one home, do you?' he said. 'Not girl or boy . . .'

'I've told you, I'm not gay.'

'Couldn't give a tupp'ny shit if you are.' He finished the gravy and then wiped his mouth on his shirtsleeve. He began attacking the chips. 'Just wish you had someone,' he said. 'You're a good lad. It's not right you're on your own with an old bleeder like me.'

'I like being with you!'

'Yeah, but you'd be happier with a young lady. You don't remember your grandma Doris, but she was the light of my life. Loved her from the moment we first met down the old Ilford Palais.'

'Yes, you've said. But I've never met anyone who makes me feel like that,' Jordan said. 'And it's not for the want of trying, whatever you may think. Part of the reason I won't go over to Brixton is because Nana Willi likes to introduce me to "suitable" girls.'

The old man burped. 'Well, you're a good kid,' he said. 'Them lovely God-fearing girls at them churches they have down there can't find fault with you. There's that lovely West Indian girl in *Call the Midwife*. I mean you couldn't do any better than someone like her.'

Jordan wondered whether he should even grace an observation based on a TV show with an answer, and then decided that he shouldn't. Besides, nice as the character of the God-fearing West Indian midwife in the programme was, he didn't want to be with anyone like that. He was the son of two junkies who had needed to be withdrawn from smack just after he was born. Jordan tended to pass on God. And since the discovery of the dead baby in St Paul's Churchyard, he'd been even more averse to the great whatever it was in the sky.

In spite of finding Wilko with a couple of his mates first thing, Jordan had spent most of the day with the older man. They'd both seen the pattern of stab wounds on that baby's body and, while Jordan hadn't made the connections that Wilko had, he'd known it was strange.

One wound had been to the throat, then two more at the shoulders, followed by two others at the tops of the legs. Precise, planned, equidistant stab wounds from front to back. And while Jordan had, right from the off, felt there had to be something ritualistic at play here, he hadn't known what. But he'd known that if anyone had a theory it would be Wilko.

They'd sat, Wilko smoking, Jordan slurping down coffee after coffee in the churchyard for hours, talking. Wilko had been the first to use the word 'ritual'.

'It's an old, old thing, the ritual sacrifice of a child when opening an important building,' he'd told Jordan.

'But St Paul's is centuries old,' the young man had replied.

'Oh not this case, no,' Wilko had said. 'Just saying it was something that used to be done. Some people believe there's the body of a child underneath Christ Church in Spitalfields. I dunno. The architect, Hawksmoor, was some think, a magician. He was certainly a Mason . . .'

'That's not relevant.'

'No?' Wilko had shaken his head. 'Tell me, Constable Whittington, them five stab wounds on that poor nipper's body, what would they make if you joined them all up?'

Jordan had thought for a moment and then he'd said, 'Well, I suppose a sort of a house shape, a square with a pitched roof . . .'

'No!' Wilko had rolled his eyes. 'No, joined across the body! They make a five-pointed star, a pentagram.'

'Oh.'

In Jordan's limited experience pentagrams were associated with pagans and goths, who liked to wear them round their necks or have them tattooed on their arms. Nana Willi was very anti such things and was of the opinion that pagans and goths worshipped the Devil.

'And that is a powerful thing, that pentagram,' Wilko had continued. 'If you draw it with the top pointing down it's supposed to be a sign of the Devil. Probably the most important occult symbol there is.'

He'd said he was going to speak to a friend who was a vicar. This vicar, he'd told Jordan, specialised in something

61

called 'deliverance' which was actually exorcism. It all sounded very far-fetched and Jordan wondered what the man in charge of the case, DI Brown, would make of it. Probably not much.

After Jordan had finished his dinner he went into the living room to watch TV and drink beer with the old man, and then he went to bed. But he couldn't sleep. The sight of that baby, whose skin was the same colour as his own, kept on replaying in his mind.

FIVE

Lee grabbed hold of the bloke's shoulder and forced the papers into his hand.

'Snaresbrook, next Thursday,' he said as he walked away from him. 'Be there.'

The bloke, an enforcer for an up-and-coming family of Kray-a-likes from Ongar, smirked.

'I'll think about it,' he said.

Lee wanted to go back and beat the shit out of the little toerag. Called to appear on a charge of petty theft, Billy Adams was so much more. A classic clean-freak mummy's boy, twenty-eight-year-old Billy had a record for assault on women, only some of which had stuck. That he was now up on a shoplifting charge was laughable. The greedy git had got light-fingered in Aldi, apparently.

As Lee drove away from the massive faux-Georgian

gaff Billy shared with his mum and her French bulldogs, he thought about how process serving wasn't the easy gig everyone thought it was. Getting legal paperwork to some people was dead easy, but on other occasions it could be dangerous. If Mumtaz had served on Billy Adams, for instance, it was quite likely the bloke would have slapped her. He didn't like women, only his mum, and he especially didn't like Asians. Rita, the mother, was distantly related to the Kray-a-likes, which was why Billy had got his job with them. And the Kray-a-likes, the Carney family, were pure BNP right through to their marrow.

And yet was this unpaid gig Mumtaz had in the City any safer? Wilko Wilkinson had phoned him the previous evening, after their brief meet-up in St Paul's Churchyard. He'd told him how the baby had died, and it had had a profound effect. Whereas in the past when he found things hard to take, Lee would have resorted to drink or drugs, these days when he got into a state he cleaned. His bathroom and the cooker wouldn't know themselves after the go he'd had at them at 2 a.m. Of course, whoever killed the kiddie wasn't necessarily local to the area, but why travel to bury such a small body? According to Wilko it hadn't been far down underneath the soil. He'd said that it was almost as if whoever put it there had wanted it to be found. That or they were in a hurry.

But if they had wanted it discovered, then why? Lee had never known Wilko that well and, although he knew he was interested in history, he hadn't realised he was quite so 'esoteric'. He'd reckoned the five wounds on the baby's body meant something. Five wounds of Christ and the pentagram or something – Lee wasn't a great one for that sort of thing. But then Wilko had mentioned he was pulling in George Feldman, whom Lee did know.

Father George Feldman was an Anglican priest who worked out of a church on the edge of Epping Forest. A nineteenth-century Gothic structure, St Mary Magdalene's Church was so materially neglected it could easily be described as semi-derelict. But in spite of woodworm, vandalism and the ravages of time, George Feldman faithfully ministered to his tiny congregation of ancient women, performed his pastoral duties and, occasionally, performed 'deliverance' work. More usually called an exorcist, George was one of a surprisingly large body of people employed by the Church of England to 'cleanse' haunted houses and banish demons. Lee had first come across George when he'd been involved in a drugs raid on a house in Manor Park. While the police had arrested a couple in their twenties plus an attic full of cannabis plants, George had been talking to the neighbours about all the weird noises they heard in the middle of the night. It turned out the cannabis factory and the noises were connected. And so had Lee's association with the vicar begun.

Not that they were close. George was someone Lee saw rarely, but whenever he did, he always enjoyed his company. This was mainly because George rarely talked 'God', could swear like a sailor and had a vast stock of weird and hilarious stories to tell about both his 'adventures' as a priest and his childhood as the son of an eminent Jewish barrister. George had actually been born and brought up in London's legal quarter, the Temple.

What City of London CID were going to make of the priest with his permanently stained dog collar, his absolute belief in 'things unseen' and his accent out of a 1950s drawing room farce, Lee couldn't imagine.

Carter Court and its environs had not only taken a lot of punishment during World War II; much of the area had been burnt down during the Great Fire of London in 1666. However, when the area had been redeveloped after the fire, nothing was done to change the layout of these essentially, still, mediaeval streets. After the war, when the whole area had been almost levelled by the Luftwaffe, many of the old buildings had been replaced, but the meandering quality of the tiny streets had remained.

Carter Lane, which had in the twelfth century been called Shoemakers Row, had been used as a cut-through for farmers in the east of the City, taking their animals to market. It allowed them to bypass Ludgate Hill and the cathedral completely. This had brought Mumtaz to the name 'Lud'.

Like King Arthur, King Lud was a semi-mythical character who was supposed to have founded London in 66 BC. Lud and his sons had unsuccessfully defended the city during the Roman invasion and it was said that he was buried on the banks of the now underground River Fleet, somewhere between Ludgate Hill and Fleet Street. This area was, Mumtaz felt, 'deep' London. This was where it had all started, this was where the greatest activity and suffering had taken place – an area of sanctity, violence and trades as old as time.

Mumtaz had dusted off her old digital camera so that she could take pictures of notable buildings and features. Even though everyone used their phones to take pictures, it still looked unprofessional if she was meant to be an academic.

After successfully identifying what had once been St Paul's Choir School, Mumtaz sat down on a low wall to look at her pictures. After a very few moments, and oddly she felt in a prosperous part of London, she was joined by a woman who was very obviously pregnant.

As she sat beside her, the woman, who was probably in her twenties, said, 'Sorry, gotta have a sit for a moment. My ankles are like tree trunks.'

She rubbed her legs, which Mumtaz could see were indeed swollen down around the ankles.

Mumtaz smiled.

The woman said, 'You taking photos?'

'Yes.' It was as good a time as any to try out her cover story. 'I'm conducting some research,' she said. 'I'm a historian.'

'Oh.'

'This used to be a very busy part of London,' Mumtaz said. 'I mean it still is, but what I'm talking about are trades like weaving and leather work, small-scale publishing . . .'

'Used to be newspaper offices down Fleet Street,' the woman said. 'One of my uncles used to drive his cab round here back in the eighties when all the papers had their offices there.'

'Do you come from this area?' she asked the woman. She didn't think she did. She certainly didn't sound like the other residents she'd encountered.

'Nah,' the woman said. 'Dagenham. But me and my er, my other half, we live here now. We got a flat.' Then she smiled. 'I'm Danielle, by the way.'

Mumtaz nodded. She'd decided that morning that she was going to use a name that was not obviously Asian.

'Marian,' she said.

They both went quiet for a moment then. And with only a faint sound of traffic coming from Ludgate Hill, it was almost as if time had stopped around them.

'I can't help but wonder whether you have an ulterior motive,' Barry Feldman said to his brother as the two of them walked up Ludgate Hill towards the great cathedral. 'You're like some sort of woodland creature, you never leave the forest.'

George, four years younger than his brother and in many ways still an open book to him, said, 'You know me well.'

'I do,' Barry said.

'I did buy you lunch . . .'

Barry laughed. 'Good God man, El Vino's is not the sort of place a chap just gobbles his tapas and runs. That wasn't lunch, it was an Olympic relay race.'

Barry, like their father had been, was a traditional, old-style barrister. He worked diligently and hard for his clients, but were he invited to lunch, especially at El Vino's on Fleet Street, he expected to be there until closing time. But then, Barry still lived in the Temple.

'I paid,' George said.

'Yes, and consequently I was obliged to slurp down a

very nice Cabernet Sauvignon in an order so short you'd need a microscope to see it.'

They stood in front of the great cathedral's doorway and Barry continued, 'So what now? If you think you're finally going to get me to be baptised, then think again.'

'No!'

'Then . . .'

'We need to go to the churchyard,' George said. Then he shook his head. 'But if what I've been told is right then I can feel it from here.'

Barry said, 'Feel what?'

George turned to him and said, 'Evil.'

'I don't think I've been to a pub, except with my partner, since I've been expecting,' Danielle said as Mumtaz held the door to The Hobgoblin open for her. 'They say you shouldn't drink these days, don't they? Not like my mum. Not that she got pissed you understand, but women would have half a lager or a wine when they was expecting back in them days.'

Danielle liked to talk and Mumtaz was grateful for it. Already she'd learnt that Danielle knew the 'old geezer' who lived in the house next door to the pub, the house with the blue door.

Now she was inside the pub, Mumtaz could see that not only was it smothered in St George's flags, but it also boasted some features she had thought disappeared years ago. Like the cardboard peanut holder where the more bags were removed, the more 'features' of a naked girl were revealed. Like the Pirelli calendar from 1996 . . .

With more boldness than she actually felt, Mumtaz walked up to the bar. The man behind it was young, dark and handsome in a way she classified, on no real evidence, as 'Mediterranean'.

'Morning ladies,' he said in a cheery Estuarine accent. 'What can I get you?'

'Oh, I'll have a lime and soda,' Danielle said as she fumbled with her bag. 'I'll get these,' she said to Mumtaz.

'No, no, you sit down,' Mumtaz replied. Then she said to the barman, 'And a Diet Coke for me.'

She handed over a ten-pound note while Danielle, glad to sit down again, sat.

'You do food,' Mumtaz said to the barman.

'Yeah. Pie and chips mainly.'

Lee would be glad he'd won the bet. If she told him.

'What sort of pies?'

'The usual,' he said. 'Steak and onion, steak and kidney, chicken and mushroom . . .'

'I'll have chicken and mushroom,' Mumtaz said. She called over to Danielle. 'What would you like, Danielle?'

'Oh.' She still looked flustered and a bit hot in spite of the cold weather. 'Steak and kidney please. But not many chips. Gotta try and keep me weight under control.'

'OK.'

'But let me pay for that,' she continued.

Even though this 'case' was of a non-paying variety, Mumtaz knew she could still put this on expenses. 'No,' she said. 'I can charge it to my department. Glad to have your company.'

Food ordered, she sat down opposite Danielle. Luckily

she'd chosen a table away from the bar, by the window, which meant that they could have some privacy. Other than the two women the pub was empty.

'So this "old geezer" you met . . .' Mumtaz began.

Danielle took a sip from her glass and then said, 'Lives next door to here.'

'How'd you meet him?'

'Oh I often walk around,' she said. 'Partly trying to keep me weight down, partly I'm a bit bored to be honest. I'm sorry, Marian, you don't wanna hear about all that.'

Little did she know. When Mumtaz had been married to her husband Ahmet, she had learnt all about isolation and boredom. He'd rarely let her out of the house.

'You've a right to say you feel isolated,' Mumtaz said. 'I've never had any children of my own, but I have friends who have felt really out of things when they've been pregnant, especially if they've gone to live away from their families.'

Danielle smiled. She was an attractive young woman and Mumtaz noticed her eyes had teared up when she mentioned 'family'. She said she came from Dagenham, a largely white area where the working-class families tended to be close.

'Anyway,' Danielle said, 'this old bloke I think does actually come from here. So he might be useful for your project.'

'Did you speak to him or . . . ?'

'He come up to me,' she said. 'I was here, in Carter Court. All the people my partner knows round here reckon this pub's a bit rough, but I didn't know where it was, so

I went looking. The old man was coming out of his house and wondered what I was doing here.'

'You told him?'

'Yeah,' she said. 'He said I looked different to the others.'

'Different?'

'You must've noticed how most of the women round here look as if they're going to a garden party,' she said. 'The blokes all cycle and the woman float about in flowery dresses. I'm not like that.'

Danielle, that day, was all about denim. Even her long blonde hair was swept up in a denim scrunchie.

'The old bloke reminded me of me granddad,' Danielle continued. 'Same name too, Arthur. He said his family had always lived round here. They used to make candles.'

'Candles?'

'Long time ago. Maybe for the cathedral? I dunno. But Arthur himself, he told me he used to catch eels. But then that all stopped for some reason . . .'

There were still some remnants of crime-scene tape around that flower bed but, other than that, there was nothing to see.

'Was it murder? Or rather is it?' Barry asked George as the two men walked towards the site of the child's burial.

'My information is that it is an unlawful killing,' George said.

'I still don't see why you're involved,' Barry said. 'Where's the ghost or the poltergeist?'

'It's about evil,' George responded. 'If you knew how that child had been murdered . . .'

'So tell me.'

'I can't! You know that!'

George knelt down and began to silently pray.

Barry had never understood religion. Their parents had been secular Jews, so religion hadn't been part of their lives as children. As an adult Barry, at least, had forgotten all about it. Their sister, Eve, had become a Buddhist and then given that up in favour of a life of hedonism. Only George had got the religion bug which, he said, had grown out of his political activism. He'd been a right leftie back in the 1980s, always protesting about something. He'd been particularly exercised by the miners' strike and had spent a lot of time in the coal towns of South Yorkshire. He was supporting pickets at the Orgreave Coking Plant in June 1984 when the police attacked them. Following what turned into a violent confrontation, seventy-one pickets were charged with riot which, back then, attracted a life prison sentence. George was never the same after the Battle of Orgreave, during which he said he'd experienced an epiphany. Theology college followed and then the priesthood and Barry still, more than thirty years later, did not understand.

George rose to his feet. He said, 'I'm going into the cathedral. You can come or not. It's up to you.'

Last time Barry had been into St Paul's had been on a school trip when he was seven.

'What do you intend to do there?' Barry asked.

'Speak to people, clerics.'

'About what?'

'About what happened here,' George said.

'I expect the police have already done that,' Barry said.

73

'They have.' George was on the move, Barry following. 'But not in the right way.'

Detective Inspector Scott Brown liked to give the impression of being a Jack-the-Lad, and it was true he did have the morals of an alley cat and a penchant for binge-drinking, but underneath all that he was a bit shy. And DS Pinker was sassy, which made it all so much worse.

'That area's stiff with cameras, guv,' she said when she came to Brown to talk CCTV around St Paul's.

He as usual wanted to have everything about any case he worked on wound up yesterday.

'I've still got a shitload of recordings to go through,' Melina Pinker continued.

Thirty and half Greek, Pinker had the sort of golden Mediterranean looks that Brown found alluring. She, however, had made it known a long time ago that middle-aged macho men were not her thing.

He leant back in his chair and put his arms behind his head.

'Luckily we can see the comings and goings from the churchyard from four different angles,' she continued. 'Plus up Ludgate Hill and round the Tube station. Putting that all together is gonna take some time though.'

'Initial impressions?' he asked.

'Not much round the target time,' she said.

'You see anyone carrying anything?'

'No, just newspapers,' she said. Then she paused for a moment.

'What, DS Pinker?' Brown asked.

'Guv, I know that uniform have been doing door to door . . .'

'For what it's worth. Hardly anyone lives round there.'

'Yeah. But,' she said, 'wonder whether we're looking at someone who knows where the cameras are. Someone local or someone from the cathedral.'

'That's all possible,' Brown said. 'Although no one was in the cathedral, according to their statements.'

'There's the footage from inside the cathedral too, sir.'

'Yeah.' He rubbed a hand across his face.

She pulled a chair across from an unoccupied desk and sat down.

'Sir,' she said, 'about this exorcist . . .'

'He's not an exorcist, Detective Sergeant, he's a deliverance minister.'

'Same thing,' she said. 'Wilko told me.'

'Well, Wilko wants to keep his involvement in this case to himself,' Brown said.

'Yeah, but . . .'

'Father Feldman has expertise in the field of the occult,' Brown said. 'As you know, Pinker, there are aspects of this crime which could be connected to some sort of ritual stuff.'

'I thought you'd discounted that, guv.'

'I think it's a remote possibility . . .'

'But not zero?'

Was she one of those women who always looked for the sensational in everything, a conspiracy theory nut? If she was, he'd just gone off her.

'Nothing's ever zero,' Brown said tetchily. 'Get on will you, Detective Sergeant.'

75

She returned to her desk. He'd brought the priest in because Wilko had asked him to and everyone liked Wilko. A strange old git, but he knew his patch even if he was a bit mad. Also Brown, deep in his soul, wondered. He'd seen that tiny slaughtered corpse with its precisely placed wounds. An Englishman through to his marrow, Brown was nevertheless concerned about the divisions that had arisen in the country, especially since the Brexit vote. He'd unashamedly voted to leave the European Union, but he hadn't foreseen the trouble and even violence that vote had caused. And some of it definitely had a weird, almost religious dimension. Wilko had said, 'There's a whiff of sulphur in the air these days. If we ignore it, we're fucked.'

Scott Brown was inclined to believe he, at the very least, had a point.

He had thought it would be pleasant to combine a visit to St Paul's Cathedral with a nice lunch with Barry, but as usual, any contact with his family had descended into their mockery of him. Barry had banged on about the nature of Anglicanism when they'd entered the cathedral. Not that he knew anything. Claimed to not be able to understand how George could dress and behave just like a Catholic priest, while the priests in the cathedral were more like evangelical preachers.

Years ago he'd explained about High and Low churches and what the differences between them were, but either his brother hadn't listened or he'd been incapable of understanding. George was an Anglo-Catholic, one of a group of Anglicans spiritually and sometimes physically tied to Rome. Not that it mattered when it came to his familial relationships. They didn't care, and he was glad when his brother had left him alone with the young priest who introduced himself as 'Call me Harry'.

No clergy had been in the cathedral in the early hours of the previous morning. They'd all managed to account for their movements to the police. George said he was accusing no one of anything, but had maybe some members of the clerical team not felt in the days leading up to the child's burial that something strange was happening?

Harry said, 'What do you mean, strange?'

George had tried to articulate the occasional fringe of darkness he saw out of the corner of his eye, both inside and outside the great church. But the young man didn't seem to know what he was talking about. That or he was trying to avoid the subject. Ditto his colleagues. It was only when George was leaving the cathedral and he noticed someone was following him that things changed.

Out on the main entrance steps, George turned to the tall, grey, elderly priest and said, 'Can I help you?'

The man, who didn't introduce himself, said, 'I felt it. What you talked about, the evil.'

George walked over to him.

'How did you feel it?' he asked. 'What happened?'

The priest, a little flustered now, said, 'I knew it was coming . . .'

'The death . . . ?'

'The sacrifice,' he said.

'Sacrifice? What?'

The priest backed off. 'I just knew,' he said. 'But don't

try to tell them.' He tipped his head backwards, towards the cathedral. 'Just don't . . .'

'Why not?'

He shook his almost bald, grey head and said, 'They don't acknowledge it. They see it, but they don't see it, you know?'

George didn't, but when he tried to follow the priest, the latter told him to back off and so he did.

SIX

He pronounced the word 'eels' as 'ills'. He said, 'Used to be able to catch 'em right up into West London. But you'll be lucky to find one west of Greenwich now. Not a lot of call in recent years . . .'

Arthur Hobbs looked like a garden gnome. With pink apple cheeks and a bulbous nose, he had merry blue eyes and, until twenty years before, he'd been an eel fisherman on the Thames. He was also the only other person in the pub apart from Mumtaz and Danielle.

'Pollution done a lot of damage,' Arthur continued. 'And also ills went out of fashion. People got all queasy about 'em.'

'I like eels,' Danielle said. 'You can still get them in Dagenham.'

'Oh, Dagenham, yeah,' Arthur said. 'Yeah, Dagenham.'

Then he called to the barman to pour him another pint of Best.

Arthur had turned up as the women had been about to leave. He'd called over to Danielle and asked her how she was, then he'd joined them. Mumtaz had introduced herself as Marian, the historian, which was when Arthur had rolled into his tales of eel fishing.

He said, 'So you're a historian are you then?' to Mumtaz.

'Yes. Looking at the social history of this area,' she said.

She went on to embellish her story a little; it was rarely a bad idea, adding veracity. But her mouth slipped into a word it wasn't meant to say. 'My dadi, er, my mother-in-law has always had a keen interest in social history.'

This was true – but not in England, back in Bangladesh.

Did Arthur look confused? Would she have to make something else up to cover?

'Lot of history round here,' Arthur said bluntly.

Mumtaz felt her heart rate ease down.

'Do you know how long your family have been here?' Mumtaz asked.

He sniffed and moved his shoulders backwards slightly. 'Five hundred years.'

'Five hundred years!'

'Oh yeah,' he said. 'Same house too. Live next door to this pub.' He looked at Danielle. 'She knows.'

'He does.'

Mumtaz said, 'But that's a . . . Well, it looks like a Georgian house . . .'

'The front of it is,' Arthur said. 'But there's bits as date back to the 1550s. Candle-makers we was, my family. Made candles for the cathedral we did.'

'That's amazing!'

Was this the 'in' Mumtaz had been hoping for? She said, 'Has anyone ever come and photographed . . .'

'You can see the old bits from above,' Arthur said.

She waited for him to volunteer some more information, but he didn't. Eventually she said, 'You're just the sort of person I need to speak to, by the sound of it.'

But he just smiled.

'I mean,' she continued, 'you must know so much . . .'

'I do, but I like my privacy,' he said.

'Yes, well of course, you would be anonymised.'

Then he went truly left field and Mumtaz hoped her face didn't register her shock.

'People like yous don't come to pubs like this,' he said.

He was still smiling, but was it just her imagination or did his eyes look different now? Not in a good way . . .

It was however Danielle who replied. 'Oh that was me,' she said. 'I've been here before remember, when I met you? I thought Marian might be interested in this place as it's old and that.'

But Arthur didn't respond, just carried on drinking his pint until it had all gone. Then he said, 'Well, best be on me travels, ladies.'

And then he left.

Another one, Lee thought.

Sixty-something, broken nose, called Gary, from

Epping. Lee tried not to be bored because it was all work, but what was it with these men? This Gary's wife, his third, was called Fallon and she was twenty-five. Lee would put money on the chances she called him 'babe'.

'I thought when she had Harrison she'd settle down,' Gary said miserably.

'Your son?' Lee asked.

'Yeah, he's three. Had him just before we got married. Fallon wanted to look good in her wedding dress.'

Gary produced a photograph of a white blond boy who looked a little bit like the prime minister.

'So what does Fallon do?' Lee asked.

'Looks after the baby,' Gary said. 'I give her everything. Shopping gets delivered, we have a cleaner, she's got her own motor . . .'

'Does she go out in the evening when you get home?'

'No.'

Lee cleared his throat. 'Mr Connor, when do you think your wife is meeting this man you claim she's having an affair with?'

'I don't know,' he said. 'If I knew that I wouldn't need you, would I?'

It was a fair point.

'Sometime when you're not around,' Lee said.

'Yeah.'

'Which is?'

Gary shrugged.

'I'm self-employed. I'm in and out. Never know from one day to the next.'

He was a plumber by trade. But no ordinary plumber.

Gary Connor was plumber to the East End glitterati – Chigwell-based old white gangsters, top-end Asian landlords, a couple of Eastern European knock-off fag and booze millionaires. Not that he did the work himself any more. Gary had blokes for that. He hadn't touched a ballcock himself for decades.

'One of my customers wants a new hot tub or a leaky pipe fixed, I have to be there,' Gary said.

'So,' Lee continued. 'Do you suspect anyone . . .'

'Oh, did I not say? It's me brother,' Gary said. 'Me young one, Dillon.'

'And you know, how?'

'I've seen 'em,' Gary said. 'Every barbecue we had last summer, they were sniggering in corners. Round the back of the hot tub, in the loggia . . .'

'Kissing? Touching?'

'Nah. Just . . .' He shrugged. 'Cosy.'

'Anything else?'

He thought for a moment and then he said, 'Nah. Not really. A feeling . . .'

This was not an unusual occurrence. At least half the obbos the Agency mounted on supposedly cheating spouses turned out to be no such thing. Usually involving older men with younger partners, the suspected other man or woman was generally younger too. However, in Lee's experience, the offender was rarely a family member. He said, 'I have to ask, Gary, when do you think your wife is cheating on you if your work schedule is so uncertain? You said she looks after your child all day long on her own, when would she get the time?'

83

'Dunno,' he said. 'That's what I'm paying you for, to find out. I'm backed up with appointments for the next few days. I'll be out from around eight, probably 'til six. I've told her, the missus. So if anything's happening, it'll be happening then. Can you start tomorrow?'

'Who are you really?'

Mumtaz stopped. They'd been walking away from the pub when the younger woman had asked her.

'I'm Marian,' Mumtaz said.

'Yeah, your name probably is Marian, but why are you here?' Danielle asked.

Mumtaz knew only too well never to underestimate girls like Danielle. She'd been to school with a lot of white, East End working-class girls and most of them, despite their often risible reputation, were as sharp as tacks. What had given her away?

Danielle took Mumtaz's arm. 'I saw you running in the fog two nights ago,' she said. 'I was looking out my window. You turned to see whether someone was behind you. I recognise your face.'

She could deny it. In fact she should deny it.

'Is it something to do with that pub?' Danielle persisted. 'You a copper?'

'No,' Mumtaz said. The Hobgoblin did look as if it might be somewhere British National Party members might feel welcome, but even if that were true, that was not currently her concern.

'I used to work for a firm of solicitors,' Danielle said. 'And one time we had a historian come to us about the history of the building where we worked. He made an appointment with my boss. We knew where he come from and everything first.'

She'd avoided naming a particular college or university department, which had been foolish. Or rather it would have been alright had Danielle not been so on the ball.

They turned into Carter Lane.

'If you don't want to talk about it in the street, you can come up to the flat,' Danielle said. 'Henry, that's my partner, is at work.'

Father George was a strange-looking man. Of uncertain age, he was tall, stooped and wore clothes that were entirely black apart from his dog collar. Scott Brown felt embarrassed just having him in his office. Luckily, however, they weren't alone. The young PC who had found the child's body had been seconded to CID and had been called in to join their conversation, thank Christ. Jordan Whittington was a friend of Wilko's and appeared to be much more comfortable with all this metaphysical stuff.

'I felt it as soon as I walked into the churchyard,' Father George said. 'Evil.'

'How did it manifest?' Jordan asked.

'You know it when you come across it.'

'Yes, but how does it make you feel?' the young man persisted.

Scott was floored by mumbo jumbo. Didn't know what to do with it. Couldn't convince himself it had any relevance. Of course murder scenes made people feel shivery. Didn't mean there was a ghost in residence.

Didn't mean ghosts or whatever even existed.

The priest frowned and then he said, 'Watched.'

'As in . . . ?'

'As in overlooked by something one cannot see,' he said. 'Something malign. And when one prays, one knows to one's very core that this malign influence is blocking one's words to the Almighty. As if someone is shouting when you try to listen to the television.'

The office fell silent. Then the priest continued, 'That area around the cathedral is the oldest part of London. It's where the city was originally founded by the pagans. King Lud, a semi-mythical king who defeated the Romans the first time they tried to invade. When they were successful the Romans themselves established temples to their gods in that area, including Mithras. All sorts of obscene ceremonies used to take place in Mithraic temples to propitiate the god. And although Christian shrines have been raised on many of those sites, a memory, if you like, can remain behind.'

'Father,' Jordan said. 'Could it be that someone was actually watching you, do you think? I mean, I know you may disagree, but humans are animals . . .'

'In a sense.'

'And so we do have the same instincts that other animals do. We get a tingling feeling on the back of our neck, the hairs rise on our arms . . .'

'I can't rule that out,' Father George said. 'It would be ridiculous of me to do so.'

Scott Brown felt himself inwardly sigh with relief. Now they were on his territory.

'Tell us what happened?' Jordan said.

Brown had looked up Jordan Whittington's CV. He had a degree in Applied Psychology, apparently. Whatever that was. He was clever.

The priest said, 'I'd had lunch with my brother. We went to El Vino's on Fleet Street.'

'Did you drink?'

'My brother did. I don't, apart from Communion wine. Then I walked to the cathedral, with my brother, and we talked. As I approached the front entrance, I began to feel it.'

'This being watched.'

'Evil, yes,' he said.

'And your brother?'

He smiled. 'Barry is an atheist,' he said.

'Yes, but . . .'

'No, officer, my brother felt nothing. In fact he pooh-poohed my view that anything untoward was happening. Even when we walked into the churchyard, even when we came to the site of the child's temporary grave, Barry was unmoved.'

'But not you?'

'Oh no,' he said. 'As I told you, I tried to pray but the feeling was so strong, it felt as if God was being cut off from me. I didn't say anything to my brother. I knew he wouldn't understand. He left to go back to his Chambers and I went into the cathedral.'

Brown asked, 'Why?'

'Sergeant Wilkinson had told me that the cathedral had been empty that night, and I wanted to confirm that was true.'

'And did you?'

The clerical team had been interviewed by both Wilkinson and CID. Their stories had been consistent with each other. St Paul's had been empty.

'I did and I didn't,' the priest said.

'What's that mean?'

'All the clerics I spoke to confirmed they had seen, heard and experienced nothing. However, one I did not speak to, who only came up to me as I was leaving the cathedral, while not disputing that, had a rather different take,' he said. 'He said that "they", meaning his fellow priests, had turned their minds away from the reality of the situation.'

'Which is?' Jordan asked.

'That a sacrifice has taken place,' Father George said.

The room fell silent again and then Scott Brown said, 'A sacrifice to what?'

'I don't know,' the priest said. 'All I do know is that is what it is.'

'A sacrifice?'

'A ritual sacrifice, yes,' he said.

'I can't tell you anything,' Mumtaz said.

Danielle's flat was very cool. Minimalist, it was decorated in cool shades of pale sage green and grey. The floors were real wood, not laminate, and the furniture was upholstered in smooth grey leather. It was also uncomfortable. Even so, Mumtaz was jealous. This made her small flat look like a junk shop.

'I'm in the area on behalf of a client . . .'

'Yeah, but is it a crime someone's done?' Danielle asked.

Pregnant, bored and home alone most of the time, Danielle was needy.

'It's a matter of concern to my client,' Mumtaz said.

'So not something criminal then?'

'No,' Mumtaz said.

Why had she told her she was a PI? Was it because she liked her? Was it because she felt sorry for her? Or was it perhaps that she saw something in Danielle that reminded her of herself when she was married? Stuck at home, ignored for the most part, wondering what she was for . . . Or was it a sign of her inexperience?

'So when I saw you and you were running . . .'

'I was disorientated by the fog,' Mumtaz said.

'But you were scoping out the area?'

'I was familiarising myself with it, yes.'

Danielle offered her a biscuit to go with the tea she'd made earlier for them both, but Mumtaz declined. They were chocolate and, once she started eating them, she knew she couldn't stop. Danielle had no such qualms and took four out of the packet.

'So, that old man, Arthur,' she said. 'Is it anything to do with him?'

Mumtaz paused for just too long. 'No.'

'Because as soon as you started talking about his house, he changed,' Danielle said. 'That's why I said it was my idea to go to the pub. The way he looked at you was, well it was strange. Not like the way he looks at me. He's a funny old thing. When I first met him he invited me to his house, saying it was old and that. Don't s'pose he'll ask me again . . .'

Full disclosure was impossible, and Lee had taught her from the start that involving civilians directly in a case was a strict no-no. But if Arthur Hobbs had somehow rumbled her then she couldn't have anything to do with him again, not directly . . .

Danielle said, 'I dunno why he was so keen to have me round his place and not you. Unless he knows who you are of course . . . But he just met me on the street that first time. Pregnant, hanging about like some street kid . . . I mean if he's so proud of his heritage, why didn't he want to speak to you? You're a much better bet than me.'

An idea began to form in Mumtaz's mind. But she didn't say anything. She wouldn't be able to until she'd spoken to Lee.

'And anyway,' Danielle said, 'can't be that up his arse about his privacy, not with all the blokes in and out his place.'

What did men carry whilst walking through central London in the early hours of the morning? One school of thought would probably state that just about anything was the answer. In an infinite universe that had to be true. But in reality those things, as observed on CCTV footage by DS Melina Pinker, boiled down to newspapers, sports bags, umbrellas and beer glasses – full or empty. The few women in evidence carried hand- or shoulder bags and also the odd umbrella. However, no woman had walked through St Paul's graveyard the night the baby's body had been discovered. In fact only two men had actually been caught on camera traversing the space. In both cases the images were unclear and neither of the men in question were carrying anything.

Pinker put her chin in her hands. The baby had been small. Just under three kilos. Could a small baby like that be effectively hidden inside a coat? Maybe if it had been already dead?

Following one subject using footage from several different cameras wasn't easy, but it did seem as if one of the men had spent longer inside the graveyard than the other. Melina asked the technician to bring up the first footage they had of man number one on the screen and then freeze the frame.

'Can you enhance this so we can see his face?' she asked.

The technician shrugged. 'Dunno until I try,' he said. 'You'll have to give me a bit of time.'

'How long?'

'Couple of hours?'

'Make it an hour and I'll buy you a bag of doughnuts from Tesco's,' Melina said.

Lee was parked up outside Gary Connor's massive house. Tucked away, or rather not so much tucked as Christ knew how far from the Abridge Road, technically Gary's palace was in Chigwell. Modern, clean-lined, set in several acres of manicured lawn, Walnut House was a testament to what could be done with steel and glass to ensure that both of those materials looked really unpleasant.

Of course, there were massive electric gates in front of the massive driveway up to the house. The gates and the front of the property bristled with CCTV cameras. But by Gary's own admission, the back way onto his estate was an open book. Accessed via an old unmade track, the far reaches of Gary's empire were covered by a wood.

Gary had told him, 'I never knew where I could site cameras in all that.'

Had it occurred to him to get some advice? He'd just shrugged and moved on to the next thing when Lee had asked.

Lee was about to drive off and explore where he'd be positioning himself for the obbo the following day when Mumtaz called. She told him what she'd done, about this girl Danielle, and he'd had to stop himself losing his shit. As calmly as he could he said, 'We don't tell anyone what we're doing and I mean no one.'

'Yes, but she's not dim,' Mumtaz said. 'And she covered for me with the man who owns the house with the blue door.'

'If he made you too, then you're not having a good day,' Lee said.

This whole thing had been fucked from the word go.

'Listen!' she said. 'I agree. Not good. But I think we can salvage something out of this.'

'What?'

'Danielle is pregnant, at home and bored,' she said. 'She wanders around the local area, nursing swollen ankles, looking at things. She's very observant. She told me she's seen men going into and out of that house.'

'So?'

'So the old man, Arthur Hobbs, told me he is very jealous of his privacy.'

'Maybe he doesn't like women,' Lee said.

'He likes Danielle,' she said. 'He invited her in when he first met her.'

Lee didn't say anything. He really wasn't that concerned about what he privately in his head called The Case of the Kid with the Nosebleed.

Eventually Mumtaz said, 'I've told Danielle I can tell her nothing. She accepts that. If I haven't queered the pitch for her, then she can get in – and she will.'

'Then you'll have to tell her about the kid,' Lee said. 'You can't.'

'No and I won't,' Mumtaz said. 'But if we wire her up . . .'

'A pregnant woman? Have you lost your fucking mind?'

'Lee, she's a working-class, Dagenham girl.'

'What do you mean?'

'Meaning she's no one's fool,' Mumtaz said. 'And anyway, if you're right about this business then there's nothing to be afraid of, is there?'

'Mumtaz, a baby was killed less than two hundred yards from Carter Court.'

She thought about this for a moment and then said, 'You think there's a connection?'

'I think it's always a good thing to keep an open mind,' Lee said. 'Your dad's teenage mates may well want to keep all this under wraps but depending on what we find, that may not be possible. This Danielle know that a baby's been found dead?'

'I don't know,' Mumtaz said.

'Then find out,' Lee said. 'If she doesn't know for some reason then maybe you should tell her.'

He ended the call. Then he sat for a moment thinking. After that he made a call – but not to Mumtaz.

SEVEN

Without preamble, Habib Farooqi's mother burst into his bedroom and shouted, 'How long have you been on that bloody phone?'

It had been a while. Loz was getting himself into a right state over the kid at St Paul's, Kym's dad and everything else.

'I don't know,' Habib told his mum.

Loz on the other end said, 'Ring me back.'

Habib ended the call. His mother said, 'I know you like to talk to Lawrence but you see each other all the time. Why do you have to be on the phone too? Eh?'

'Oh, he's just . . .'

'Put the phone away and do your homework!' She made to go and then said, 'And give me the bloody phone!'

'Oh . . .'

She ripped it out of his hands and then left.

Habib had heard nothing from Mrs Hakim. Maybe she'd decided that there was nothing to investigate. He had her number but was afraid to call it. Much as he'd reassured Loz that everything was alright, Habib knew that it wasn't. The state that boy had been in, they should have just called the police. If Mrs Hakim hadn't got back to him then either she'd dropped the whole thing or she'd not discovered anything. The kid could be dead by this time!

The police had found a dead baby in St Paul's Churchyard. Could that boy have been involved in that? Maybe that blood on him had come from the dead baby? Maybe he'd killed it? But then he'd asked for help . . .

Habib and Loz had bonded over worry. Years ago back at primary school, they'd both been frightened of Mrs Malyon and they'd both been horrified when they'd been put in her class. She shouted and if she didn't like you then she shouted even more. A lot of the kids laughed about it, but not Habib and Loz. Neither of them liked getting up to read to the class and that was one of Mrs Malyon's favourite things. Habib always felt his heart go really fast whenever he had to do it, and then he began to feel sick. Loz just used to wet his pants. The two of them fretted for days about reading in class. But having company did make it better. Not that reading in class was as serious as this. This was making Habib unable to sleep. Loz was a mess. And now Habib's mum had his phone so even if Mrs Hakim did call, he'd miss it.

* * *

You had to walk through a short tunnel between two old buildings to get to Carter Court and then, once inside, it was very difficult to conceal yourself. The only thing it wasn't possible to do was hide the fact that you were visiting. Or was it?

Danielle had been watching the entrance for over an hour and she'd only seen two men. They'd gone straight to the pub which, by the sound of it, was full. Arthur was at home. It wasn't much to tell Marian, if she decided to, but then she'd said that anything Danielle observed would be useful. But to whom and why? Danielle was conflicted about Marian. She crossed her arms over her chest. Henry would be home soon. He'd rung her earlier to say that he was bringing a partner in a rival firm and his wife to the flat for 'supper'. What was supper? Back home it had meant a bit of white sliced and jam before bed.

To be fair Henry had said he'd cook, which meant it'd probably be some organic thing with lots of seeds. That was OK. But it was the conversation that she dreaded. This man's wife was also a solicitor and so there'd be law talk, which she was used to. But then they'd probably discuss politics at some point, which was where it could all go a bit wrong. Henry and people like him were always so sure of themselves and she always felt that if she disagreed in any way, they'd laugh at her. Not literally but they'd exchange those looks she so dreaded, as if they pitied her. Then, sometimes, Henry would get the 'ump once the guests had gone and she'd have to say that she was sorry, that she'd spoken out of turn.

But then in a weird sort of way, she'd had a good

day and so she wasn't as wound up as usual. Maybe the 'supper' would go OK? Maybe now she could just keep quiet and let them do the talking without feeling as if her rage would consume her.

'I'm sorry mate, I know you mean well, but I think this is getting out of hand.'

Jordan felt slapped. He'd known that Scott Brown was down to earth when he'd been seconded to CID – and he knew that had only happened because Wilko had suggested it. Had Wilko himself told Brown what he'd just told him, the DI would have at least given it consideration, even if he did think it was bullshit. Wilko was one of those people you didn't actually say no to.

That accepted, Jordan knew he had to fight his own corner. He said, 'It's not just tinfoil-hat conspiracy stuff, guv. There are actual documents that relate to these tunnels.'

He'd found some documentary evidence, via City of London archives, that at one time, a tunnel had existed between St Paul's Cathedral and the old St Paul's Choir School, across Ludgate Hill. Not only that, but other tunnels existed in that area too – principally between providers of some goods and services to the church. All had, it was said, been blown out of existence during the London Blitz. Most of the buildings round about had been razed to the ground. But what if some of the tunnels were still in existence, and what if one or more of them provided unseen access to the cathedral?

'Yeah, but Constable, I've already interviewed the priests about how one gets in and out of the cathedral and no tunnels was even hinted at,' Brown said.

'Maybe they don't know they're there?' Jordan said.

Brown shrugged. 'DS Pinker's having a go at getting CCTV footage enhanced. Let's see if we can identify any faces from that.'

He patted Jordan patronisingly on the shoulder. Berk.

He'd patronised Father George too. But then Jordan had found him a bit too strange as well. Wilko knew some odd types. He'd met some PIs from Newham with Wilko at St Paul's Churchyard. Apparently randomly wandering the city, but Jordan had to wonder what they were really doing. The woman had been beautiful. It had been a while since he'd met a woman who had really excited him, but she did. He wondered what his Nana Willi would make of her, and came to the conclusion that she would probably be horrified. His family didn't 'do' Islam.

DS Pinker arrived carrying a large box of doughnuts and said to Brown, 'Come and look at this, guv. Think we might have got a face.'

Nobody really knew what the old king had looked like. And while he hoped that what he had created did bear some sort of resemblance to him, Arthur Hobbs was grudgingly aware that this carving didn't. He'd imagined wild hair, a bit like dreadlocks, which was probably fairly accurate. But whether he'd had handsome features was more open to question. Back then, before dentistry, a man in middle age would likely be entirely toothless for one thing. Hunting and fighting may have produced scars, maybe even the loss of an eye or ear.

But it was all speculative. No one could really know at this distance in time. What the mask had to do was inspire fear more than anything else, because he had to have been fearsome. A warrior king, he bore about as much resemblance to modern monarchs as a wild boar does to a domestic pig. And like a boar he would have been a thoroughbred. Born wild, free and pure, he would have anointed himself, as they did back then. No namby-pamby priest smearing a bit of oil on the head back then!

Arthur was just about to close his eyes and try to imagine how it might have been, when he remembered that the boy needed to be fed. He got up slowly from his chair and shuffled into the kitchen. The fridge didn't offer a great deal of variety, but poking around at the back he found some corned beef and a tomato. That'd have to do. He could make a sandwich for the boy, he'd like that.

They met, as they often did, in the gloom that was the interior of Ye Olde Cheshire Cheese on Fleet Street. There were several reasons why they met there. Firstly, Wilko liked the beer and the fact that the Cheese had wooden floors sprinkled with sawdust. Secondly, they both enjoyed an open fire and a plain wooden table; and finally, because there was something inherently disreputable about the place. Whether that was to do with the fact that until the 1980s most of Fleet Street's most famous hacks had patronised the pub – and got arse'oled – or because the upper storeys had been used as a brothel in the eighteenth century, neither of them knew or cared. The policeman and the priest came to the Cheese because they felt comfortable there and because of the ghosts.

Back in mediaeval times there had been a monastery on the site. Various vaulted chambers remained below street level and, while Wilko sometimes felt like drinking downstairs with a host of barely visible thirteenth-century divines, this evening he and Father George were upstairs. This was largely because they were expecting a guest.

'I dunno what he wants any more'n you do,' Wilko said as he hefted his pint and then took a long, deep swig of beer. 'He's always been a bit out the ordinary, as you know.'

Father George, already three glasses of port down, said, 'I heard a whisper that he's been having an affair with the woman who works for him.'

'Really?' Wilko shrugged. 'That's a Muslim lady. Covered her head when I saw her. Didn't think that'd be his sort, but who knows?'

'So when did he get in contact?'

'This afternoon,' Wilko said. 'Out on some obbo at the time. Funny, precarious sort of living, being a PI. Serving notices on people, looking at women asking the milkman in for a bit of how's your father and taking pictures. Like The Job – you have to put up with a load of bad behaviour . . .'

'Wilko . . .'

He looked over his shoulder and saw that Lee Arnold had arrived.

They all peered at the image on the screen. DS Pinker said, 'This is as good as they can get it. You can sort of see a face.'

To Jordan it wasn't much more than a smudge, but then he wasn't accustomed to looking at such things.

'IC1,' DI Brown said.

'Or 2,' Pinker added. 'Dark hair. I may be wrong, but . . .'

'Not carrying anything.'

'No,' she said. 'But he's clutching the front of his coat.'

'It was cold.'

'Yeah. But remember the child was newborn, guv,' Pinker said. 'Just under three kilos. Small by modern standards. And if it was already dead then he could've laid it flat against his body.'

This was how you had to be able to think in CID, Jordan thought as he felt his skin crawl. You had to be able to model the thought processes of murderers and rapists. You had to put yourself inside a disordered or desperate head.

To a certain extent that was true of life in uniform too, but in CID it was all so much more. In order to be successful, you had to employ speculation and then, in some cases, run with that speculation to reach a range of conclusions, none of which might be correct.

'Do you get age from this image?' Brown asked Pinker.

'Technician reckons thirties to fifties, guv.'

Brown raised his eyes. 'About as useful as . . .'

'Guv, he's saying the bloke's from early to late middle age.'

'Alright.' He waved a dismissive hand at her. This was obviously not as useful as Brown had hoped. He said, 'Get an artist in. Sometimes they can make out things we can't.'

Then he left the office with, 'Going down the boozer.'

Alone with Melina Pinker, Jordan said, 'This artist . . .'

'We use several,' she said. 'Geezer who lives over Trinity Buoy Wharf is about the best, I think.'

Trinity Buoy Wharf was a well-known artistic colony over on Bow Creek. Jordan had once wandered over there with some of his mates as a teenager. If he remembered correctly, some of the artists over there lived in old shipping containers. Why anyone would want to do such a thing was beyond him, but then he thought that was probably because they were posh.

On the basis that Father George was a priest and Wilko was, well, who really knew what Wilko was, but he was no fool, Lee told his drinking companions everything about the Boy with the Nosebleed case.

'It's probably got fuck all – sorry, Father . . .'

'Oh, please don't worry!'

'Nothing to do with this dead baby, but you know once you've been in The Job it comes hard sometimes not to pass intel like this on,' Lee said. 'Mumtaz is all for keeping this close because of her young clients but I'm not happy. I mean, it is probably nothing . . .'

'You sound as if you're trying to convince yourself as well as us,' Father George said.

Lee smiled. 'I dunno, to be honest, Father. I don't do all this evil and ghosts and stuff you guys and Mumtaz do. I can't handle all that. It's just that . . .'

'If there's been something out of the ordinary going on around a crime scene, we need to know about it,' Wilko said. He frowned. 'These boys said this kid had blood on his face?'

'Yeah.'

'Hands?'

'Not really sure,' Lee said. 'By that I mean, they aren't. The whole encounter was a glance, not much more. Like I said, there was some old bloke at the end of the corridor looking at what the kid was doing. There was some blood down his front . . .'

'Mmm.'

'On the face of it, sounds like possible child abuse to me,' Father George said. 'Although one must be wary of pointing the finger wrongly in such cases.'

'Part of the reason why we're going so easy,' Lee said.

'George, look where this is,' Wilko said.

The two men locked eyes for a moment and then the priest said, 'Well, yes . . .'

'I'll get another round in,' Lee said as he got up to go to the bar. 'Same again?'

'I think so.'

Lee himself was, after a long-term love affair with alcohol, teetotal and so 'his' would just be a Diet Pepsi. He also knew that his two companions probably needed some time alone. And he was right.

'As soon as you told me about the baby, I feared the worst,' Father George said to Wilko.

'That house in Carter Court goes way back,' Wilko said.

'He never lived there though, did he?'

Wilko shook his head. 'Not that I know of,' he said.

'But I think it's safe to say he practised in the cathedral.'

'He was chancellor.'

'The old queen must've known he'd carry on when she appointed him.'

'Elizabeth the First was always fascinated by the Dark Arts.'

'It's an origin and a meeting point for so much,' Wilko said. 'It *is* London! It's always been the epicentre and now it's becoming the focus again!'

'Focus for what?'

Lee put their drinks on the table and sat down.

Wilko looked at George and then at Lee and said, 'I dunno for sure where you stand on the future of the United Kingdom, Lee . . .'

'Seriously?' Lee shook his head. 'I think we have to see how it goes after we leave Europe.'

The United Kingdom had voted to leave the European Union back in 2016. Now, on the eve of departure, which was due to take place in January 2020, prophets of both doom and the inauguration of a new British Empire were thick on the ground. Lee Arnold was neither, although he had voted to remain inside the bloc.

'If you had to take a punt?' Wilko asked.

Lee drank and then said, 'Shitshow.'

The other two men nodded.

'Why?'

'The father is besotted with the boy. Only son, isn't it . . .'

Mumtaz was familiar with what her father was saying. She'd been to school with the vast Rahman family – eight girls and one very spoilt, very fat brother doted on by his parents and his sisters.

'But Baba,' she said to her father, 'surely that means that if Habib has done something wrong his father will forgive him?'

'Of course!' Baharat Huq said. 'But it's dishonourable what the boy did. Selling on the street like a tinker! That much I do know, even if that's the limit of it! Farooqi is a pharmacist, a man of substance! Habib knows this! He knows that people will point at his dad and say, "There goes the pharmacist who can't control his family!" You know this.'

'Do I? Do I really?' Mumtaz said.

Her father sighed. 'I am not one to say you should stay in your own community all the time,' he said. 'You know that is not me, but sometimes I think maybe you do spend too much time . . .'

'Baba, I am not about to tell the world about the pharmacist Farooqi!' Mumtaz cut in. 'But you know the boys should have told what they saw to the police. I don't feel good about—'

'I don't want to know! What they saw is not for me to know!' her father said. 'I will be judged when I die but don't give me more worries now! There will be a simple explanation, whatever it was that happened, there will.'

'I'm not so sure,' she said. 'You know a baby was found dead in St Paul's Churchyard?'

'And that has what to do with Habib and Lawrence? Is that where you are investigating?'

'Well . . .'

'They are good boys! Lawrence is a bit of a dreamer but . . .'

'I'm not saying a dead baby has anything to do with the boys,' Mumtaz said. 'I don't think that for a moment. But I am uneasy, Baba.'

'In what way?'

Mumtaz knew that the only reason she could talk to her father so easily was because she wasn't with him. On the phone and therefore at a remove from his piercing gaze, it was simpler somehow. And she didn't really know what she was talking about.

'I'm not entirely sure,' she said. 'All I can say is that it's odd. The case itself, the area the incident happened in . . .'

'Oh, tell me no more!' Baharat Huq said. 'You must talk to Lee about these things!'

'I know, but . . .'

'He is a good man, he cares for you.'

'We're very different, Baba,' she said. 'It's not straightforward.'

'Isn't it?'

'No.'

'I think it is,' he said. 'He would do anything for you, that man.'

'Yes, but . . .'

'No,' her father said. 'Listen to your father like a good girl! I have never in my whole life known things to be so bad in the world as they are now. And I lived through Partition. The world burns and floods because of the global warming and still the politicians and the captains of industry do bugger all. In twenty years' time we will all

107

burn to a crisp! Then the Brexit rubbish! Food shortages to come! Everyone at each other's throats! Silly people going back into the past to Empire time and suchlike!'

'I know this, yes . . .'

'Yes, so we must stick together,' Baharat said. 'If someone cares for you, and you care for them, you must persist. There are so many dangers now. I don't know what's happening to this world, but it is not good and I don't understand any more.'

He had never been pessimistic and Mumtaz hated the way he had become so over the years. And if she were honest, she felt that way too. The world was dangerous yes, it always had been, but there was something toxic in the way that some responded to this now. It was as if empathy, particularly for those deemed 'other' in some way, was dying.

'I don't often talk about being Jewish,' Father George said. 'I changed my religion a long time ago. But I remain ethnically Jewish and so I remain sensitive to anti-Semitism.'

One of Lee Arnold's grandfathers had been Jewish. Like a lot of East Enders his background was tangled and ethnically mixed.

'I know a few rabbis and they all say the same thing,' George continued. 'They've never seen so much anti-Semitism in their lifetimes. It's not all about Palestine. There's a whole, home-grown . . .'

'Little Englander?'

'More'n that,' Wilko said.

'What, you mean the "bring back the Empire" stuff?' Lee asked.

'More'n that,' Wilko said.

'Like what?'

Wilko took a deep breath and said, 'You know Hitler wanted to make Germany what he called "racially pure"? And you know that more recently the Serbs . . .'

'Ethnic cleansing?' Lee said. 'Here? No, you're shitting me!'

'You think we're immune to such excesses?' George said. 'Lee, don't fall into English exceptionalism. We can do these things, same as any other nation. Look at all this anti-immigrant stuff that gets peddled these days.'

'That's a long way from . . .'

'Lee,' Father George said, 'I don't expect you to accept this but Wilko and myself, we have been noticing things for some time.'

'Racism?'

'Sort of,' George said. 'Well, yes, but we've been picking up an undercurrent of ethnic myths . . .'

Lee shrugged. 'Like what?'

'Like the idea of the once and future English king.'

'Not Arthur, before you accuse us of getting all Hollywood. No, much older than that, linked to the pre-Roman invasion of the country. A notion of the survival of a purely English race.'

'So bollocks,' Lee said.

'Bollocks can be dangerous,' Wilko said. 'If you know what I mean. What we're talking about are people on the far right of Hitler. They're few, as far we can tell, but they are fanatical and they do believe that they are the genuine real-deal original Brits. They're also very likely to be manipulated by less delusional, more political, actors.'

'What do you mean?' Lee asked.

'I mean they ain't got no limits, this bunch,' Wilko said. 'Which means that if more conventional right-wing actors want something really out-there done, then look no further.'

'And then there's the occult . . .' George said.

Lee raised a hand. 'Hang on! Hang on! If you're gonna go all weird on my arse then I'm gonna need a fag!'

The three men got to their feet and, drinks in hands, they went outside.

'Wilko, I've known you a lot of years,' Lee Arnold said. 'And you've always been interested in this stuff. I remember you telling me about the Highgate Vampire when I first met you. Where's your proof for this?'

In the early 1970s alleged vampires had been apparently 'sighted' in north London's Highgate cemetery. It had of course turned out to be a hoax, but a lot of people had really believed that the undead walked abroad in the cemetery at the time. To be fair Wilko, a child at the time, hadn't – but the case had left him with a 'nose' for the occult, or so he liked to tell people.

'Where do you think?' Wilko said.

'Wilko and I have identified troubling sites on the Internet,' George said.

Lee laughed. 'Mate . . .'

'You may scoff, Lee,' George continued. 'But we're not

talking about websites you can just go online and stumble across.'

'Oh.'

The priest meant the so-called 'Dark Web', where there existed portals into the netherworld of extremism of all stripes, including misogyny, pornography, religious mania and racism. Lee knew that the police monitored activity on it to some extent, but he wouldn't have pegged old Wilko as a computer-literate adept.

George, in part, answered his question. 'Wilko keeps his ear to the ground.'

'It's amazing what some of them kids coming into The Job from university can do these days,' Wilko said as he drew heavily on his fag.

'And then there's me,' George said.

Lee, also dragging hard on a fag, looked at the priest.

'Deliverance work is, shall we say, throwing up some unusual cases these days,' he said.

'Like?'

'Like those whose peaceful existences have been disturbed by the invocation of toxic entities, by those who would do them harm.'

'And in English?' Lee said. Father George sounded like Mumtaz in full-on psychologist flow.

'Some of my black parishioners have been frightened out of their wits, and threatened by, events in their homes they cannot explain,' he said. 'And while I have no doubt that many entities beyond the grave can be horrifically racist, I also have no doubt that those who are invoking these forces are racist too.'

'So the spirit of Oswald Mosley sent to do a bit of poltergeist work by the BNP family next door?'

Father George smiled. 'Something like that,' he said. 'And maybe, something like this murdered mixed-race baby too . . .'

EIGHT

'What did Brown say about the tunnels?' Wilko asked Jordan Whittington when he came on shift the next morning.

Jordan was early and had bowled into the canteen to get his morning coffee when he'd come across the older man. Sitting down opposite him he said, 'Not much. To be honest though I think it's Father George who's wound him up the most.'

'Why?'

'Oh, come on Wilko,' Jordan said. 'All that exorcism stuff is a bit much. If Father George's parishioners have got a beef with their neighbours then they can make a complaint to us.'

'You know it's not that easy,' Wilko said.

'It is!'

Wilko sat back in his chair. 'Listen Jordan,' he said. 'I know everyone here thinks I'm a bit of a weirdo. To your credit you've always given me a listen . . .'

'You know so much about London,' Jordan said. 'It's like sort of a secret history. And I do think you've got a point about this baby. There is something weird about how it was killed. But I don't get this fear you have, mate. I don't. I think that maybe you're reading things into stuff that isn't there.'

'Think I'm a tinfoil-helmet merchant.'

'No! But you have to admit it is all a bit conspiracy-theoried up. I know there's been a lot of that lately, given the current climate . . .'

Wilko sighed. Then he wrote something down on a piece of paper in his notebook and handed it to Jordan.

'Be round my place when you get off later,' he said. 'Got something to show you. I'll even make you a spot of tea.'

'This is insane,' Habib Farooqi said to his best mate Lawrence. 'You can't nick off your mum!'

They were outside the school. Loz was smoking a fag while Habib was shoving handfuls of chocolate barfi into his mouth.

'Your mum's going to go proper mental if she's got no money!' Habib said.

'I know!'

'And what about your little brothers? What if your mum's got nothing for tea? How much did you take?'

'A ton.'

114

'Hundred quid?' Habib shook his head.

'Kym wants a grand,' Loz said. 'Me mum had just got her child benefit, innit.'

'Shit, Loz!'

'Can't we go back to selling that cream again?' Loz asked. 'I mean we never done nothing wrong. It was just we saw that boy . . .'

Habib still had some of the contentious capsaicin cream. But that wasn't the point.

'No,' he said.

'But man, I'm a Samsung Galaxy and another grand down.'

Then Habib saw something, or rather someone . . .

Lee had gone straight from his flat to his obbo job in Chigwell, leaving Mumtaz in charge of the office on Green Street. Nobody, or almost nobody, was expected to call, but she had paperwork to catch up on.

It was just gone midday when Mumtaz's mobile rang.

'Is that Marian?' a familiar female voice asked.

'Yes?'

It could only be Danielle.

'It's Danielle,' she confirmed. 'You know, from . . .'

'Of course,' Mumtaz said.

'Just wondering if you're gonna be around today or . . .'

Mumtaz had wondered that herself. Given that Arthur Hobbs had been hostile, she had thought she might give EC4 a rest. But then there was still the issue of the boy . . .

'I met that old man, Mr Hobbs, this morning,' Danielle

115

said. 'I'm going round his house this afternoon. I thought you might like to know.'

Had Mumtaz said, albeit inadvertently, anything that might have made Danielle think she was afraid for someone in that house? She couldn't think of anything.

'Why's he invited . . . ?'

'He seems to like me,' Danielle said. 'I s'pose we're a bit similar in that neither of us is posh. Not like most of them round here.'

'Yes, but why has he invited you?' Mumtaz repeated.

'He asked me before,' she said. 'Said we could have a cup of tea together, look round the old bits of his house. I'm so bored . . .'

Mumtaz felt the hairs on her arms stand up. This was making her anxious even though she didn't know exactly why. After all, why shouldn't an elderly man invite a young woman into his historically unique house? Except that Danielle wasn't interested in history, she was merely a bored young woman who was pregnant – and vulnerable.

She said, 'I've serious doubts whether Mr Hobbs will allow me to come with you.'

'No, he won't,' Danielle said.

'But maybe I'll take the Tube over,' Mumtaz began. 'To be on the spot . . . For you . . .'

'For me?' Danielle laughed. 'What, you think he might kidnap me or something? I could probably get him down with one punch!'

'No, I . . .' But she wondered. Why was Hobbs interested in Danielle and how had he managed to work out that Mumtaz wasn't who she claimed to be? Had she maybe come across him before? Professionally? Had that one small slip of the tongue she'd made in the pub given her away? And why did the old man unnerve her so much? She had no actual proof that it had been Arthur Hobbs who had silently terrorised Loz and Habib when that bloodied boy had answered the door to them. It was very likely to have been him, but . . . She'd not, so far, seen a blond boy, like the one Habib had described to her on the streets of EC4 – but then maybe he was still in that house . . .

'Anyway, that's what I'm doing,' Danielle said and she ended the call.

Loz hadn't seen her and so when Habib said they'd better both get to school, he jogged inside the building and disappeared off to his form room. Habib, however, only followed him so far. As soon as he saw that Loz was way ahead of him, Habib went back out into the street.

And there was Kym Franks, the supposedly pregnant love of Loz's life, smoking a fag and flirting with a boy called Imran who was eighteen and liked everyone to think he was a drug dealer. Habib, who was an astute judge of character for a fifteen-year-old, thought that Imran probably just smoked too much weed.

'Kym?'

She looked round when he said her name.

'What?'

'You pregnant, innit?'

Habib didn't talk like this at home because if he did, his dad would go mad. Even Loz, who spoke 'street' all the time, would have a go if he heard him. 'Man!' he'd say. 'You don't speak like that, stop!' However, on the street, one did use 'street' in order to survive.

Kym, a large white girl whose face was so made up it was almost a mask, said, 'You callin' me a skank, Farooqi?'

Imran, whose family Habib's dad had once described as 'a bunch of free-loading arseholes', smirked.

Kym poked him spitefully in the ribs with an elbow. 'Ow!'

'Ain't no skank,' she said. Then she turned to Habib. 'Where'd you get that from? Bumboy Loz?'

'You told him you was . . .'

She put her hands on her hips. 'That twat tell you he knocked me up?' She laughed. 'He can't get it up, so how he knock anyone up, clever boy?'

'So he . . .'

She sucked her teeth.

'You told him you were pregnant,' Habib said. 'You asked him for money! Said you'd get your dad . . .'

'I don't need no dad to take care of me!' she said. 'I'm a independent woman! What shit you talk, bumboy!'

Imran, who had been watching this exchange, said to the girl, 'You want me to deal with this?'

He was probably planning to shag her.

Kym said, 'Nah, man.'

Habib persisted. 'So you knocked up or ain't ya?'

Kym grabbed him by his collar, which caught Habib off guard. Up close she was even more frightening than she was far away.

'What kind of woman do you think I am, cunt?' she said.

Habib said nothing. It was better that way. He wasn't bothered about Imran but he knew that Kym could do a lot of damage with those sharpened false nails of hers.

Eventually, after staring deeply into his eyes in a flagrantly evil manner, Kym pushed him away.

Habib walked as casually as his shaking legs would allow into school, thinking about what he had learnt. Which was basically nothing. Kym could or could not be pregnant. Obviously she wanted to shag Imran, who was a looker in spite of his stupidity, and she probably wanted him soon, as in that day. So she'd hardly admit to being pregnant in front of him, especially not by Loz. But that didn't mean that she wasn't. It also didn't mean that she *was* either, which was annoying. After robbing his mum's purse, what would Loz do next to get money for that bloody girl?

Habib was not a brave young man, but at that point he took what he would later describe as an 'executive decision'.

So far, so sodding predictable. While the front of Gary Connor's property bristled with CCTV cameras, the back which fizzled out into woods did not. But nobody had crept through the trees so far. Lee wondered whether Gary had something against his younger brother Dillon – apart from a perceived jealousy regarding his wife. Dillon at thirty-five was much closer to Fallon's age. Maybe they simply shared a taste in music? A lot of these older geezers with trophy wives lived in a state of complete paranoia. Lee fully expected to discover absolutely nothing.

He'd seen Fallon once or twice in the garden that morning, with Gary's kid. Yes, she was young and firm of body, but her face was so made-up and possibly Botoxed it was difficult to tell what she might really look like.

He thought about Mumtaz. It was difficult to think of anyone so different from Fallon Connor. But she was considerably younger than him, so was he in some ways similar to Gary? He didn't like to think that he was, but if she found someone else, how would he feel? He tried not to think about it and instead wondered what she was going to do when she went to EC4 to catch up with that Danielle woman.

Even if Danielle turned out to be a useful contact, Mumtaz had made a mistake by admitting she wasn't who she claimed to be. She knew very little about this woman. Had she possibly been swayed by the fact the woman was pregnant?

Of course, that whole situation would come to nothing, but what if it didn't? What . . .

But then Lee was distracted. Someone was walking through the trees at the back of Gary's garden. And Fallon was standing at the back door, looking . . .

Brown had sent him over to the artist's studio to get him out of the way. That was certainly how Jordan felt about his trip over to Trinity Buoy Wharf. The enhanced photographs of the man seen entering St Paul's Churchyard the night the baby was murdered had been emailed over to someone called Jago Sullivan, an artist. Jordan had imagined that this bloke would just sketch out his impression of this man and then email that back, but according to Brown, someone had to babysit the artist.

Jago Sullivan worked in a part of the wharf known as Container City 1. Basically a load of red-painted shipping containers welded together into a low-rise tower block of artist's studios complete with glass balconies. To Jordan it was a rather studied iteration of industrial boho accommodation and he doubted whether the units were cheap to rent. The artist himself, as predicted, had the sort of accent that cost a lot of very expensive schooling, even if he did look as if he'd just rolled out of bed and smelt of skunk weed.

After a somewhat stilted introduction, Jago took Jordan into his studio, which proved to be a very tidy, almost clinical space dominated by ranks of expensive computer equipment. Jago, it seemed, was a digital artist.

'I've had a look at what Melina sent over and I've come up with this,' Jago said as he led Jordan over to a large Macintosh screen.

It was clearly a rough sketch but it did involve some detail.

Jordan said, 'How'd you get from that smudge to this?'

Jago lit a roll-up and said, 'If I told you, I'd have to kill you.'

Jordan smiled. 'Yeah, but seriously, I can't see anything in that enhanced image.'

Jago brought up the picture DS Pinker had sent him

and then pointed out areas of the face where colour tones altered, albeit slightly. It wasn't easy to spot and as Jago explained how he came to the decisions about the face that he did, Jordan couldn't follow all of it. At the end, the artist said, 'This isn't definitive. Something containing so little data can't be, but I do my best. Melina knows that.'

Perhaps uncharitably, Jordan wondered whether this bloke and Melina Pinker were an item. But then he made himself concentrate on the image Jago had drawn. It was then that he saw what he had at first interpreted as a vicious configuration around the man's nose and mouth. It was actually a pipe.

Danielle wasn't answering her phone. Perhaps she was inside the house with the blue door?

Mumtaz sat nursing a cappuccino in a tiny cafe on Carter Lane, not entirely sure why she was there. If Danielle was inside the house with the blue door, then maybe she wasn't taking calls for quite legitimate reasons? But then who didn't answer their phone these days? Her father had recently told her about some man his own age who had answered, or attempted to, his phone during prayers at the mosque. That was insane, but it was also how the world was sometimes.

When she'd finished her coffee, Mumtaz walked out into the damp afternoon air and began to head towards Carter Court. Had she been wrong not to report the boy Habib and Loz had told her about to the police? Between her own need to keep the boys' illegalities secret and Lee's straight-up denial that the incident was anything to worry about, she'd nevertheless been niggled at by doubts.

A newborn baby had been murdered in this area. An innocent child brutally stabbed by someone who was either evil or unhinged. And yet because EC4 was such an exclusive and thinly populated area, there was no talk on the streets about it. Had something like that happened at home in Forest Gate, there would have been at least muted discussion in the newsagents along Woodgrange Road. Here there was little, that Mumtaz could discern, by way of community and she found it unsettling. It was also clear that Danielle found it unsettling too. She wondered whether, in the normal course of events, someone like her would even think about visiting an old bloke like Arthur Hobbs. Maybe she found him interesting? It was all quite normal really and yet, if that were the case, why did Mumtaz feel so uneasy about it?

Almost without any volition on her part, Mumtaz's feet led her to Carter Court and then she stopped. The pub, The Hobgoblin, was shut by the look of it and the court was its usual silent self. Mumtaz was wondering what she should do, when she noticed that the front door of the house next to the pub was open . . .

The picture Gary had supplied of his brother Dillon made identifying the intruder easy. Young, he was probably, Lee surmised, a stepbrother – tall, shaven-headed and loose-limbed. Had Gary's dad perhaps taken a younger wife at some point? Wearing a grey tracksuit with a pair of slightly rotten-looking trainers, Dillon Connor looked like the sort of bloke often seen slouching towards a football match with his hands in his pockets.

Lee raised his phone and took a photograph. A couple of seconds later, Fallon Connor came out of the house and ran into Dillon's outstretched arms. They kissed in a way not usually expected of a brother and his sister-in-law.

In one way it was tediously inevitable, while in another at least it proved that old Gary wasn't losing his marbles.

NINE

There was image after image. All small, all in black and white, all showing something that was beyond abomination. Jordan knew about the Holocaust but he'd never seen images as visceral as these before. These captured evil. Pictures of twisted, agonised corpses, of half-burnt bodies hanging out of incinerators, the bewildered, starved faces of the few survivors.

Wilko put a cup of tea down in front of Jordan and said, 'My dad took them. 1945.'

'What was he doing there?' Jordan asked.

'He was a soldier,' Wilko said. 'Eleventh Armoured Division. They liberated Belsen Concentration Camp. That was some of what they found. My old man never got over it.'

'Yes, but . . .'

'He took them pictures so it wouldn't be forgot. When I was a kid I wondered how it ever could be. Taught all about it at school.'

'So was I,' Jordan said.

'Which is good.' Wilko nodded. 'But you know that some people, more'n you'd think, say that it never happened. Jews, Gypsies, gay people, anyone who opposed the Nazis, six million, disappeared? Where the fuck do these clowns think they went? And what makes me go cold is that this denial is something that's growing. The coming of Trump, of Brexit, it's all on a continuum, fear and hatred of the "other", blaming the "other". And this is where it always leads – death.'

Jordan put the photographs down and drank his tea.

'When I saw that dead kiddie, I knew,' Wilko continued. 'You know the Nazis were well into the occult?'

'Were they?'

'Hitler was a superstitious type. Thought he could begin a thousand-year white supremacist Reich if he could harness the ancient magical powers attributed to Jews.'

'Do Jews have, er, magical powers?' Jordan felt stupid even asking the question.

Wilko shrugged. 'Dunno. Ask Father George. I know we've had magicians and alchemists in this city for centuries, most famous of which, Dr Dee, he weren't Jewish. But he wanted power even if he didn't have nothing against any particular group of people. Occultists and dictators, if you're really unlucky you'll get both kinds in one body, like Hitler. And boy, you know that if

126

you look at these conspiracy theories people put out these days, it's all there.'

'What? Magic stuff?'

'Yeah,' Wilko said.

'Wilko,' Jordan said, 'do you actually believe in magic? I mean if you think that baby's death was part of some sort of ritual, do you think it actually can work?'

'Ah, there's a question.' Wilko sat down. 'I do not know, boy. I think it's possible, but that don't mean it's real. You can argue that magic is just the way in which ancient people tried to impose some sort of order on their lives. That and religion, which is just another kind of magic in my opinion. But . . . What I do know is that people who want to force their views on others will do anything to make that happen. Our system of democracy should stop that happening, but as we're learning there's ways round that. Like religion – ISIS and all that – and magical thinking, as in lazy conspiracy theories to explain things too complicated for a lot of people to be arsed with.'

'So what you gonna do?' Jordan asked. 'I mean Brown's on it. We do have an image of a person of interest now.'

'Some geezer in the churchyard, yeah I know.'

'I feel there's a "but" coming, mate.'

Wilko sighed. 'Yeah.' Then he said, 'Come on, I've cooked some chicken thing for our tea. I'll tell you all about it.'

And then he put the photographs away in a drawer.

* * *

Poor old Gary. Lee didn't know him well, but he'd been around him long enough to realise he wasn't the sort of geezer who liked people seeing him cry.

It had been Gary's idea to meet at the King William. Lee had always felt dodgy about hooking up at a pub, but Gary had insisted. Luckily they'd managed to get a table in a corner, although Lee had noticed a couple of blokes up at the bar looking in their direction.

'I really thought she was the one, you know?' Gary sobbed as he clutched his bottle of Peroni as if his life depended on it.

Lee felt he should maybe run through the photographs he'd taken of Fallon and Dillon together, just to make sure that Gary couldn't fool himself the whole thing had been some sort of mistake. In spite of the cold weather the pair had had sex in the garden. But then they were young. Lee thought better of it and put his camera away.

'Proper mugged me off, the pair of them,' Gary said.

'I'm sorry, mate,' Lee said. 'You asked me to do the job . . .'

'And you done it,' Gary said as he put his hand in his pocket and peeled a handful of fifty-pound notes off a large roll of cash. Handing the money over, he nodded. 'Ta, mate.'

'Sorry it had to work out like this,' Lee said as he sipped his Diet Pepsi. 'Really rough part of the job . . .'

'And he's such a plum!' Gary said as he wiped his eyes and then rubbed his fingers over his buzz-cut head.

All Lee wanted to do was go home via the kebab shop on Woodgrange Road, but Gary clearly wanted to talk.

'I know I look like the sort who'd have words about foreigners moving onto my manor and all that, but that ain't me,' Gary said. 'I'm not no racist. Half the blokes who work for me are black. My old dear's neighbours are Albanian. Lovely people. Keep an eye on Mum for me they do, get her a bit of shopping down Lidl . . . But Dillon! Course he's only me stepbrother. Our dad married his mum when the old man decided he didn't want our old dear no more. Parrot.'

That Gary had done something similar himself wasn't mentioned. Lee nodded.

'And I give that boy a job and . . .' Gary threw his hands in the air. 'I mean, I like footie as much as the next bloke, but he's a hooligan.'

'Who is?'

'Dillon! Keep up!' Gary necked his beer and then raised his hand to the bar to signal to the barman for another.

The beer arrived very quickly. Gary was well known in these parts.

The big man continued. 'I've paid blokes off who want to give the muppet a good hiding. One of my own men. Dillon got into it with him, giving it "Paki" this and "Paki" that! I was embarrassed, you know? I know Iqbal's mum and dad! Lovely people. That's when I sacked the fucker. Brother or no brother. I told that old slag of a mother of his that I wouldn't have it and she just laughed in my face. Fucking trash, the lot of 'em! I told my dad at the time, you marry her and you'll have nothing but ag! But the soppy old twat was besotted! And he'd got her knocked up with Dillon. Bleedin' south of the river scumbags and you know what they're like?'

'Where from?' Lee asked.

'Bermondsey,' he said as he shook his head. 'He's a fucking Lion.'

Lee shook his head.

The Lions, as Millwall Football Club's fans were known, were sworn enemies of West Ham supporters like Gary, and Lee. Famous for their acts of violence, at the height of football hooliganism in the 1970s and 80s they were also known as the Bushwackers.

'So what you gonna do?' Lee asked.

'Dunno,' Gary said. 'I should give the little cunt a good hiding, but then what will that do? I won't lie, I want to.'

'Yeah.'

'As for Fallon?' He shook his head. 'If it weren't for Harrison, she'd be out that door. But I love that boy. There'll have to be consequences. No fucker mugs me off and gets away with it. But I'll have to think it through.'

Gary knew that Lee was an ex-copper and so he'd hardly tell him what he had planned for the unfaithful Fallon, particularly if it involved violence. Lee doubted that it would, given what he knew about Gary, but just in case he said, 'But no rough stuff, mate.'

And then Gary began to cry again.

Scott Brown looked at the artist's impression Jordan Whittington had got from Jago Sullivan and said, 'Who smokes a pipe these days?'

Melina Pinker, the only other officer keeping late vigil with her boss, said, 'Puff-heads?'

Brown shook his head. 'No,' he said. 'Or rather yes, but look at what he's smoking. That's no stoner's pipe. Look at the size of it!'

The pipe, once identified, had turned out to be large. The bowl was carved into an unintelligible shape which appeared as a sort of off-white smudge.

Melina peered at the image. 'Could be a meerschaum pipe, guv.'

Brown narrowed his eyes. 'Blimey, that's a word from the past,' he said. 'But now you come to say it, that light colour . . . My granddad had some meerschaum pipes, think he might have nicked them when he went to Germany to fight the Nazis.'

'It's a kind of clay,' Melina said. 'You see a lot of meerschaum pipes in Turkey. But I think they're mainly for tourists. Souvenirs, you know. Jago reckons he can make out smoke though. So this bloke's smoking . . .'

'Fucking weird,' Brown said. 'I mean like, where do you even buy pipe tobacco these days?'

Melina, who always felt that Brown rather overdid the fitness fanatic schtick, said, 'Er, from a newsagents, at a garage, in the supermarket . . .'

'Yeah, but . . .'

'I did look up actual tobacconists in the City,' Melina said. 'Ones that sell cigars, pipes and snuff. They're few and far between but there are a couple of newsagents. SOCO picked up the usual bunch of dog-ends at the scene . . .'

'But no loose tobacco.'

'Not as far as I know.'

'Mmm.'

'Guv, the image is going to press.'

'Yeah, but it's not brilliant is it?'

Then she said, 'Guv, what about these old tunnels that Wilko talks about?'

'Oh, Christ, not you an' all!' Brown said. 'So where'd you suggest I start looking for them then, Detective Sergeant? Underneath the local Pret? Or maybe I should go into a nearby dry-cleaner's mob-handed and see what's in their cellar?'

Melina looked down at the floor. 'I just thought . . .'

'You just thought that you'd like to have a bloody exorcism.'

'Well what else do we have, guv?' Melina said. 'Some dodgy image of a pipe smoker and, so far, some possible sources of DNA. But if that doesn't match anyone on the system . . .'

'I've said for donkey's years that everyone in this country should be in the system so we don't have situations like this,' Brown said.

Melina stayed quiet. She could see the value of a national comprehensive DNA database, but it still gave her the shudders. Wasn't that something that dodgy regimes run by dictators wanted to do?

Habib was round at Loz's flat. His little brothers were watching telly in their bedroom while Loz's mum was pulling the living room and kitchen apart looking for her lost money.

In Loz's room, Habib was trying to make his mate give the money back.

'Kym's not pregnant,' he'd told a miserable Loz once the two of them were alone.

Loz said, 'She told you?'

She sort of had, and anyway Habib had decided that she wasn't. It was what he truly believed. And it was what he told himself.

Now, however, they were in the arena of Loz's bottomless paranoia.

'I dunno,' he said after he'd had some time to think about it. 'I mean, what if she is?'

'She isn't,' Habib said.

Kym had told him that Loz couldn't get an erection. But he couldn't say that to him. You only accused blokes of not 'getting wood' if you really hated them. Anyway, she'd been coming on to that Imran at the time. She wasn't going to tell him she'd shagged Loz, even if she had.

'You can't get all this money,' Habib continued. 'Thousands and thousands. She's taking the piss.'

'You never said that at first,' Loz said, 'not when we started making the cream.'

'No . . .'

Habib hadn't known what he'd believed back then. All he'd focussed on was the problem – and the amateur chemistry. Loz's situation had given him the opportunity to make actual medical stuff and he'd loved it. That he'd been helping Loz, and possibly some old people in pain too, had been quite secondary to playing Marie Curie in his mum's kitchen.

'Loz, you have to get that money back to your mum,' Habib said. 'She's crying and everything.'

Loz's mum was not a woman who cried easily and so both the boys knew that it was serious.

'Yeah, but if I do that then I've got nothing to give Kym!' Loz said.

Habib lost it. 'She's taking you for a mug!'

'You say that, but what if she ain't?'

And then they were back to where they'd started again.

A couple of boys sat outside the kebab shop on the pavement. Lee ignored them. They weren't drinking, weren't loud, even if they were stoned off their nuts and grease from their doners had solidified round their mouths.

Inside a middle-aged man was getting chips while a large white woman with very fat arms stood miserably in a corner clutching her purse.

Lee went up to the counter and spoke to Haluk the Turkish Cypriot proprietor. A disappointed-looking man in his fifties, Haluk said, 'Evening Lee, what can I get you?'

He could have had something like a chicken shish for a change, but Lee had been lusting after a large doner ever since he'd been in the pub with Gary. He said, 'Large doner, all the trimmings please, mate.'

Haluk nodded and Lee stood to one side to let a young black girl behind him make her order. Then he took his phone out and tried to ring Mumtaz again. But her phone was still dead. Not just unavailable, stone bloody dead. Had she perhaps broken it? If she had, then that was more bloody expense. But then he knew that by even thinking that he was indulging in what she would call a 'displacement activity' – something designed to push his fears for her to one side.

But then how much trouble could she get into scoping out some old house in EC4? Then he remembered the dead baby and, while he was paying Haluk for his kebab, he tried to call Mumtaz again. Still he got nothing.

He brought another number up on his phone and called it.

'That bloke walked into the churchyard,' Wilko said as he ladled a helping of chicken casserole 'thing' into Jordan's bowl.

'He didn't go into any local shops or bars,' Jordan said.

'Maybe he was already pissed,' Wilko said. 'He get picked up by cameras further west?'

'We think he came down High Holborn. If that is him. But before that . . .' Jordan shrugged. 'Like he just sort of appeared and then disappeared . . .'

'Maybe he did.'

Jordan pulled a face. 'Wilko . . .'

'Oh it's been known!' the older man said. 'You won't remember it but a girl called Genette Tate disappeared in Devon in 1978. One minute she was seen riding her bike, next minute her bike was in the middle of a road and she was gone. Never been seen or heard of since. There's places under the earth, behind buildings we don't pay no attention to, places to hide, to sometimes come and go and sometimes to die. You can use every camera in the world, but you'll never find them because you have to know where to look and that can be difficult.'

'You back on the tunnels?'

'Not just me, boy,' Wilko said. 'You know St Paul's

has always been right at the heart of the City. Everything has passed through that patch of ground: Paganism, Catholicism, Protestantism – witches, traitors, magicians, royalty . . .'

'Wilko, yeah, I know this, but even if some sort of ritual has taken place it's probably just deluded people . . .'

'There? In that place?' Wilko shook his head. 'No, boy, it's ramping up again. Look at the Dark Web. That's where the poison spreads the most, but look at people around you too, at politicians. Hate's gaining ground, just like it did in the nineties in the former Yugoslavia. And same as there, the roots are old. Even houses of God can go bad and that place has.'

'St Paul's?'

'Years ago, people were tried in there, put to death in the churchyard. It's my belief unholy ceremonies took place there. It's my belief they still do.'

Jordan frowned.

'Me and Father George been watching the development of nationalism and the dark arts for many years . . .'

'Centred on St Paul's?'

Wilko took a laptop computer down from a shelf and switched it on.

Mumtaz's flat was dark so Lee went to their office on Green Street. But she wasn't there either. He tried her phone again, to no avail, thought about calling Shazia, rejected the idea on account of the fact he didn't want to alarm her, and then began searching Mumtaz's computer for any information about this Danielle she'd met in

EC4. But he couldn't find anything.

He hadn't spoken properly to Mumtaz since he'd had that odd conversation with Wilko and Father George the previous night. They both seemed to be convinced there was some connection between the house with the blue door and the death of that baby in St Paul's Churchyard. Typical of them both, there had been talk of mysterious tunnels leading to and from the cathedral. And because it was a beloved and, in its different incarnations, a truly powerful national symbol, this had been tagged to nationalism. Wilko and George claimed it was rising and both believed it was being assisted by occult forces.

Five years ago, Lee would have just dismissed this as bullshit. But these days he wasn't so sure. A kind of nationalism based purely on emotion and belief was certainly gaining traction, and conspiracy theories involving deeply magical thinking were almost mainstream. Figures from the past were revered to the point of madness in some quarters – Churchill, King Arthur, even monsters like Henry VIII and Mosley. All of this was boosted by the Internet, mainly on social media platforms, and, more worryingly, by the so-called Dark Web where those who didn't want to be found resided.

Lee lit a cigarette and then went to the tiny galley kitchen at the back of the office to pick up an old saucer to use as an ashtray. He never usually smoked in his office – it was illegal – but his inability to get in touch with Mumtaz was worrying him. Idly he began sorting through bits of paper on her desk. Though she was by nature a tidy person, he'd noticed her become more messy as she attempted to balance her work, her home life and her relationships with her stepdaughter Shazia and with Lee. In reality the two of them got very little time together. It made him feel sad even though Lee knew that, at the present time, there was no way around it.

Eventually he found an envelope covered in all sorts of words, including 'Danielle' and beside it the word 'Saint'. Was that her surname? Was that even a surname? Lee sat back in Mumtaz's chair. She'd told him she was going to EC4. She knew he didn't really approve but she'd done it anyway; she'd been light on details.

The police, as far as Lee knew, had interviewed the few local people in the area plus the clergy in the cathedral about the dead baby. Not that Mumtaz had gone to the cathedral but . . . He brought up the cathedral website. In reality he did it to give himself something to do. But then he saw something that made him draw in breath. Now how had the police missed that?

For a man still in his twenties, Jordan didn't have a great deal of interest in tech. Like everyone he had a mobile phone and a computer, he even had a Twitter account, but it wasn't something that he thought about often. In terms of online crime, there were other officers who dealt with that. And while he'd seen the odd off-colour website online, particularly when he'd been a teenager, he'd never seen anything like this.

He looked away from the screen, up at Wilko and said, 'This is nuts.'

'Think that's bad, you should see some of the US sites,' Wilko said.

Jordan looked back at the screen. 'This is incitement to racial hatred,' he said. 'Reminds me of those Al Qaeda sites.'

'No different,' Wilko said. 'Islamic fundamentalism, white nationalism, it's all a racist, misogynistic pack of lies. Laughable to you and me but deadly serious to those who believe it, as well as those in the political establishment who want these arse'oles to vote for them. They cosy up and it's all going on under our noses, while certain elements in our governments say we have to listen to this bollocks because it's "freedom of speech". It's bullshit.'

'Yeah, but what about St Paul's?'

Wilko sat down beside his guest. 'Ah, well that's a bit more difficult to define,' he said. 'There you have to trust me to a certain extent. Or rather you have to trust Father George. He's a nose for the bad shit and if he tells me that somewhere's not good, tainted like, then . . .'

His phone rang and Wilko picked it up. As Jordan watched him listen to the person on the other end, he was struck by how grave his face became.

TEN

Lee was woken up by the sound of his phone pinging. He had a text.

Raising his head up from Mumtaz's desk was painful and he was horrified by how strongly the office smelt of kebab and fags. He hadn't meant to fall asleep, but after he'd called Wilko at nearly midnight it had just sort of happened.

He picked up his phone and brought up his texts. He felt a huge rush of relief when he saw that the new text had come from Mumtaz. It said, *Sorry been out of communication. My husband's mother is sick and so I've gone to be with her. Back as soon as I can.*

Mumtaz's husband, Ahmet, was dead. His mother, he thought, lived in Bangladesh. Shazia, Mumtaz's stepdaughter, had told him that her grandmother hated

Mumtaz. She blamed Mumtaz for her son's death, with some cause as it happened, and had never thought her good enough for her son.

He called Shazia. It took her a while to pick up. Having finished her degree in criminology at Manchester, Shazia was now living back in London with her boyfriend, Krishnan. A uniformed police officer, Krishnan had recently taken his detective exams and was waiting to hear whether he had been successful. Shazia was due to go to Hendon Police College in 2020. They were young, in love and they rented a tiny, if homely flat in Rotherhithe. Whenever Mumtaz or anyone called them, the couple seemed to have just got up or were still in bed.

'Shaz?'

'Lee?' She sounded sleep-sodden. Lee looked at his watch. But then it was only 7 a.m.

'Sorry,' he said. 'Didn't realise it was so early. Did I get you up?'

'No,' she said. 'Krish has just literally left for work and I was about to get myself some breakfast.'

'Shaz,' he said and then he wondered what he should say. He didn't want to alarm her.

'Lee, is everything alright? Is Amma OK?'

'Yeah, yeah . . . Look Shaz, I don't want to pry or nothing . . .'

'Lee, Krish is as lovely as he seems,' she said.

Her father, Ahmet, had been a desperate and brutal man: a gambling addict, he'd been deeply in debt to a criminal gang who eventually exacted part of said debt by killing him. Mumtaz, his second wife, had watched him bleed out after being attacked on Wanstead Flats. Both she and Shazia had suffered sexual abuse at Ahmet's hands. Lee had over the years become very protective of both of them.

'Yes, I know,' Lee said. He liked the young man a lot. 'No, Shaz, it's about your dadi . . .'

Dadi was her father's mother.

Shazia's voice became cold. Her father's mother had all but rejected her, especially now that she was living in 'sin' with a Hindu. 'What about her?'

'She's ill, or . . . ?'

'She's never been well in her life,' Shazia said. 'Been dying ever since I can remember. She never does it though. If she is ill, it's just situation normal. Why?'

'I heard she might be unwell.'

'From Amma?'

'Er, yes.'

'You sound unsure.'

One day she was going to make a good detective.

'You know what your amma can be like,' Lee said. 'She's . . .'

'Is everything alright, Lee?'

As far as he knew, it was and he said so. Shazia said, 'What's this about Dadi? Not that I give a shit, you understand.'

He told her. Not about Mumtaz going missing, just about how she had told him she'd gone to see her mother-in-law.

'I can't see why,' Shazia said when he'd finished. 'Even with Dadi living in Birmingham now, Amma wouldn't go to see her and Dadi wouldn't want that. Anyway, Auntie Shamima wouldn't let Amma in even if Dadi wanted to see her.'

'She your dad's sister?'

'Yes. Right bitch,' Shazia said. 'If she's moved Dadi over here from Bangladesh you can be sure she's only done it for one reason, and that's to get her hands on Dadi's house in Dhaka, or the money she got for it when she sold up. But I don't know, Lee. Amma knows I don't give a shit about any of Dad's family. Ring her on her mobile.'

But he didn't. Maybe Shazia would, but he doubted it. She took no risks when it came to contacting her father's family and would disapprove of Mumtaz having anything to do with them. Lee just hoped he hadn't made Shazia feel uneasy about Mumtaz. He would hate to think he'd alarmed her over nothing. But to just go off in the middle of a job was uncharacteristic and he felt uneasy. His phone call to Wilko had been disturbing too. What he'd told the older man had upset him. Wilko had promptly gone off into his bonkers theories about St Paul's.

DI Scott Brown sat on the corner of Jordan's desk and said, 'Hate to say it, but you're right.'

Jordan looked up.

'About churchyard closing times,' Brown said.

'Oh.'

The previous evening Wilko had taken a call from that Newham PI, Lee Arnold, telling him that the gates into and out of St Paul's Churchyard closed at 4 p.m. during the winter months. So why had they been open the night the baby died, and had the police asked St Paul's staff about this?

'Seems they were supposed to have been shut, but they weren't,' Brown continued.

'So who was supposed to do that?' Jordan asked.

Brown sighed. 'Now there's the point,' he said. 'We don't know.'

Jordan frowned.

'Apparently they, the clerics, are going to investigate and get back to me,' Brown said.

'Don't they have, like, routines for such things, guv?'

'Seems not,' Brown said. 'Although I personally don't buy that. Anyway, I said I need to hear from them today. Not very happy about it they weren't, but then . . .' He shrugged. 'Meanwhile, not exactly being on the ball about church stuff, I'd like you to get into contact with Father George, try and find out if he thinks this is normal – although why I'd use the words "Father George" and normal in the same sentence . . .'

Brown walked away, leaving Jordan alone with some very strange thoughts. After his dinner with Wilko the previous night, he'd been left wondering about what was real and what wasn't. Wilko and Father George seemed to be convinced the world as they knew it was being attacked by right-wing occult forces. Certain members of the clergy were also involved. But then weren't the priest and Wilko peddling conspiracy theories themselves?

When the so-called 'culture war' had started in the wake of the Brexit vote in 2016, the 'sides' involved had seemed pretty straightforward. Either you were a hard-working, patriotic, working-class, often older person who wanted to leave the EU, or you were a liberal, educated, rather up-yourself type who wanted to remain. Orchestrated, so some felt, by the same upper classes who had always controlled everything, Brexit, it seemed, was designed to benefit both the very rich and the very poor. But it was more nuanced than that. Above the level of those who had simply voted with their guts, some had vested interests on both sides of the equation and many of those were not always who they seemed.

Jordan scrolled through the numbers on his phone until Father George's came up.

Long, long ago when she'd been a teenager, Mumtaz had broken her ankle. She'd fallen down the stone stairs that led to her parents' basement. The bones of her tibia and fibula had snapped and she'd had to go to hospital to have her leg set. Afterwards she'd been on morphine for a couple of days. She remembered how that had felt very well. She felt like that now.

She knew intellectually that she had opened her eyes, but there were no further clues. She couldn't see. Not a thing. Had she gone blind somehow, or was she somewhere so completely dark . . . ?

She put a hand down to where she felt her legs were and felt them. They definitely existed. She poked them with her fingers and experienced some pain. This was good, but where was she and why?

Pushing against a hard, slightly gritty surface, she sat

up. She remembered seeing the pub in Carter Court, The Hobgoblin. It had been quiet. She'd looked at it as she had walked towards a blue door and then . . . nothing.

But had the blue door been something real or something from the dream she'd just had about a massive cityscape that existed in a vast hole, like a bomb crater? God, she'd been terrified! It had put her in mind of an old film, *Blade Runner*, where Harrison Ford had whizzed around a dystopian skyline in a flying car.

And then she remembered. Not how it had happened, she had no idea about that. But what had happened. She'd been pushed and then she'd flown through space.

There was, George Feldman often thought, a lot to thank God for. Trees were a popular choice; friendship, comfortable shoes, cheesecake and now a telephone call from a young police officer he barely knew.

He excused himself from Mrs Chalmers' enormously oppressive lounge, not to mention her low opinion of her new neighbours ('hippies!') and walked out into the old woman's large, dark hallway. As soon as Jordan Whittington spoke, George felt an imaginary cold finger run up his spine.

'The clergy are saying it was an accident,' Jordan said. 'They say they've got no formal procedures for shutting the cathedral at night.'

'Who says this?' George asked. 'Do you have a name?'

The young man paused for a moment, possibly looking at notes. Then he said, 'It was a secretary from the office of the Very Reverend Canon Palmer. It's him, according

147

to my boss DI Brown, who is responsible for the building and therefore its security as well as its upkeep.'

'That's true,' George said.

'Do you know this Canon Palmer, Father George?'

'No, I don't.'

The old priest he had seen when he'd been to the cathedral, with his brother Barry, had not been a canon. He'd been too grey, unkempt and ground down to attain high office. The modern church needed slick, not eccentric faces these days, as George knew only too well. But who had the old man been and why had he talked, without prompting, about evil and sacrifice?

Jordan said, 'Because we're possibly going to have to go back into St Paul's and question the clergy again.'

'Mmm. Of course.'

'I've a list of those the team questioned before. DI Brown's given them until this evening to get back to us by phone. But if they don't, then I have to go out and speak to them in person. Thing is, if you could spare the time to come with me . . .'

'Of course I will,' George said. 'Although how you will explain my presence, I don't know. I am not Father Brown and this isn't the Cotswolds.'

The popular G. K. Chesterton novels about a crime-solving Catholic priest called Father Brown had been turned into a TV series years ago. It was now a staple of afternoon television.

'I'm out of my depth,' Jordan admitted.

'Does your superior know about my presence?'

'Of course,' Jordan lied. DI Brown had asked Jordan

to consult Father George, not potentially take him along. But when Brown had spoken to him about the clerics at St Paul's, Jordan had got the distinct impression they were not keen to share their processes and procedures with anyone.

Did George know he was lying? Jordan felt that he probably did, but the priest agreed to accompany him anyway. Which was the main thing.

George, for his part, felt cold when he ended the call. Everything he had picked up about the cathedral, everything he'd discussed with Wilko seemed to have a concrete base in what the young officer had told him. And that was disquieting.

Lee liked Mumtaz's family. He liked her parents, her brothers and her daughter. Furthermore, he cared about them – which affected his job. And that was wrong. He knew he should just phone up her father and ask him whether or not she was with her mother-in-law. But if he did that he would upset the entire Huq family. Hate was not too strong a word to use about the way the Huqs felt about the Hakim family – Shazia aside. Through Ahmet they had brought pain and shame to Mumtaz and her family, and there was no contact between them. Indeed, Baharat Huq had once told Lee that if 'those snakes' ever tried to get back in good odour with any of them he would take out an injunction. So if he told Baharat where his daughter was, there could be consequences. And so it came to pass that all of Lee's misgivings about becoming emotionally involved with his business partner came crashing into his mind.

And he still didn't really know where she was.

Because he'd been a serving police officer himself, Lee knew that because she hadn't been missing for twenty-four hours, the police wouldn't look for her yet. They would also argue that in light of the text from her phone, she wasn't missing. They would suggest Lee contact her mother-in-law. But if he did that and she was there, then that would probably be interpreted by Mumtaz as interference on his part. It wouldn't matter were she just an employee, but she wasn't. She was the woman he loved. And she was fiercely independent.

However, Shazia knew and maybe she would call Mumtaz? But then he knew she wouldn't if she thought she was with her grandmother. And anyway, why would Mumtaz go to see the old woman? She owed her nothing. As far as Lee could tell there was only mutual hatred between the two. Why had she gone there?

He took his phone out of his pocket and sent her a text. *Why are you with your mother-in-law?*

The house was full. Men like his dad and women like his grandma. People his teachers always tried to avoid on parents' evening. Mr Becker, who taught English, probably thought they were drunk or on drugs. He was teetotal and never stopped going on about it. But these people weren't drunk or on drugs; they were the way they were without any sort of help from addictive substances – most of them.

The boy had dreams. In a room with no windows, unable to distinguish night from day, he observed things that could be real and they made him sick. He couldn't eat, no matter what he was brought. And that was because when all this started what he'd seen had been real and he couldn't get it out of his head.

He'd always thought his dad was just an arse'ole, a bit of a loud 'I am', a wanker. He'd never imagined what he had proven himself to actually be. His dad was a cunt and what was more, he was probably the most twisted cunt the boy had ever met.

Once freed from the strictures of Mrs Chalmers' gloomy parlour, George Feldman had the rest of the day to himself. He knew he should really use the time to compose his weekly sermon, but he really didn't feel like sitting on his arse for hours on end, staring into space. He rang his brother Barry, then got on the Tube and got off at Chancery Lane.

'This time I decided to take no chances,' Barry said as he rose to his feet to greet his brother. They met in a restaurant of Barry's choice, an Argentinian place, famed for its excellent beef.

'No more little bits of things on sharing plates,' Barry continued. 'I've a mind towards chateaubriand and a bottle of Merlot to kick things off . . .'

George shrugged. 'Whatever floats your boat.'

They both sat down and Barry ordered the wine.

'You're around and about a lot these days,' Barry said. Intense beefy smells from the kitchen were making his stomach growl with hunger. 'Still trying to root out evil in St Paul's?'

'Something like that.'

George wanted to be on the spot if and when Constable Whittington called. He also wanted to wander. Although heavily bombed in World War II, the streets around the cathedral were ancient in origin and of course what was underneath them was moot.

He'd heard things about the tunnels from another exorcist, or 'deliverance minister' as his 'low' church's more traditionally Protestant colleagues insisted upon calling it. The Rev. Stephen Masters was vicar of a church in Hertfordshire where guitars were a regular feature and people often spoke in 'tongues'. All very American to George's way of thinking. But then all sorts attended the occasional meetings of the south-east's exorcist community.

'Call me Steve', as the Rev. Masters had insisted everyone do, said he'd seen documents alluding to Wren's original architectural designs for St Paul's – which included for sure one underground passage leading to the Choir School, as well as the remains of some older subterranean structures associated with the mediaeval cathedral. This, the precursor to Wren's church, had burnt down in 1666 during the Great Fire. And it was this cathedral that 'Call me Steve' believed was the source of what he described as the 'resident evil' present in the building.

When the UK had been a Catholic country under Queen Mary I, the cathedral had been inhabited by the Holy Inquisition. Within its walls, people had been questioned about their faith, about their interactions with alleged demons and witches. Rooms and passageways underneath the cathedral, it was believed, had been used as interrogation and torture chambers.

George and Barry shared a large tenderloin cut of beef, after which the priest felt distinctly stuffed. That 'Steve' George remembered reminded him of that young priest 'Call me Harry' in the cathedral. Sitting back rather wearily in his chair he asked his brother, 'Are you having anything else?'

'Well, another bottle of Merlot won't go amiss,' Barry said. 'And I may glance at the dessert menu.'

George knew of old that his brother would do far more than just glance. It was already almost three and Barry was clearly in for the duration of the afternoon. There were worse places to wait for a phone call, although George really wanted to get out and stretch his legs. He said, 'I think I may have to push on soon.'

Barry sighed. 'You've never been what one might call a trencherman, have you?'

'Not really. But it's been nice spending more time together lately.'

'Even if your real motive is the pursuit of evil?' Barry asked.

George rose to his feet. 'I can't ignore it,' he said. 'If I did that, I couldn't live with myself.'

Gary Connor had paid his bill. As far as Lee was concerned that was the end of it. But now here he was on the phone.

Lee had been on an obbo when Gary had first called and so he'd ignored it. A very nice elderly lady from Leytonstone had wanted to know what her toy-boy husband had been up to at a house in Canning Town. She wasn't going to be pleased.

Once he'd spoken to the woman, Lee phoned Gary.

'It's Lee,' he said. 'What's up, mate?'

This time it was Gary's turn to be otherwise engaged, but he did at least answer.

'Fucking temperamental jacuzzi in Loughton,' he puffed – probably wrestling with some valve. 'Wanna put some more work your way.'

'Fine by me,' Lee said. 'What's the coup, mate?'

'I'll put it all in an email later,' Gary said. 'Basically, you'll be working out Dagenham.'

'Sweet.'

DI Brown and DS Pinker dived out as soon as the results came through. All info about men smoking pipes was temporarily pushed to one side. It wasn't that often a DNA test came back a direct hit, but on this occasion that had happened. The dead child's DNA pointed directly at a man currently banned for multiple drink-driving violations. Brown and Pinker were off to south London to question him. The rest of the team followed up on leads pertaining to men at or near the scene the night the child had died. Jordan, deputising for Brown, waited for the clergy to call him from St Paul's.

He wasn't comfortable around religious 'types'. All that airy-fairy spiritual stuff left him cold. On the few occasions he'd been to church with Nana Willi, all that speaking in tongues and falling on the floor business had done his head in. He'd no doubt his mum's family got a lot out of it. They were always so happy in church and what they learnt there really did inform their lives. They were always out and about doing good things in the community and Nana Willi particularly was the soul of generosity, to both those close to her and complete strangers. But still, Jordan couldn't make himself like the pastors who led the worship in that church. They were far too snappily dressed and had cars only rich people drove. He didn't buy the argument that as community leaders they could 'hardly be seen driving around in old rust buckets', as Nana Willi always argued.

The clerics at St Paul's, however, were of another order. Very 'establishment', in spite of a sort of slightly casual attitude Jordan did not trust. Father George was really weird but, in a way, Jordan felt more at ease with him than any of the others. Maybe it was because he was friends with Wilko? Not that he'd probably pass a sanity assessment himself. But Wilko, for all his strange facts about London and his odd beliefs about the place, did care. Whatever he was, his motives were good – which was something Granddad Bert had always taught him was 'a measure of a person'.

Brown's phone rang then, making Jordan, who had been almost asleep were he honest, jump.

George Feldman's first experience of St Paul's Cathedral had happened when he was ten. Unlike his brother, he'd not been taken on a school trip to the cathedral, but had visited with his father. At the time, and just as Barry still did, the Feldman family lived in the Middle Temple of the famous London Inns of Court. Close to the cathedral, Feldman senior had one day taken it upon himself to visit the massive church with his youngest son. Back then the place had still been scarred by centuries of London smogs, and so George recalled the building as a vast black hulk. Inside it had only been lit by candles, which had given George's first exposure an eerie feel.

However, it was the area around the cathedral that had really made an impression on George that day. In their attempt to bomb the cathedral during World War II, Hitler's Luftwaffe had destroyed many of the streets around the great church, including what had once been the centre of the city's publishing trade, Paternoster Row. In the 1960s when George and his father walked those streets, Paternoster Row had been rebuilt as a drab ode to concrete known as Paternoster Square. His father had hated it and had avoided walking through it, preferring instead to take George across Ludgate Hill into the little tangle of streets that still retained some of their original buildings.

And although many of those buildings were in a poor state of repair, there was at least an authenticity to this area, centred around a street called Carter Lane, that spoke to George of a Dickensian London he had never known. Back then it had been dark, slightly frightening and threaded with mist from the river.

Today much of that had changed and Carter Lane had gained many new, much brighter buildings in between the old. With few people about, however, it still had a slightly menacing feel. It produced in George almost the exact same sensation of tingling dread that he had experienced as a ten-year-old boy.

George walked into the tiny space that was Carter Court and looked at the old pub that stood opposite the entrance. The Hobgoblin. In an area so freighted with symbolism it was difficult to look at the name of this pub without getting a shudder down the spine. Hobgoblins were spirits associated with homes and were, since the coming of Christianity, considered disruptive and mischievous, if not downright evil.

However, this pub was a Victorian structure and so it had been named relatively recently. George couldn't remember the place from his youth, but then that was a long time ago.

'Hello.'

He hadn't noticed the young woman now at his side. She was heavily pregnant.

'Oh, um . . .'

'Pub's open if you want a pint,' she said. Then, probably because she noticed his dog collar, she added, 'Not that you . . .'

'Oh, I can assure you that priests do drink,' George said.

She smiled. She had a pretty face.

George's phone rang. He said, 'Excuse me.'

She walked away, towards the pub, as George took the call from Jordan Whittington.

'Shaz . . .'

Lee Arnold hadn't meant to call Mumtaz's daughter

157

again, but now he wasn't just anxious, he was frightened.

'What is it?' the girl asked. He could hear other people talking and laughing in the background. She was probably out with mates.

'I've still not heard from your mum,' Lee said. 'Can you give me your grandmother's number so I can check up on her?'

'She's OK, Lee,' Shazia said. 'Apart from having to listen to Dadi's shit, she's fine.'

'Probably,' he said. 'But . . .' How much should he tell her? He didn't want to make Shazia paranoid too.

'Look, I'll do you a favour and call Dadi,' Shazia said. 'If Mum is there and some random white bloke asks for her then the old girl will give her shit.'

It was a fair point. Also, if he did call and Mumtaz was fine, which she probably was, she'd be angry with him for checking up on her.

'Thanks Shaz,' Lee said. 'To be honest, can't think why she might be there anyway . . .'

She laughed. 'You're so not Asian, are you,' she said. 'So they're still Mum's in-laws until she marries again. Of course she's gonna jump if they ask her to do something.'

Being thin was something Loz had always felt gave him an advantage in life. Habib, who struggled to keep his weight down, thought that being thin was a gift from God. However, on this occasion, Loz did find himself wondering whether it was some sort of curse. Kym, pregnant or not, was a big girl and when she pinned him to the wall outside school, he knew he was going to struggle to free himself.

As she pushed her face into his, reminding him of the one time they'd had sex in her dad's garage, Loz cringed in fear.

'Where's my money?' she hissed. 'You really want my dad to come round yours and batter your mum?'

'No . . .'

'So where's—'

'How do I know you're really pregnant?' Loz blurted. Why he hadn't asked this a long time ago was precisely why his heart was hammering now. Not only did Kym have a violent dad, she was violent herself.

She paused for a moment before she failed to answer.

'What you say to me, batty boy?'

Although white, she liked to use the same slang as some of the local black girls. 'Batty boy' was a derogative term for a gay boy.

Loz, for whom logic wasn't usually a default position, nevertheless said, 'I can't be gay and get you up the . . .'

'You a baby daddy now so you need to pay!' Kym said. 'And even if you don't want no child, you still need to pay for an abortion, you get me?'

Loz said nothing. He'd put the money he'd nicked from his mum's purse back.

From somewhere he managed to get it together to say, 'How do I know you're telling the truth?'

This was the second time he'd challenged her and this time his audacity made her suck her teeth in fury. She also loosened her grip on him, which allowed Loz to run.

ELEVEN

After an unknowable amount of time, Mumtaz managed to find her handbag. Crawling on hands and knees on a rough and uneven floor, she eventually tracked it down to somewhere in front of what felt like a wall. There was still not even a pinpoint of light and so she had to go through the bag to find out what was in there using only the sense of touch. Predictably her phone had disappeared. Whoever had put her in this place had obviously taken it.

Had they just simply destroyed it, or had they taken it in order to use it for something? And anyway, who were 'they'? As far as Mumtaz could remember she'd walked into the house with the blue door, Arthur's house, because the blue door had been open. Then – falling. Nothing before, only this incessant darkness after.

Once she'd investigated her handbag again and having still found that her phone was missing, Mumtaz decided she would try and stand up. Maybe if she could follow this wall along she might find a door. But standing proved to be more difficult than she had imagined; her first attempt at getting to her feet resulted in her knees giving way and she fell back down onto the floor.

They had been expecting them. As Father George and Jordan walked into the cathedral, they were met by a posse of clerics headed by the Very Reverend Canon Palmer and the young priest 'Call me Harry'. Apart from those two there were two middle-aged men, one white, the other black, and a small elderly white woman.

Canon Palmer made the introductions – although George could still only remember 'Call me Harry' and so it was a bit pointless from his perspective. Introductions made, the Canon suggested they all repair to the chapter house next door for tea and more private surroundings. Jordan, who clearly didn't understand the ways of the Church, looked alarmed. To him it seemed as if the clergy were digging in for a long session. But as they moved out of the cathedral, George whispered to him.

'It's just what they do,' he said. 'It won't take for ever.'

The chapter house was a red-brick building, also designed by Christopher Wren, which was used by the cathedral staff for meetings. Ushered into a large room lined with dark wood, George and Jordan were offered tea, biscuits and cake before they all sat down to talk.

The canon opened the proceedings with, 'I understood

from DI Brown that he would be attending.'

'He's detained,' Jordan said. 'Sends his apologies.'

'Mmm.' He smiled. 'Well, Constable, Father George, I do feel, I must say, that I don't know what I may be able to add to what has already been said on this matter of the gates to the churchyard. I have questioned my staff and while we are all very sorry, of course, that this omission took place, it was merely an error.'

'Who is responsible for closing the gates at night?' Jordan asked.

According to Brown, the cathedral staff had told him there were no set procedures for this activity. Brown had found that difficult to believe.

'The security of the cathedral precinct is the responsibility of us all,' the canon said. 'Although strictly all security matters devolve to me . . .'

'So you were responsible,' Jordan said.

The clerics looked uncomfortable. But the canon smiled. 'We are only human.'

Jordan looked at Father George, who said, 'Canon, with respect, I find it difficult to accept that a building as precious as this doesn't have security procedures set in stone. My own church, a small parish church . . .'

'With respect, Father,' the canon said, 'a parish church is a small—'

'Small it may be, but I still open the gates when the time on the board outside states, and I close them at the appointed time too. It's important.' Then something occurred to him and he said, 'Where's the old priest?'

'Old priest?'

163

'When I came a couple of days ago there was an old priest,' he said. 'Spoke to me just after you talked to me, Harry.'

'Call me Harry' smiled and then said, 'I saw no old priest I'm afraid, Father George. I must have missed him.'

'We have no old priest here,' the canon put in.

'Maybe he was visiting?' Harry said.

George was on the point of alluding to the old priest's fears but knowing it would do no good, he kept his counsel.

Jordan meantime had been thinking. He said, 'Canon, if as you say, both you and your staff are responsible for cathedral security, and while you have kindly given us a list of those on duty the night of the murder, I wonder whether each one of those people including yourself, could tell us exactly what you were doing when you were meant to be securing the building?'

The canon smiled. 'We can,' he said. 'It will take a little time . . .'

'I wondered whether we might do that now. Here.'

No one spoke or moved. Smiles already on faces became frozen.

The canon said, 'We can, although as I am sure you will appreciate, Constable Whittington, recalling an event, some days ago, that had little meaning at the time requires some thought. Personally I think that maybe a period of reflection may be in order, certainly for myself. In addition, I imagine you would like a written account, for your records?'

'Well, yes, I . . .'

'Good. Well that's agreed.' He stood. 'Gentlemen, ladies . . .'

164

The other clerics stood now and George felt his heart sink. The canon had taken control. Jordan's lack of experience and lowly rank had allowed him to assert himself in a way that was playing out as a mild rebuke of the young officer. It made him feel both angry and chilled to his core. This was what the Church did when it was protecting itself: it captured the narrative.

Jordan, standing now, said, 'Er, well thank you . . .'

'You are most welcome.'

It was then that George said, 'Canon, may I ask a favour before we go, please?'

'You may.'

'Constable Whittington doesn't know the cathedral well. I wondered whether I could show him round.'

'The cathedral is closed,' the canon said.

'Yes, but . . .'

'I'll show you round,' the small elderly woman said.

'Mrs Hardwick . . .'

'It'll be my pleasure, Canon,' the woman said.

He remained motionless for a moment and then he made a tight smile and said, 'That's fine then. Good evening, gentlemen.'

The canon bowed and then led his staff out of the room without another word. Alone with George and Mrs Hardwick, Jordan, looking helpless, said, 'So what now?'

George, smiling at the elderly woman, said, 'I think we'd like to start with the crypt if you don't mind, Mrs Hardwick.'

* * *

'They got my sample mixed up with someone else.'

DI Scott Brown sighed. 'They' always did it seemed. Apparently police DNA sample results existed in a sort of 'results salad', where they were all chucked in and swirled about to create a large mess-bowl designed to entrap the innocent.

Brown leant across the table towards the tall, skinny middle-aged man and said, 'Colin, I can take another sample from you now if you want.'

Colin Macbeth's eyes darted everywhere except Brown's face and then he said, 'Yeah. So do it.'

This happened a lot. Someone reeking of guilt, usually a man, fronting up to an investigating officer about something he knew he could only lose. But then of course that sample too would be 'lost', 'contaminated', he would have been fitted up in some way.

Brown said, 'Listen Colin, you're not the first bloke to have put his dick inside someone he shouldn't . . .'

'I don't know nothing about no baby!'

'Maybe you don't,' Melina Pinker said, 'but you're its father.'

'I'm not!'

Brown switched tack.

'Look,' he said, 'we need to find the mother. We're not ascribing blame for the child's death to either parent at this stage, but they may know . . .'

'I don't know who killed it!' Colin said. 'I've got nothing to do with it!'

'This was a newborn,' Brown persisted. 'Its mother may need medical help. Maybe she's been attacked by whoever took the baby. You thought of that? Maybe the killer has taken her somewhere, is holding her hostage? Maybe she killed the child herself? All we need from you is a name, Colin. A name and we can release ya.'

'I don't know!' He shrugged. 'I don't!'

Brown looked at Pinker and sighed. It was going to be a long night.

Lee Arnold was in the car on his way home when Shazia rang. He pressed to receive the call and said, 'Shaz.'

'Lee, she's not there,' Shazia said. She sounded worried and so she should be. If Mumtaz wasn't with her mother-in-law, then where was she?

'I called Amma's dad,' Shazia continued. 'He's no idea where she is. I told him not to tell her mum . . .'

'Good thinking,' Lee said. Mumtaz's mother would collapse if she knew what was going on. Bad enough that old Baharat had to know. But at least now they knew that Mumtaz was missing rather than just hiding somewhere for some reason.

'Lee, what are we going to do?' Shazia said.

Lee looked at the time on his phone. Wilko was still on duty.

'I'll report her missing,' he said.

'Where was she that you last know of?' Shazia asked.

'The City,' Lee said. He changed course and headed for Bishopsgate Police Station.

'Oh, Lee, what can I do?'

'Nothing,' he said. 'Is Krish home yet?'

'No,' she said. 'In about an hour.'

'Tell him what's happened and keep in touch,' Lee said.

'I'm off to Bishopsgate now. I've an old mate there who'll make sure they get onto it.'

'Lee, do you know . . .'

'I've got a few leads,' he said. 'Just let me get on with it, Shaz. Soon have her home.'

He ended the call. Now chilled to the bone by shock, he turned the car heater up and switched his radio off. He needed to concentrate so he didn't have an accident, because he was shaking.

Jordan left a message for DI Brown and then followed George and Mrs Hardwick into St Paul's Crypt. Like Wilko, George was of the opinion that the crypt was the source of underground tunnels which, if true, could mean that whoever killed the baby may have got into the cathedral complex via those. It was typical Wilko, fanciful as hell. But it did make sense, especially in the context of the old pre-Wren cathedral. Surrounded by buildings occupied in service to the great church, the tunnels could have provided a much-welcomed respite from the stinking conditions prevalent in mediaeval London.

George let Mrs Hardwick show them around. They saw Nelson's tomb, a stern-looking black marble sarcophagus originally made, she said, for Henry VIII's one-time champion, later enemy, Cardinal Wolsey. Apparently Nelson's body had been sent back to England for burial in a barrel of brandy. Apparently some of those accompanying the corpse had helped themselves to his ad hoc embalming fluid and got roaring drunk. It was all very interesting, but Jordan was keen to get back to the station to find out about the man Brown and Pinker had gone to question.

He heard George say, 'What I'd really like to see is the OBE Chapel, if you don't mind.'

'Of course.' The elderly woman had a nice smile. 'It's at the eastern end along here.'

They followed her through vaulted ceilinged passageways and along marble paths until they came to a small chapel.

Mrs Hardwick said, 'This is the Order of the British Empire Chapel. The Order itself was instigated by George V in 1917 to honour people not eligible for gallantry medals in the Great War. The banners on the right are those of the Sovereign, on the left of the Grand Master of the Order.'

'Fascinating. May we look around?' George asked.

'Of course.'

He grabbed Jordan's arm and pulled him towards the small altar, while Mrs Hardwick sat down in a chair and appeared to contemplate a stained-glass window.

Once they were behind the altar, George said, 'We're looking for something that could be a door or hatch . . .'

The chapel was quite unadorned and so it was difficult to see where something like that might be hidden. Jordan saw George discreetly pull up the altar cloth with his foot. *Why here?* Jordan wondered but he didn't say anything. The next person who spoke was Mrs Hardwick.

'If you're looking for a tunnel you won't find one,' she said.

George stopped in his tracks. She walked over towards them.

'They were all sealed many years ago,' she said.

So they had existed!

'Well, more correctly, some were sealed while others collapsed during the Blitz,' she said. She smiled. 'I share your concerns.'

George frowned.

'About the child that was sacrificed,' she said. 'You know, before this was a church it was a pagan temple. Sacrifices were made to the gods of the original Britons here. People then knew no better. Now they do, which has turned what was once ignorance into something quite darker.'

Jordan said, 'What do you mean?'

'I mean I share Father George's fears,' she said. 'And those of Father Edward.'

'Father Edward?'

'The priest you saw, the old one.'

'So he is attached to the cathedral,' George said. 'I knew it! Why did the canon lie?'

'Because the canon doesn't hold with ghosts,' the old woman said. 'Silly man.'

Mumtaz would never know what made her stop on the edge of that precipice but when she sat down next to it, she could feel the pull from its endless, infinite darkness. Scrabbling for things that had fallen out of her bag, she found what felt like a pound coin and threw it down into the void. It took three seconds to register any sort of noise which, when it came, was a splash. Water.

So what was she in? A well? A room containing a well? And where was this place and what was meant to happen now?

* * *

170

The duty brief, when he finally turned up, was a lad who looked as if he was about sixteen. All done up in a suit and tie, he was a million miles away from the usual 'duty', who tended to be middle-aged, fat and heavily lined. They were always divorced.

Mr Walters, by contrast, was a very eager beaver indeed and looked as if he might well still be a virgin. He was keen to keep Colin Macbeth out of trouble and had clearly advised him to say nothing. Brown and Pinker had been subjected to the 'no comment' routine for a good half hour when they took a comfort break.

They both went to the bog and then had five minutes in the canteen with some wretched coffee and a bag of chocolate buttons which they shared. While they sat miserably and silently opposite each other, Wilko arrived.

He pulled a chair out and sat down next to Brown.

'My old mate Lee Arnold's just turned up to report a MisPer,' he said.

'He that PI used to be a copper up Forest Gate?'

'Yeah. His business partner's gone missing on our patch,' Wilko said.

'Where?'

'Last known Carter Lane.'

Pinker said, 'Near the cathedral?'

'That's the one. Lee says they've been looking into a sighting of an injured boy in Carter Court, house next to The Hobgoblin.'

'So why didn't they report it to us?' Brown said.

'It was kids what reported it. They were selling hooky gear door to door.'

171

'So, did they find . . .'

'Nah. And now the person looking into it, this Mrs Mumtaz Hakim, has gone missing.'

'How long?' Pinker asked.

'Over twenty-four hours,' Wilko said.

'She's a grown woman.'

'Someone,' Wilko said, 'sent a text from her phone to Arnold's telling him she's with a relative in Birmingham. But she's not and now her phone has disappeared completely.'

'Father Edward has been seen many, many times over the centuries,' Mrs Hardwick said. 'He generally turns up when things are particularly bad. He was around a lot in World War II.'

'I spoke to him,' George said.

'Oh yes, he speaks,' she said. 'If he didn't speak, how could he warn us?'

'Warn us about what?' Jordan asked.

'Evil,' Mrs Hardwick said simply. 'It never takes a day off, as it were, but when it pertains directly to the cathedral itself, Father Edward usually takes a hand.' She put one of her hands on George's shoulder. 'And you being an exorcist, you were the perfect recipient for a Father Edward message. Old Canon Proctor was a great advocate for Father Edward and always took his pronouncements seriously. Not like this one. What did he say to you, Father George?'

'He said that evil had come to this place. To be honest I'd felt it myself by that time. He said that no one in the cathedral would acknowledge it.'

She nodded.

'And he mentioned sacrifice.'

'Mmm. Well, you saw how the canon and his team reacted,' she said.

'Yes, but couldn't the person Father George spoke to just be a visitor?' Jordan asked.

'No,' she said with absolute certainty.

'But how . . .'

'I just know,' she said. 'What you have to understand is that those currently working within the cathedral do not hold with anything as "mediaeval" as ghosts or as troubling as sacrifice. They are good people, committed to the care of the poor and needy and to the worship of God, who I think they see as a rather pleasant, vaguely left-wing man from Esher. What they fail to appreciate is that the world is no longer a sun-filled garden from *The Good Life*. They live in a benign past that never happened. Those of whom Father Edward speaks also live in a past that never was, the difference being that their delusion is decidedly toxic.' She held a hand up to Jordan and continued, 'And before you ask me to elucidate, young man, I can't. I don't know who these people are, where they are or why they killed this child. Or rather I imagine they killed the poor little thing because she was mixed race. What I do know is what both ritual magic and that which purports to be ritual magic look like, and so I know that this is the latter. But it's no less dangerous for that.'

'So you don't believe that the clergy here are colluding in whatever this is?' George asked.

'No,' she said. 'At least not consciously. Although I do fear they may know who did do this.'

'So they're shielding them?'

'They don't know these people have done anything wrong,' Mrs Hardwick said. 'They're just congregants, you know. Christians who always put a little something in the collection plate and who never rock the boat.'

TWELVE

Wilko had been given two special constables only, on account of the fact that EC4 was sparsely populated and Mumtaz was an adult MisPer. That Lee came with Wilko on the house to house wasn't known to the City Police's more senior officers. Besides, while the specials concentrated on the swanky new flats in the area, Lee knew where he and Wilko should go.

Carter Court was entirely in darkness except for the lights from The Hobgoblin. Although nobody was outside the pub, it seemed to be pretty lively inside.

Wilko said, 'Sounds like they're having a good time.'

If Lee wasn't too much mistaken, the music they were hearing sounded like some sort of obscure punk. It jarred in an area like this and, as they passed the pub, Lee caught a glimpse of a lot of men drinking and smoking –

indoors. That remained illegal as far as he knew.

Wilko knocked on the blue door and they both waited.

'I don't know about all this ghost stuff, Father George,' Jordan said once they were out of the cathedral walking towards St Paul's Tube station. 'I mean, with respect, I know you . . .'

'Oh, I don't necessarily believe it myself, Constable,' George said. 'Just because I do what I do doesn't mean I'm not critical about the existence of these things. I'll be honest, I've never seen what you'd call a ghost, although I have been around some very lively poltergeists.'

'And yet you sense evil?'

'Oh that's another matter,' he said. 'Ghosts are not evil in themselves. This is different. Of course the man I met may have been a ghost, I'm not ruling it out, but I think he was someone like me, someone who picks up on these things.'

'So was Mrs Hardwick mad?'

Father George shrugged. 'What is mad?' he said. 'Personally, I don't think so. I think she's just someone who knows things. The way she volunteered to be alone with us so quickly makes me tend to think that her motives are genuine. And like her, I am inclined to believe that the motives of the clerics are in no way sinister. They want to preserve what they see as the benign status quo, not rock the boat.'

'So you think the cathedral was left unlocked on purpose?'

'I don't know,' George said. 'Maybe, but not in order to allow that terrible thing to happen. They are too detached,

176

I feel, for that to be possible. And of course their story about having no set procedures for locking up may be true, but I doubt it, not these days.'

'Why these days?' Jordan asked.

Father George laughed. 'And there you show your youth, Constable,' he said. 'Back in the 1970s and 80s, way before you were born, there was no such thing as Health and Safety, no forms to fill out telling organisations like the NHS how you rated their service. Things just, for better or worse, jogged along. There were more industrial accidents in those days, but hey, at least you had no forms to fill out did you?'

'No, but . . .'

'Now fewer people die but, over the years, people my sort of age have continued to moan about things like Health and Safety, which they construe as something that limits their freedom. They also regard it as emanating solely from the European Union, which is not the case,' George said. 'And so hence we have the current destructive culture wars. Not just in the UK, but in the USA too. And there's big money behind it – just not for the ordinary person on the street.'

'And you think the priests are in collusion?'

'No,' he said. 'No, they're clerics, they don't like change, whatever that may entail. What they don't realise is that change is coming whether they like it or not, and not all of it is going to be for the better.'

'No?'

'No,' he said, 'because sometimes change means going backwards and that's a very bad thing in my experience.'

Jordan smiled. 'You really do talk like Wilko a lot of the time, Father George,' he said.

George, who had started to head for St Paul's Tube Station, looked back over his shoulder and said, 'If you see Wilko before I do, tell him to ring me will you, please?'

Was this gnome-like old man the one Loz and Habib had seen with their boy with the bloodied face? And while gnomes couldn't, to Lee's way of thinking, be trusted, there was also something of the cheery Father Christmas about Arthur Hobbs too. Mumtaz, he remembered, had found the old man unsettling.

In answer to Wilko's question about Mumtaz, and after he had seen her photograph, the old man said, 'I seen her about but I don't know her.'

'She knew you,' Wilko said. 'Joined her in the pub together with a lady called Danielle. Pregnant apparently. You know her, Mr Hobbs?'

He thought for a second and then said, 'Nah.'

'So you can't point us in the direction of the lady who might know where Mrs Hakim is?'

'No,' he said. 'Don't know nobody round here now, not these days. All City types they are now, round here. Don't talk to me.'

'What about the blokes in the pub?' Lee asked.

'What, The Hob?' he laughed. 'I dunno mate, I don't go there.'

'Mrs Hakim said you went there when she was having lunch with this Danielle.'

'Oh, I'll go and get meself a pie there sometimes . . .'

Wilko said, 'Looked like your sort of place to me, Arthur.'

'Ain't.'

'I see no "City types" in there tonight.'

'Dunno about that.'

'You sure you haven't spoken to Mrs Hakim?' Wilko held the photograph up again. It was always as well to give people the chance to change their minds. If indeed Arthur Hobbs was changing his mind.

Eventually the old man said, 'As I say, I see her about but I don't know her and I ain't eat with her. Ask young Bradley, he's usually on the bar at The Hob during the day. He'll tell you.'

'We will. And Danielle?'

'Don't know her neither,' the old man said. 'Like I say, nobody round here talks to me no more.'

Was it young Mr Walters who had changed his mind? Did he, during the comfort break, tell Colin to throw them some red meat? It could be a good tactic sometimes. But Brown, if not Pinker, didn't trust it or him.

'I dunno what her name was,' Colin Macbeth said. His head was down, as if in shame.

'Where'd you meet this woman?' Brown asked.

Macbeth shrugged.

'You had sex with her,' Brown said, 'you must know where you met?'

'I was pissed.'

'Even so!'

Colin Macbeth lapsed into silence.

Pinker said, 'Colin, I'm assuming this was in the right time frame? About nine months ago?'

'Yeah.'

'So beginning of this year?'

'Yeah.'

'So where . . .'

'Look, my missus and me, we was going through a bad time at the beginning of this year,' he said. 'Wendy, my other half, she had a hysterectomy, made her weird.'

'In what way, weird?' Pinker asked.

'She . . . Well, she went off it, you know . . .'

'She lost interest in sex.'

'Yeah. Don't excuse it, I know. But . . .'

'You say you'd had a few,' Pinker said. 'Where's your local?'

This seemed to stump Colin Macbeth.

'I may be wrong, but you look like the sort of bloke who has a local,' Brown said. 'I mean, we can ask around . . .'

'Jolly Sailor,' Macbeth said.

There you go. Where's that?' Pinker asked.

'Southwark Park Road.'

'So maybe you met this girl there,' Brown said.

'What was she like?' Pinker dived in.

'Young.'

'Young? How young?'

'Not too young if that's what you mean!' Macbeth said.

'So what's too young then, Colin?' Brown asked.

Images of those she loved came into the utter blackness to torment her. Her parents, Shazia, Lee. Against a matt-black background she could see them easily and she wondered what they were thinking. To them she must have just disappeared. Lee had known where she'd gone but it was doubtful he knew this place.

In her calmer moments, Mumtaz had reasoned that 'this place' had to be connected in some way to the house with the blue door. Was it underneath it? In a building close to it? Was this in fact some far-flung part of Arthur Hobbs's house? He'd told her the place was massive, that it comprised rooms that went back to as early as the fourteenth century.

And what about Danielle? She'd told her as much as she'd been able, in fact a bit too much, about what she'd been doing. And Lee knew about her. Surely if he was looking for her, he must have remembered the name Danielle?

If she concentrated, Mumtaz could hear water. Not rushing water but more like the sound water makes when it laps against the shore. Was she close to the Thames? The old man's house was near but not exactly close to the river. And yet who knew what ancient tributaries flowed under the city? She remembered that legend about that pre-Roman king, Lud, who had been buried on the banks of the Thames. Was his body down here with her somewhere?

Nobody had come with either food or drink for her, and so she felt that she was probably not being held hostage for some reason. She'd just been left here, in a dank black room with a deep well. The only possible reason she could think of: because someone wanted her dead.

* * *

'He's called Henry Blizzard, he's a brief,' the young constable said. 'His partner, the woman he lives with, she's pregnant.'

'And who told you this again?' Wilko asked.

The lad looked down at his notebook and said, 'A Mr Alexander Perry. Him and his wife live next door. I tried calling on Mr Blizzard but he was out.'

Lee said, 'Where'd they live?'

'It's called The Wren, sir,' the young man said. 'Block of apartments on Carter Lane.'

'Sounds about right from what Mumtaz told me,' Lee said.

There had been no reason for them to question Arthur Hobbs further after they left the house with the blue door. But then they'd moved on to The Hobgoblin. As soon as Wilko, in full uniform, had walked in, the place had taken on a hostile air. But then a lot of people were smoking and so when he didn't so much as mention that, it came as a relief. Those inside the pub even took Wilko and Lee to meet the barman, Bradley, who had no recollection of Arthur Hobbs meeting with any ladies.

Lee, for his part, had cast a critical eye over the punters. They were, he noted, all men, which was odd in the twenty-first century. Young, middle-aged and old, on the one hand they were a mixed bunch, while at the same time they seemed to be of a type. It was a type, furthermore, that looked out of place in the City. They were like him – their accents, the way they stood, some of their mannerisms. Working-class London, even if there were more than a few Rolexes on show. Money, though often discriminating on the basis of class, didn't always.

No one had seen or heard of Mumtaz. Wilko had allowed them to carry on smoking in peace. He'd told Lee it was because he 'didn't need the ag' but maybe, at some time, he might need the goodwill not slapping a fine on the place might bring. Who knew?

Now they were inside a building named after a famous architect, looking at a Mr Henry Blizzard. Probably in his mid-thirties, Mr Blizzard was a dark, good-looking man. What Lee would have called his 'flat' was a cool, pale, minimalist place. Clean to the point of clinical – Lee admired it. He'd only managed to kick his addiction to booze, many years ago, by cleaning his own place to within an inch of its tired, late-Victorian life.

'Mr Blizzard, do you have a partner called Danielle?' Wilko asked.

Mr Blizzard frowned. 'What's this about?'

'Can you just answer the question, please?' Wilko said.

Blizzard, a solicitor, considered his options and then said, 'I do. Why?'

Wilko took Mumtaz's photograph out of his pocket and showed it to him. 'We're looking for this lady,' he said. 'Called Mumtaz Hakim. She's missing, last seen in this vicinity. We've reason to believe Danielle may have spoken to her.'

'I see.'

'We tried to call earlier but you were out.'

'We went to supper,' Blizzard said. 'Covent Garden.'

'Can we speak to Danielle?' Wilko asked.

'Well, she's lying down, she's pregnant . . .'

'We won't take long.'

He left, leaving the two of then standing in the bright white living area. Wilko looked at Lee and whispered, 'Sounds promising.'

'Mmm.'

Dust seemed to have been banished completely from this space. Did Danielle clean all the time? Surely this was professional work. Lee began to feel his skin crawl.

Blizzard returned with a small blonde woman who was probably in her late twenties. She was hugely pregnant and had very swollen ankles.

Wilko said, 'Sorry, to disturb you, Miss er . . .'

'Saint,' she said. 'Danielle Saint.'

Jordan's grandfather had gone to bed, which was good. If he was in bed he'd stop phoning him up all the time, wanging on about how he'd missed his tea which was now in the bin. Back at Bishopsgate, the young man used his time to Google myths and legends related to St Paul's Cathedral. Father George, as Wilko had once told him, tended to have a profound effect on everyone who met him. His enthusiasm for the history of EC4 had been infectious. But Jordan wasn't just back at the station to use his computer. Brown and Pinker had a suspect under interrogation, a man thought to be the father of the dead baby.

According to his colleagues the interview had been going on for several hours. Only latterly had the man availed himself of the duty brief. But that was all that anyone knew.

Jordan was reading a piece about how Old St Paul's had burnt to the ground during the Great Fire of London when Brown and Pinker arrived. The whole investigative team, including Jordan, gathered around them.

Brown said, 'The fifty-six-year-old man we now had in custody has been released.'

Someone said, 'Shit! Isn't he that baby's father?'

'He's submitted to another DNA test this evening, in addition to the one we have on record. But,' Brown said, 'he has admitted that he could be the child's father. Bunked up with a woman whose name he can't recall about nine months ago, round the back of a pub called The Jolly Sailor in Bermondsey. He claims to have had no further contact with this woman after that night. Now he, Mr Colin Macbeth, reckons this pub is his local, so I want us in there.'

'In there how, guv?' one officer asked.

'I don't know yet, Dean,' Brown said. 'We have to tread carefully.'

Jordan said, 'So you don't believe him then, sir?'

Brown looked at Pinker and then he said, 'I may be wrong, but I'm disinclined to believe him, yes Whittington.'

'Why's that, sir?'

He looked at Pinker again, who this time said, 'All you need to know is that Macbeth is a person of interest. We need to find as much out about him as we can. We also, and this could easily get lost amongst our desire to find this child's killer, need to be aware that its mother is out there too and she could be in trouble. She's a black woman; DNA suggests she is probably of Caribbean heritage and she's probably quite young. Any contacts between Macbeth and a woman like that are of interest to us.'

Jordan said, 'Did this man talk about this woman's race at all, sir?'

Brown shook his head. 'No,' he said. 'Admittedly I didn't say anything about that to him, but I also think he's keeping that to himself.'

'Why?'

'Fuck knows,' Brown said. 'But my gut's telling me, it's deliberate. I've no idea why. But I think it means something.'

'And if the new DNA sample proves he isn't the father, what then?' an officer called Mabel Onoja asked.

Brown smiled. 'It won't,' he said. 'Trust me.'

When they got back out onto the street, Wilko and Lee lit fags.

Lee, who had been sitting on what he knew during their talk with Danielle Saint, said, 'So she's the Danielle Mumtaz met.'

'She says not,' Wilko said. 'How can you be sure?'

'Mumtaz has a habit of writing down random bits of information on post-its in the office,' he said. 'Mess of it, but what can you do? So I found one with Danielle's name written on it, plus a load of other scribble and then the word Saint.'

'So it weren't written as like her surname?'

'No. But bit of a coincidence, don't you think?'

Wilko smiled. He didn't believe in coincidence any more than Lee did.

'What did you make of the boyfriend?' Lee asked.

'Mr Blizzard . . .' Wilko shook his head.

Both men had thought that Henry Blizzard would be more concerned about his pregnant girlfriend, but he hadn't been. In fact his attitude towards her had been formal if anything, and quite cold.

'Posh – much posher than her,' Wilko said. 'Bit obsessive compulsive if you ask me. You see the state of that place? Like a fucking operating theatre! Not that you probably noticed . . .'

Like most people who knew Lee Arnold, Wilko was aware of his 'clean' thing.

Lee said, 'I was lost in admiration, Wilko.'

'You would be.' He shrugged. Then he continued his description of Blizzard. 'Professional – brief, ain't he? Good-looking bloke. Jewish.'

'Jewish? Christ, Wilko, not every brief . . .'

'No! Doughnut!' Wilko said. 'Mezuzah! One of them little cylinder things with some parchment in them Jews attach to their doorposts. One large as life as we come in the front door.'

'Was there?'

'Yes,' Wilko said. 'Blimey, you call yourself a PI.'

'I just want to find Mumtaz,' Lee said.

This was all moving way too slowly for him. He just wanted to find Mumtaz and then forget about boys with blood on their faces and dead babies. All he wanted was her. And Wilko knew it.

'Fond of her, are you?' the older man asked.

Lee looked away. 'You could say that.'

'Nice lady,' Wilko said. 'Intelligent.'

'Yes . . .'

'Pretty too,' he said.

Lee didn't say anything. This was taking it out of him. He wanted to just push his way into Arthur Hobbs's house and look for her.

Because he knew she was there.

The boy put his plate down on the ground and then drank from the can of Coke the old man had brought him. When was his dad coming to get him? He didn't like this place. Putting aside the things he'd seen here, it was because of this place that his dad had turned into some sort of raving lunatic.

Although that wasn't strictly true. His dad had always been a bit of an idiot. He was the dad who lost his rag at Sunday kids' football and embarrassed himself. He was the one who'd caused all that trouble at school when it was time to choose options for GCSEs. Loads of boys had opted to do Food Prep and Nutrition. His mum had been delighted. Chefs at the top of their game earned a bucketload. But his dad had caused a massive scene, shouting his mouth off about how only 'funny' boys did 'cooking'. He meant gay boys. He hated them, called them 'poofs' and 'bumboys'. His mum told him to shut up, accused him of being a dinosaur. She was too good for him. He'd thought she should leave years ago.

Maybe if he ever got back to her and told her what the old man had done, she would? The thought of his mum brought tears to his eyes, but he was determined not to cry. What would that achieve? Soon the old man would be back to take his plate away. Generally he had someone with him, one of them. But if by chance he didn't, maybe he'd tackle him. It was that or pretend he was suddenly on board with what they'd done, and that was risky.

If he wanted to get out of this place, he'd have to fight for it.

THIRTEEN

Lee Arnold had gone straight from EC4 round to the flat Shazia shared with her boyfriend Krishnan. Krish as a serving copper knew all too well about the legal impediments around gaining entry to a suspect's property, even if Shazia raged about the injustice of it.

'If Amma's in that house, you should be able to go in!' she yelled.

Her boyfriend held her close. 'Babe, Lee can't just go barrelling in,' he said. 'Not even this Wilko can do that. What evidence is there?'

'That was where Amma said she was when she disappeared!'

'Doesn't mean she's in that house,' Krish said.

'Wilko's gonna try and get a warrant,' Lee said. 'It hinges on whether there's reasonable grounds for suspicion.'

'Reasonable . . .'

'Sssh.' Krish rocked her in his arms and said, 'Come on baby, you know how these things work . . .'

She pulled away from him. 'My mother is missing, Krishnan!' she said. 'How the fuck would that make you feel?'

And then she cried. After further assuring her he was doing everything he could, Lee left to go back to Forest Gate, where he fell into his bed exhausted in the early hours of the morning. Now awake again, he took his first coffee of the day into his living room and sat down. No news from the coppers it seemed. His stomach was tied in knots. Where was Mumtaz? He opened his laptop on the coffee table to the sound of Chronus singing 'I'm Forever Blowing Bubbles' and regretted ever having taught the bugger to talk.

He opened his emails and saw that Gary Connor had, as promised, sent him something. Apparently his wife, Fallon, when confronted with the pictures Lee had taken of her and Gary's stepbrother snogging, had taken Gary's kid and decamped to Dagenham. Now with the brother, Dillon, and his mum Cindy in a house in Dagenham Heathway, Fallon had started divorce proceedings against Gary, citing her main reason as his 'continual use of violence' against her. If a lie, and Gary said that it was, it was a low blow on her part. Fallon had struck first, probably with a view to getting her hands on both Gary's millions and his brother. At least that was what Gary believed. Now he wanted to pay Lee to keep 'an eye' on Dillon, Fallon, the baby Harrison and Dillon's mum. But

192

mainly Dillon. If Gary was right, his stepbrother was a nasty bit of work. A racist, a thug and a benefits cheat. Not the sort of person Gary wanted raising his son. Not the sort of person a court would deem suitable to do so. There was an address and the registration number of Dillon's car, plus the name of his current 'off the books' employer. The kid apparently worked on a fruit and veg stall.

Habib saw her first. Not that there was any actual bruising; it was more that Kym's face had changed shape. And she looked as if she was about to cry. Her false lashes even glistened with moisture.

Not a popular boy with his contemporaries, Habib found it difficult to find anyone who knew Kym who would talk to him. But then there was Mercy.

'Oh Habib, she's really upset,' she said when he asked her what had happened to make Kym look so miserable. 'A boy she was seeing told her dad lies.'

Everyone, without exception, liked Mercy. She was a clever, kind, generous and beautiful black girl who could be funny and even cheeky sometimes but was also an out and proud Christian. Even those kids who envied her, trusted her.

'What lies?' Habib asked.

'About her getting pregnant,' Mercy said. 'She's not.'

'Isn't she?'

'No!'

Mercy clearly hadn't caught the news about Kym and Loz.

'Imran Riaz, who left last year, told her dad that Kym had let some loser have sex with her and now she was pregnant. But it's just not true,' Mercy said.

'So what did her dad . . .'

Mercy placed her head close to Habib's and whispered, 'Her dad beat her up. Tried to kick the baby out of her, Kym said.'

'But there is no baby . . .'

'No! Of course not. But you know what Kym's dad's like, he's mad. That's why she looks so . . . weird.'

'Why?'

'He punched her in the face,' Mercy said. 'Imagine your own dad punching you in the face!'

The Jolly Sailor was one of those pubs that opened early. This was just as well considering the fact there were punters standing outside from 9.30 a.m. onwards. As soon as the doors opened at ten, a group of five men, plus Jordan Whittington, went inside.

When the young officer had left home earlier his grandfather, Bert, had wondered why he looked such a state. His hair uncombed, wearing his oldest jeans, a raincoat that Bert recognised as one of his own and a pair of trainers slated to be taken to a charity shop, he looked as if he might accost passers-by for some loose change. But Bert knew better than to ask and so Jordan had left home without attracting comment.

He went up to the bar and ordered a pint of cider. Not some poncy Belgian brew in a bottle, but a pint of the bog-standard cheap cider alcoholics frequently resorted to when they were down on their luck. He flung some coins on the scarred counter and then sloped off to the 'beer garden' round the back – a soggy patio featuring wet garden furniture – to join the other men. All the other punters smoked. Jordan could take it or leave it, but he'd come armed with a small packet of tobacco and some Rizlas and so he set about making a roll-up.

The old man had brought him breakfast. He'd asked about his dad and when he was coming to get him but had received no reply. The man had been alone, but he'd lost his nerve and so he'd just taken the gloopy-looking scrambled egg on toast from him and then got on with the job of eating.

There was so little down there. But then that was part of his punishment, the boredom. Being a 'poof' had consequences. He needed to say that he wouldn't be a 'fairy' again, but he knew that he wouldn't. His dad was trying to make him in his own image and he wouldn't do it. What was more, if he did ever get out of this place, he'd go straight to the police.

He finished his scrambled eggs and drank some of the bitter tea the old man had brought him. Today the miserable old sod had just plonked the stuff down and then buggered off quickly. Soon he'd be back again to collect the plate and the cup. He looked at the door that was the only way in and out of the chamber, and it was then he noticed it was very slightly open.

* * *

195

They all knew each other and so The Jolly Sailor early doors brigade looked at Jordan with some suspicion. He was so unlike them. Firstly he was young, secondly he was black and thirdly they didn't know him. But he had something that one of them, a bloke who called himself Fitzy, wanted. He had tobacco.

Most of the others were down to their last strands of baccy and so Fitzy, who spoke with a Scottish accent, could beg and plead as much as he liked – he wasn't getting any. A tall, thin man with one wrist in a plaster cast told him to 'Get your own, you mean old cunt!' Jordan watched the man edge closer to him. Smoking a thin 'one strander', Jordan wanted to give the impression of an ex-con. Although smoking had been banned in UK prisons for some time, there was still a roaring trade in black economy baccy as well as vape fluid inside. Smokes were used as currency, exchanged for food, drugs and sexual favours.

His baccy on the table in front of him, Jordan watched while Fitzy hovered. The other men talked about some hostel in Rotherhithe. Fitzy, his need eventually overcoming any suspicions he may have had, said, 'Pal, can I get some of your baccy?'

As Jordan looked up, one of the other men called out to him, 'Don't give him nothing, son! He's a mean old bastard!'

But Jordan pushed the tobacco pouch towards Fitzy, who said, 'You're a gent!' and then sat down.

He rolled himself a smoke in silence while the other blokes muttered amongst themselves. When he finally lit up he breathed in and closed his eyes in what looked like bliss. Having downed their pints, the other men went inside to get more booze.

Fitzy looked at Jordan and said, 'They just got their benefits.'

'Ah.'

Then he said, 'Not seen you round here before.'

Brown had told Jordan to play it cool. He said, 'Not been here before.'

'Ah.' There was a pause, then the Scotsman said, 'So . . . you new then, eh?'

Jordan said nothing at first and just looked at the other man with blank eyes. Then he said, 'Yeah.'

'Mmm.'

Fitzy smoked and drank and so did Jordan. Then the other men returned. While they drank their pints, again quickly, and got ever more plastered, Jordan and Fitzy sat in silence. There were, Jordan reckoned, other reasons why the men shunned Fitzy that went well beyond his alleged meanness. As a person who might know something useful about The Jolly Sailor, Jordan wondered whether Fitzy was actually a good bet.

'Lee?'

He was on Dagenham Heathway when his phone rang, opposite the Tube station, walking towards the shopping centre where Gary Connor had said his brother had a stall. A mixture of almost countrified single-storey shops selling tans, vapes and takeaways contrasted with the actual shopping centre – where Dillon Connor worked –

which specialised in cheap stuff. It was just as well it did, because very few people who lived locally could afford much. In spite of high house prices, Dagenham was still a place where a lot of people were poor.

'Wilko,' Lee answered. 'What's happening?'

'I took it all the way to the top, but no joy,' the older man said.

He'd failed to get a warrant to enter the house in Carter Court from his boss, Superintendent Cryer.

'Funny handshake brigade,' Wilko said by way of explanation.

It was well known that a lot of policemen, particularly senior officers, were also Freemasons. Personally Lee dismissed a lot of the wilder conspiracy theories punted around about them by some people, especially Wilko, but he took his point. Although whether the Masons were involved in Mumtaz's disappearance was doubtful to say the least.

Lee, who although engaged in work for Gary Connor, knew he'd drop it in a second to find Mumtaz, said, 'I have to get in there. Tonight she'll have been off the radar for forty-eight hours.'

'I hear you,' Wilko said. 'She is officially missing.'

'Wilko, something bad's happened. You know it, I know it . . .'

'Yeah, you're—'

'I know I'm right!' Lee said. 'My reasons may be mainly in my gut, while yours are about alchemy and fucking religion . . .'

'Look,' Wilko said. 'I get off at four. Meet me at Liverpool Street, the Costa opposite Platform 13.'

198

'And do what?' Lee asked. Although he'd got to Dagenham without any bother, now he was listening to Wilko he was agitated again. What was he even doing at work?

'Get inside that house,' Wilko said.

'How?'

'I'll get a mind bigger 'an either of ours onto it,' Wilko said. And then he cut the connection.

Lee, stationary now, put his phone back in his pocket.

'Oi, mate!'

Instinctively he looked around to see whether someone was calling out to him. But it was just a taxi driver, parked on the pavement, getting a man in a caftan and welly boots to move out of his way.

Mumtaz was thirsty. She was hungry too, but that need was not as urgent as the one she had for water. Also, hearing water lapping about down below somewhere was torture. She knew she was high above it and that reaching it, as in throwing herself down into it, probably meant she would die. But wasn't that going to happen anyway?

She'd heard nothing except the lapping of the water and could see only complete blackness. At least if she launched herself into whatever was below, she might have a chance of survival.

Had whoever had thrown her inside this place meant her to tumble into the void? No one, as far as she knew, had come to check on her. Perhaps they thought she was already dead? Her head hurt like hell and felt sticky as if it had bled. Maybe if, against all her instincts, she called out

199

or screamed or something, then someone would come and perhaps she could overpower them? Could she? Really?

Although she couldn't see herself, she knew she was bruised all over – and with her legs hanging over the void, how could she stand? For all she knew this empty space could be like a moat and almost completely surround her. Even if someone did come with a light of some sort, how could she get up on her dead, damaged legs quickly enough to be able to run?

'Do you hold with Scottish independence, boy?' Fitzy asked.

Now on only his second pint, he appeared to be more pissed than the other men who were onto, Jordan reckoned, their fifth. Or was he just stereotyping Fitzy's behaviour because he was Scottish?

'I don't do politics,' Jordan said.

Fitzy playfully punched his shoulder. 'Everyone does politics, pal,' he said. 'Just by living you're doing politics, ya ken?'

Jordan said nothing but one of the other blokes called over, 'Ah go back to Jock-land then, you fucking twat! Go back if you don't like it here!'

'Don't worry I will!' Fitzy roared.

'So fuck off now then!'

The other men laughed. Fitzy took another gulp of cider and then leant to one side to take a sip from a hidden hip flask.

'Fucking English,' he muttered.

The other men were joined by a couple of women, also

cider drinkers. Pissed before they arrived, they smelt of damp and old fags. Spotting Jordan, the older of the two said, 'Tasty!'

They all laughed. Jordan wasn't going to get the measure of this place by hanging out with these people. All hard drinkers, if not alcoholics, they were lost in their own subculture of addiction. Where they drank was irrelevant – or so it seemed.

Fitzy helped himself to more of Jordan's tobacco and said, 'Look at them old slappers there!'

Jordan said nothing. If the women were indeed on the game there was probably a good reason.

'Sort of scum you get in here,' Fitzy said as he lit up.

'So why'd you come here?' Jordan asked.

Fitzy clearly didn't like these people and they didn't like him.

He looked at his glass. Yes, the cider was cheap and if you didn't mind that it tasted like a chemistry set, that was probably good enough . . .

Fitzy shook his head. 'It's open early,' he said. 'When you've had a night in a hostel you need an early drink.'

Jordan nodded his head. He knew what some of them were like. A load of men trying to rub along together while some of them screamed, wanked and fought each other. No wonder so many chose the street.

Then a woman came into the beer garden who didn't look like the others. In late middle age, she wore a stylish white angora coat, high leather boots and mirrored sunglasses. All the men, including Fitzy, raised their glasses to her. After a moment taken bathing in their adulation, she said to Jordan, 'Give us a moment, will you please, dear.'

Her voice was as posh as her clothes.

He said, 'A moment to . . .'

'Fuck off,' the woman snarled. 'This isn't a place for the likes of you, boy.'

Jordan felt cold. Fitzy leant across the table and said, 'You'd best hop on, boy. She's right, this ain't no place for you, not now.'

Once outside, he closed the door behind him as quietly as he could. He was in a corridor. Dank and damp, it felt as if it was near water, which made some sense. Narrow and squat, the passageway was made of stone and, as he walked tentatively along it, lights came on automatically. The floor was made of earth which mercifully made no sound as he trod on it.

Where was he? All the places he'd been to under the house before had possessed walls dressed with plaster and some of them had windows, albeit high up. His dad had hinted to him that the place was bigger than he thought.

He'd told him, 'You can hide an army down here.'

Which was exactly what they wanted to do.

He'd been to the Shrine. They'd taken him there but he didn't know where it was. That had no windows that he could remember, so maybe this was somewhere near there. Weirdly he didn't feel afraid. Even with the knowledge of what they could be capable of – he just wasn't. Even though he knew his dad wouldn't save him.

It wasn't until he remembered what the old man had once said about the tunnels that he began to feel anxious.

He'd told him, 'They're older than the cathedral. There's layers too. The deepest British level, the Roman, mediaeval, them the Inquisition used, the ones what Wren put in. Go deep into the earth they do, deep and wide. Some of them lead onto other tunnels and chambers and some do not. Some lead nowhere, just to death.'

It almost made him turn back, that memory, but what would that achieve? Nothing, and if he didn't try what would that make him? Like them? And besides, if he was down there, maybe there were others and maybe they might know more about this place than he did.

He jogged to the end of the corridor and found himself at the T-junction. Now left or right?

He heard a cough back down the corridor he'd just jogged along and plumped for left. The lights on the walls went out as he moved onwards, switching off behind him.

FOURTEEN

Lee recognised Dillon Connor immediately. Plonking oranges into plastic bowls beside an Asian guy doing the same with onions. If anyone was in charge it was an older white bloke who was serving a woman on a mobility scooter. To see such a stall inside a shopping centre, placed in front of a couple of empty shops, wasn't uncommon these days. Who except the big chain stores could afford to rent out these big and expensive units? Boots the chemist had a place in the Heathway, plus some phone shops and cheap clothes outlets, but that was about it.

So here, as Gary had predicted, was Dillon's benefit fraud. If indeed he was claiming Income Support. Lee had to remember that Gary was furious with his brother and with good cause. The scrote was shagging his missus, a woman Gary clearly loved.

Lee wandered into Percy Ingle's the baker's and ordered tea and a bun. Just outside the shopping centre, it allowed him to keep an eye on the stall. He sat down.

Where was Mumtaz and what was she doing? Was she hurt? Missing adults were always a problem for the law. To some extent adults had to be free to disappear if they wanted to. That was still, in spite of the proliferation of CCTV and the ubiquity of mobile phone connectivity, a corner stone of a democratic system. But it had its problems. And there were practical implications. A lot of adults went missing every year. Many were found and many were not. Did the police even have the resources these days to find everyone?

The sound of an enraged female voice outside lifted him from his reverie. He looked out of the window and saw an older, bleached-blonde woman shouting at the bloke who ran Dillon's stall. He could hear her yelling, 'Why should he bother to help you out if you don't fucking pay him?'

The bloke said something Lee couldn't hear. Then the woman said to Dillon, 'You're a fucking mug, you are! You let him mug you off, you only got yourself to blame!'

And then she stomped off towards Boots.

Lee looked around at the other coffee and tea drinkers sitting down in Ingle's. They'd all watched the 'show' outside. One of them, an elderly man, raised his eyes up to heaven and then muttered, 'Scumbags.'

A large middle-aged woman laughed and then said, 'Never was a family so wrongly named!'

Several other people laughed. It was only later that Lee learnt what that meant.

*   *   *

It was a relief to be getting away from The Jolly Sailor. Replaced by two 'proper' CID officers, Jordan Whittington walked to Bermondsey Tube Station and made his way back to Bishopsgate. He'd not heard anything about Colin Macbeth. The posh woman in the angora coat had taken a couple of the homeless men away with her when she left the pub. Jordan caught that she was giving them some sort of casual work.

He'd settled down to write his report when DS Melina Pinker slipped into the chair next to his and said, 'How'd it go?'

'It's mainly a sports pub,' Jordan said. There had been four big TV screens around the large single-pub bar – all off when he'd visited.

'So what did you see?'

'A few homeless men,' he said. 'Early doors alcoholics by the look of them. Some woman about sixty took a couple of them off to do something. Don't know for sure if it was paid work. She was hostile to me.'

'Did she threaten you?'

'No,' Jordan said. 'But she didn't look like the sort you'd like to cross.'

'Reckon it was because you're black?' Pinker asked.

'Could be.' He shrugged. 'Then again maybe not. Maybe it was just because I was a new face. As I said, she took some men somewhere and they seemed eager to go. I'm assuming she was paying them . . .'

'Possible benefit fraud,' she said.

'Maybe,' Jordan said. 'But if Macbeth drinks there, I think it's safe to say he's not that fussed about quality beer or mixing with the polite middle classes. The Jolly Sailor is a straightforward, plain ordinary bloke's pub. Nothing wrong with that, my granddad likes places like that. But what he doesn't like is a boozer that is heavily scarred by numerous fights and uncomfortable due to neglect. And The Jolly Sailor is both of those things.'

Hidden around a corner and stationary now, he heard the old man go into the room they'd kept him in and then come out again. He heard him say 'Fuck'. Holding his breath, he listened for footsteps he knew he wouldn't be able to hear and looked for the lights in the corridor he'd just come from to switch back on, but they didn't. He left what he felt was a long time before he allowed himself to peep around the corner. As soon as he did so, the light came on behind him and he could see a short distance in front of him. It looked as if the old man had gone. Probably to report back that he had escaped. That wouldn't go well for the old git. Good. He hoped they chopped his fucking fingers off.

He turned back and began to walk along this new corridor. Dank and hot, like the one he'd just left, there were little pools of water on the dirt floor. In places it looked as if the stone walls were oozing sweat. When he got to the end of the corridor there was no choice but to go down a series of stone steps and so he descended. It was hotter and even more cramped down there and this time he was presented with three ways forward. He was about to plump for the corridor in the middle when he heard the sound of crying, coming from his left.

* * *

Wilko had given him an out and so he didn't have to do it. But George Feldman was intrigued – and concerned. Something was deeply amiss at the heart of the capital and he wanted to know what it was. The child's death had made a statement. Now that needed translation.

Over the years he had discussed the many ways in which the history of the city might lie in wait for the unwary underneath its streets, the blood that every year soaked further and further into the substrate, all but disappearing. But losing none of its power.

Now at last, or so it seemed, there was something he could do. But it was risky. That said, he had given his word to Wilko straight away and now he was committed. It was Wilko's belief that a network of tunnels and chambers honeycombed the underground city. Places concealed by time, hidden from builders of modern structures and Tube lines.

A long time ago, when he'd been a child living with his siblings and his parents in the Temple precinct, he'd had several experiences in the basement of their building that he, even now, found hard to explain. In those days his mother hadn't had a washing machine of her own. An old twin-tub, used by all the families resident in their building, was down in the basement. Sometimes George would accompany his mother to the washing machine and occasionally she'd meet another woman down there. They would talk, leaving George to explore the basement on his own. Even now he remembered the noises he heard down there. Creaks and whispers, groans like those of the damned, wind howling through empty chambers . . .

He'd never forgotten it. He'd also never forgotten how he'd tried to tell his mother about it and she'd told him not to 'say mad things'. Only once had she explained, when she'd said to him, 'People like us can't talk about things like that, it's dangerous.' What she'd meant, he still didn't really know, but he could still recall how his skin had crawled afterwards.

The left-hand tunnel was short but wide. He had to bow his head to avoid scraping his skull on the vaulted roof. Again, there were lights set into the walls. As he passed along towards an end he couldn't see, the crying became louder. What other poor sod did they have down here? What sort of state would they be in when he found them? The crying ceased.

He stopped for a moment. Although his feet made no noise, his heart was pounding so fast he could hardly hear himself think. When he stopped, it slowed. He listened for the crying. But it didn't reappear. Rather it was replaced by a snuffling and whimpering sound. It wasn't far away. He held his breath . . .

Lack of oxygen burnt the back of his throat and his tongue felt thick and dry. He was just about to gag when he heard that the whimper came from the right. From the first, maybe the second door on his right. He moved soundlessly forward and turned the handle of the first door. It opened into utter blackness.

There always had been and probably always would be 'those' families. Given to loud altercations, dodgy motors and a bit of light violence, everywhere had one of 'those' families. In reality a big, largely poor place, like Dagenham, probably had a few. The Saints, however, were quite exceptional.

Originating in south London, Pat Saint had moved to Dagenham in the eighties as a single mother of four. She'd moved to the Heathway and taken up residence in a house behind the shopping centre. A bit of a 'goer' by all accounts, she'd been a regular at several of the local pubs, which was where she'd met Gary Connor's dad, Jim. Entranced by her apparently very obvious charms back in the day, Jim had even taken on her kids in order to be with her. Then she'd got pregnant with Dillon and Jim had left Gary's mum. He'd died some years later, leaving Gary and his brother Mick to try and persuade Pat not to let Dillon run wild. They'd failed. Then Pat's eldest son Ryan had come back home to live with his mum and a full-scale problem family had evolved. Apparently, or so the locals told Lee Arnold, when Pat wasn't getting drunk and shagging local men, Ryan was nicking their motors. Dillon was, so far, mainly into petty crime and benefit fraud. No wonder Gary was so worried about Fallon and Harrison.

And what about Danielle Saint, the girl who lived with the brief in EC4? Same name, and she came from Dagenham. What were the odds? And Lee hadn't believed her. Mumtaz was sometimes disorganised but she was always accurate, and so if she'd written 'Danielle' and 'Saint' on a post-it there had to have been a reason.

The old man he'd been speaking to said, 'You after the Saints, are you?'

Lee said that he wasn't. He'd just been interested in

211

the shouting woman he'd seen outside.

'Course it's only Pat's lot that are like that,' the old man continued. 'The others are alright.'

'The others?'

'Only reason Pat got to be here when she left her first husband was because her Rodney lived here.'

'Her Rodney?'

'Her brother,' he said. 'Married a local girl and the council give them a house. Rodney's quite a different kettle of fish, quiet and that. I reckon he was pissed off as anyone when Pat moved here too.'

'This Rodney,' Lee asked, 'he have any kids, does he?'

The old man smiled. 'You are sniffing around, ain't you son?' he said. 'Not that I care. If you manage to get rid of Pat and her boys I'll buy you a pint. He's got girls, has Rodney. Five.'

There was a gasp.

He could see nothing and so he fumbled beside the door for a light switch. Left side first then the right, where he found something. He flicked it downwards.

She gasped again, the woman sitting on the floor. It was a large room and he could hear water. The woman, who had long black hair, was shielding her eyes.

'Who are you?' she said.

He could now see she was sitting with her legs over the side of something. He said, 'John.'

Tentatively, at first, she took her hand away from her eyes. She was dark, maybe even Asian. She was shaking. What had they done to her?

'Why are you . . .'

'No, why are you here?' the woman said. 'If you mean to kill me . . .'

'No!'

She jumped at his vehemence.

'No,' he said more calmly. 'I'm not like them.'

'Like who?' she said.

'Who are you?' he asked.

Her eyes were now accustomed to the light and she looked straight at him, saying nothing.

Eventually John closed the door behind him and said, 'You're sitting on something. What is it?'

She looked down.

'There's water at the bottom,' she said.

'Like a well?'

'Or a . . . It's like sitting on a jetty or something . . .'

He walked over to her and saw that she was sitting on the edge of a deep, black drop. He also saw her cringe as he got near.

'It's alright,' he said. 'I'm not going to hurt you. I'm not like them.'

'Then who . . .'

'I'm John,' he reiterated. 'They've had me down here for days.'

'You talk about "they",' she said. 'But who are they?'

John sat down beside her and said, 'They're Luddites.'

'Mr Feldman doesn't wish to be disturbed.'

One of the many things that had put George Feldman off becoming a barrister, like his father and his brother, was the

213

idea of having to liaise with a clerk. These people, usually men, were in charge of the business side of a barrister's practice. Usually 'shared' by up to twenty lawyers, clerks ran their gentlemen's diaries, negotiated fees with clients and kept their charges safe from unwanted attention from the hoi polloi. This latter charge included the barrister's families.

George's brother Barry's clerk was called Tim and he was at least as old as God.

'I need to see him,' George persisted.

Tim eased himself arthritically behind his desk and said, 'No can do, Father. Mr Feldman wishes to be alone and so he'll be alone.'

George leant on Tim's desk, which smelt of beeswax and Dickensian levels of privilege.

'Tim,' he said. 'All I'm asking is that you ring him and . . .'

'No phone calls.'

George threw his hands in the air and then just pushed past Tim's desk and burst into his brother's office.

A tremulous voice called out, 'Father Feldman!'

But by that time he was standing in front of his brother, who had a sherry glass in one hand and a decanter in the other. Looking up at George, he said, 'Oh for God's sake! What does a man have to do to get some peace?'

Tim, pushing George out of his way, stood in front of Barry's desk, cringing. 'Mr Feldman, sir,' he said, 'he pushed past me and . . .'

Barry sighed. 'My brother is a man of the cloth,' he said. 'Liaising with the Almighty makes them natural

214

liberty takers.' Then he smiled at his clerk. 'Not your fault, Tim. But if you want to make up for it, two coffees – one without sugar – please.'

'Luddites? What, you mean people who smash up new technology?'

John still didn't know who she was and so he said, 'Not exactly. But you still haven't told me who you are. I'm not saying anything else until you do.'

She sighed. He was young and blond and he was possibly the boy Loz and Habib had seen when they'd knocked on the blue door to sell their dodgy arthritis cream. He obviously didn't like these 'Luddites' and he was only a kid . . .

She said, 'I don't know if you remember, but a couple of young boys came here last week. They were selling pain cream.'

'A white lad and an Asian boy, yeah,' he said. 'I was, I had . . .'

'You had blood on your face and you looked scared . . .'

'Are you a copper?' John asked.

'No,' she said. 'My name's Mumtaz Hakim and I'm a private detective. Those boys are known to me. They came to me and told me about you as opposed to going to the police because what they were doing, selling home-made pain medication – is illegal. They felt you might be in trouble.'

'You could say that!'

'So what is this, John?' she said.

Suddenly overwhelmed, he began to cry.

Mumtaz swung her legs away from the drop below and bum-shuffled towards him. She had so little feeling in her feet, she didn't dare stand.

'John?'

It took him a few seconds to stop crying. In reality he just wanted to cry until he died. But now she was here and so he knew that wasn't an option.

When he could speak again he said, 'We have to get out of here or they'll kill us.'

Fallon and Harrison Connor lived in a pimped-up council house. It seemed that Pat Saint had a liking for grey-washed walls, oversized porches and stone elephants. Lee had seen the boy at the window and what he assumed was his mother's arm, pulling him away from it. They were definitely in residence. He called Gary, who cried.

When the plumber had pulled himself together, Lee told him about seeing Dillon on the fruit and veg stall and Pat's performance when she came to visit him.

'I've a mind to dob him in to the Social,' Gary said, referring to his stepbrother. ''Cept I don't do that.'

Lee thought that in all probability Gary probably employed the odd bloke on benefits himself.

'So what do you wanna do then?' Lee asked.

He heard Gary sigh. 'Dunno really,' he said. 'She wants a divorce, Fallon. Says she loves that little prick . . . I need time to think if I'm honest, mate. This has all been so quick . . .'

'I know,' Lee said.

'I mean, I don't think I need you to do no more for the moment, Lee . . .'

'It's OK, Gary. Whenever—'

'I mean, send your bill and—'

'Gary . . .'

If Gary was going off-grid for a bit, he'd have to ask him now or never.

'What?'

'You ever meet up with your stepmother's family?'

'Why?'

'Just curious,' Lee said. 'Their surname, Saint, not that common. But I've come across a couple recently.'

Gary laughed, mirthlessly. 'Lucky you!' he said. 'Right bunch of shysters.'

'Pat Saint has a brother? Rodney?'

'Oh he's not so bad,' Gary said. 'Bit of a nothing, old Rodney.'

Lee said, 'He's got daughters . . .'

'Yeah.'

'You don't know whether he has one called Danielle, do you?'

'Why?' he sounded guarded.

'Curious . . .'

'So you're not gonna tell me?'

'About the size of it,' Lee said.

Gary sighed and then he said, 'He does, as it goes.'

They both looked around the side of the door and into the darkened corridor.

'Do you know where we are?' Mumtaz whispered.

'Under the house,' John said.

'Yes, I know, but where?'

He looked back at her and then closed the door, softly.

'I've not got a clue,' he said. 'They say, that's Arthur and me dad, that these tunnels stretch for miles.'

'Where do they go?'

'Dunno. Some of them don't go anywhere, they're blocked up.'

'Great. Do they use them? Your dad and Arthur?'

'Oh yeah,' he said. 'The Shrine's down here and so them and the others are down here all the time.'

'The Shrine?'

Now she was up on her feet again, Mumtaz felt more awake. She wasn't ready to run as yet, but she did feel as if she would be able to walk some distance.

'It's ancient,' John said. 'It's what all this is about.'

'All what is?'

He sighed. 'This is gonna sound mad,' he said. 'The Shrine's like their church.'

'These Luddites?'

'Yeah. That's what they do,' he said. 'They worship King Lud, an early British king. He was king before the Romans came. The Luddites believe it was the Romans who contaminated the gene pool first and that if we can get back to our pre-Roman selves, we'll be great again.'

Mumtaz felt suddenly really cold. She said, 'So this Shrine – what do they do . . . ?'

John just stared at her for a moment and then he said, 'They kill people.'

218

FIFTEEN

The coffee in Barry's chambers was horrible. It reminded George of the Camp coffee they'd had as children. Made with chicory and served by their mother with hot milk. Cheap and most definitely nasty. Quite why Barry put up with such abominable stuff in the twenty-first century, he really didn't know. Maybe it was to pander to some sort of cost-saving exercise instigated by Tim. Tim probably liked it.

'I thought you'd got over all that years ago,' Barry said to George when he asked him about the tunnels underneath the City.

'You said you heard noises,' George said. 'I asked you once and you said you heard them too.'

'These are old buildings with cellars,' Barry countered. 'And there was sod all heating back in those days.'

'Mum told me I shouldn't talk about it,' George said. 'She said that people like us shouldn't.'

'Probably thought the cleaning woman would think badly of her.'

Barry lit a cigar. This was the real reason why he'd wanted to be alone that afternoon. People weren't supposed to smoke in any workplace any more, not even QCs.

'I got the impression it was because we're Jews,' George said.

'Did you?' Barry sounded most unconcerned. 'Since when did we both think about being Jews? I'm not doubting that's what you inferred, George, but I doubt very much that was what she meant. The mother I knew was an intensely superior woman who probably couldn't understand why people weren't continually showering her with flowers.'

'Barry . . .'

'Well!' he said.

'She knew there was something down there,' George said. 'There is something.'

'Something full of dirt, shit and a thousand skeletons of plague victims, yes,' Barry said.

He sighed. Like his parents, he had always found conversations about the family's Jewish roots problematic. George always seemed to think it was something that should be talked about. But he was alone in that. Barry, his sister and their parents had never spoken of it. Except once, but that had only involved Barry and his mother. And he'd tried to forget it. He'd sworn to his mother he would never tell his siblings about that day. But that was sixty years ago and she was long dead . . .

220

'Barry,' George said, 'I was afraid for a reason. It was visceral . . .'

'You were a child that believed in ghosts.'

'I was in fear of my life! And I know you heard those things too! Only once, but you came down to the washing machine with Mum and me and you heard it! I remember, I know!'

'George . . .'

'Tell me the truth,' he said. 'Just tell me.'

They stepped out into the corridor and the lights came on.

John pointed to his left. 'I come down that way,' he said. 'There's stairs at the end that lead up to where they held me. This must be deeper here and so it must be best to go back the way I come. What do you think?'

'That would seem to be logical,' Mumtaz said. 'But then again if we're closer to the water, couldn't that be a way out too?'

'Could be.' He shook his head. 'They say that the ancient Britons built these tunnels and so I s'pose you have to think about what they might have wanted to do down here. I mean they sacrificed people . . .'

'John, these tunnels are not that old,' Mumtaz said. 'I can't see how tunnels from that era would have survived. The land has risen since then. Also, I understand the cathedral authorities built tunnels, to the choir school and during the time of the Inquisition. If ancient tunnels existed they are long gone.'

'It's what they say,' John said.

'And do you believe them?'

'No,' he said. 'What I saw in that Shrine of theirs . . .'

Fearing he was about to cry, Mumtaz put a hand on his arm and said, 'We can talk about that later. Now we just have to get out of here.'

'I know.'

Had he seen one of these 'sacrifices'? Had he taken part? It seemed that his father was involved in some way. It seemed the son had very different views from his father. But that would all have to wait. Unless they got out of this place, it was all academic anyway.

Danielle Saint was, as Gary Connor put it, 'up the duff' by her boss, or so he'd heard. Word via Dillon, Gary said, while they were still speaking, was that Rodney was OK with it. But Danielle's mother was upset and Dillon's mum, Pat, was furious. Gary didn't know why.

'She works for briefs,' he told Lee Arnold. 'So I reckon she's done herself some good. I mean I know Rodney's a good enough sort but the Saints have a bad rep in Dagenham. Bloody south London scumbags. When my dad married Pat I couldn't believe it.'

'So who's Danielle's mother?' Lee asked.

'Dunno,' Gary said. 'Can't remember her name offhand, but I can find out. Something like Doris or Mabel, one of them sort of old names. She's one of 'em too.'

'One of what?'

'South London scumbags,' he said.

'I heard Rodney married a local girl,' Lee said.

Rodney laughed. 'Whoever told you that has a short

memory,' he said. 'No, Doris or whatever she is moved to Dagenham from south London when she was a teenager. She was up the duff by some geezer over there. Honestly don't know how she come to be in Dagenham. But Rodney and her hooked up somehow and he took on the kiddie.'

'A sister of Danielle's,' Lee said.

'Yeah, s'pose she must be. That eldest girl,' Gary said. 'Can't remember what she's called.'

'You know Mum came from Hackney,' Barry said.

'Yes, of course. I think we went there once, didn't we?' George said.

'I went there more than that,' Barry said. 'Before you were born. Bubbe was still alive then. I couldn't understand her because she only spoke Yiddish and Mum was ashamed. All I remember about the old woman was that she stroked my hair and admired my school uniform. Her flat was grim. It had no electricity and it was damp, all the walls were painted brown.'

'She was poor.'

'I remember asking Mum why Bubbe didn't come and live with us, and she said that it wouldn't be appropriate. She was such a snob!'

George smiled. Yes, their mother had been a most awful snob, insisting upon conventions like dressing for dinner and speaking 'nicely'. She had taken to her husband's world of middle-class Jewish gentility completely. A world where no one ever so much as mentioned being Jewish.

'What I didn't realise,' Barry said, 'was that at least half of how she was, was born of fear.'

'Of being Jewish?'

'George,' his brother said, 'when I visited Bubbe's old place for the last time you were probably about three. You didn't come and that was just as well, because when we left Bubbe's place we had to run a gauntlet.'

George frowned.

'I just thought they were thugs and at the time, Mum didn't disabuse me of that notion. Later, many years later, I found out they were fascists.'

'So when Mum talked about people like us . . .'

'Of course she meant Jews,' Barry said. 'It was 1962 and everyone wanted to believe that the fascists were dead, but they weren't and they're not and when I spoke to her about that day she told me we, she and me, had run a gauntlet of those bastards that day. She said they used to throw shit at her mother's front door. She also said that the police supported them.'

He lowered his head and continued, 'But Mum was old by that time and not entirely herself, as you may remember . . .'

Veronica Feldman had died of pneumonia in the 1990s after suffering from Alzheimer's for many years.

'Yes . . .'

'She also said that the fascists lived beneath the streets of London,' Barry said. 'In "every dark corner", she said. She also told me that you "knew". She'd tried to keep it from you but she had failed. She made me promise that I would never tell you that you were right.'

'And so I am right?'

Barry shook his head. 'No, of course you're not right!'

he said. 'She was a deluded old woman who had been frightened by the rise of fascism in the post-war East End. Of course she'd been frightened. It wasn't even as if she could have talked to Dad about it, because he would never have understood. So it festered and she got sick and . . . George, as I'm sure you know, underneath the precinct around the cathedral and probably to some extent the Temple too, is honeycombed with old tunnels. Used by the Church to allow priests to wander the old city without ending up covered in shit, where they sheltered from the plague. Some people even believe they were at one time used as holding cells by the Inquisition. Mum wasn't an educated woman. She feared what she didn't understand, and so when she heard the wind blowing through cavities underneath our building she interpreted that in a sinister fashion.'

'Yes, but . . .'

'George.' Barry held up a silencing hand. 'Mum was dementing, you are not. Forget all this. I know your religion teaches that evil can manifest—'

'It can!'

'It can't. There are just people and situations. You know that!'

George stood up. 'I'm telling you, Barry,' he said, 'Mum may not have been right about who was underneath the earth but she was correct that whatever it is, is wrong. And contrary to what Mum believed, we as Jews have a duty to flush that out into the light.'

Barry rolled his eyes. 'George . . .'

'No, no!' his brother said. 'No, I was right, and now

225

this terrible thing has happened at the cathedral, I intend to root this out!'

'And how do you intend to do that?' Barry asked.

'Give me one of your keys,' George demanded.

Barry still lived in the same apartment his parents had rented all those decades ago.

'George . . .'

'Come on! I only want to go into the old cellar!'

Barry wrestled with his trousers in order to extract a bunch of keys.

'George . . .'

'Oh, do come on!'

Barry sighed and then took two large keys from the fob and gave them to his brother.

'Satisfied?' he said.

'Thank you,' George replied.

And then he left.

Barry put his head in his hands and pondered over how alike his brother was to their mother when she'd begun to get sick.

Some serious types arrived to see Scott Brown. The DI had told Wilko to expect them. He'd described them as a 'delegation led by DI Manson'. Where they were from, Brown didn't say. Wilko surmised they were either Special Branch or spooks. All men, they were nondescript and silent until Brown came down to get them.

Wilko went into the changing rooms, got himself a very short shower and changed into civvies. The night duty had arrived and all he had to do now was hand over, and then get himself across Bishopsgate to Liverpool Street Station.

But would anyone meet him there? Really? Probably George, but then he was as mad as a bike. And he was his friend, so what did that make him?

All his adult life it had fascinated and bewitched him. Under the streets of London. He'd got it from his father. A man damaged by his war service, obsessed with the discovery of the Mithras Temple under a bomb-scarred London back in 1954. Wilko had never really understood why. All his dad had ever said was that the Nazis had twisted and weaponised their own ancient history to fit their political agenda. Had he feared that the Mithras Temple would be used for a similar purpose one day?

Later, when the old man had entered extreme old age, he'd transferred his obsession from the Mithras Temple to the person of John Dee, the Elizabethan astrologer and magician. Dee, some thought, had spent time as an inquisitor during the reign of Queen Mary, Elizabeth I's Catholic sister. By turns accused of sorcery and treason, Dee had been a controversial figure in Tudor England. It was said that during his time with the Inquisition, he'd participated in the torture of heretics. Later he was Protestant Elizabeth's personal magician. One thing was for sure: he was the ultimate survivor during what had been very dangerous times.

Father George Feldman had been the only person Wilko had ever met who understood. As a child he had been haunted by sounds from underneath the streets of London. As a man of God he interpreted these noises as presentiments of evil, maybe even the unquiet spirits of those Dee had tortured in order to save his own skin. And although it was well known that Jews, like George, had been expelled from England in the thirteenth century, it was also well known that thousands stayed on in hiding. But where had they hidden? A personal theory of Wilko's was that maybe they had used the tunnels. Had they died down there, perhaps in their hundreds? And who, if anyone, had known about them?

Wilko knew that Lee Arnold would consider such musings tinfoil-hat territory. Not only did he not do God, he also didn't do anything supernatural. And yet his woman, Mumtaz, had disappeared in EC4 without an apparent trace.

'That's all I can tell you,' DI Scott Brown said to the team assigned to the murder of the baby. 'We're off, it's over and that's an end to it.'

They'd all seen the group of serious-looking men arrive at and leave Brown's office. Neither Brown nor Pinker had told anyone who they were. But minutes after they had left, he'd told the team they were standing down.

Jordan Whittington wasn't the type of officer who usually questioned his superiors, but he'd got a bit of a taste for his secondment to CID and wasn't happy that it was at an end. And so he asked, 'Sir, is the case just dropped then? We've got some leads . . .'

'No, it isn't "dropped" as you say, PC Whittington,' Brown said. 'Our part in the investigation is at an end, that's all.'

'Yeah, but who—'

'Others more knowledgeable about this kind of offence have taken over,' Brown said.

'Who . . .'

'Never mind who, Whittington!' Brown eyed him narrowly and Jordan felt himself mentally shrink. 'You'll go back to uniform and that's the end of it.'

Later, when Brown and Pinker had returned to Brown's office, one of the detective constables came up to him and said, 'Special Branch, you know it.'

And maybe those grim men had come from Special Branch? Maybe their investigation had impinged on something the Branch had been working on for some time? Jordan knew that such things happened. But if he was right, then Wilko would have checked the men in. He'd ask him.

Leaving Dagenham, Lee drove to Newbury Park where he parked his car and got onto a Central Line Tube train. This would take him to Liverpool Street and Wilko. The old copper had told him that a mind, apparently greater than either of theirs, would get them into the house with the blue door. Lee suspected that 'mind' may well belong to Father George Feldman. If it did, he wasn't sure how much confidence he should have. George was a very intelligent man but he was also bonkers.

Anyway, in view of what Gary Connor had told him about the Saint family, Lee was actually more interested in speaking to pregnant Danielle. Although what he'd say to her, he didn't know. Just the fact he believed that Mumtaz had met this woman and that she was distantly related to 'scumbags' would hardly stand up in court, but he still wanted to confront her.

Why would she lie about meeting Mumtaz? Mumtaz had used an alias but this Danielle had apparently 'made' her and so knew her real name – and Wilko had shown her a photograph. The boyfriend hadn't known anything about it because he'd been at work.

The train pulled in to Stratford Station and a lot of people got off while a shit-ton of others got on. Lee found that his face was now dangerously close to some bloke's paunch and disappeared back into his thoughts. They'd been an odd couple, Danielle Saint and Henry Blizzard. A posh lawyer, maybe even public school educated, Jewish enough to have a mezuzah on his doorpost, and a working-class girl from Dagenham whose family were a 'problem' and, according to Gary, racist. The pregnancy had to have been an accident. Or maybe she'd set out to trap the wealthy boss who fancied her?

That was judgemental. Mumtaz would have lost her mind if she'd heard him say something like that. But Mumtaz wasn't around and underneath whatever exterior he was using today, Lee was frantic. If Danielle Saint knew anything then he was going to get that out of her, lawyer boyfriend or no lawyer boyfriend.

The corridor they were on led down still deeper into the earth. Not via stairs but a slope that snaked down, occasionally switching back on itself as it became narrower and hotter. Had they been able to see the end of it, Mumtaz and John would have known it was a dead end.

'Bollocks!'

John sat down on the dirt floor. Mumtaz, who was far from comfortable with how narrow the tunnel had become, and whose legs and feet hurt like hell, remained standing.

'Bollocks! Bollocks! Bollocks! Sorry!' John said.

'It's OK,' Mumtaz said. 'I feel the same.'

'I s'pose we have to go back the way we came.'

'Not much choice,' she said.

They both lapsed into silence. They could die in this terrible place and they both knew it.

Eventually John said, 'So those boys. What did they say about me?'

'They thought you were hurt,' she said.

He shook his head. 'I wasn't.'

'So what about the blood?'

'They call it blooding,' he said. 'They smear new members with it.'

'Where did it come from?' she asked.

'I . . . I didn't want to become a member. You have to understand that. It was me dad . . .'

'Your dad what?'

He was looking everywhere but at her now. Back along the corridor mainly.

'I think there was another door back there.'

'Yes,' she said.

Had it been that baby's blood? He didn't want to say and she could understand that. Who would do such a thing and why? It was clear that he was only going to answer in his own time and so she said, 'Do you want to try it?'

SIXTEEN

They all bought coffee from Costa and then sat outside the station opposite the Kindertransport statue so that Wilko and Lee could smoke.

'You have to ask yourself why Mumtaz might be in that house,' Lee said once they'd settled with their drinks. 'I know she wanted to find the boy and so she might have found a way to slip inside and then got lost.'

'They may have put her there,' George said.

'Who?'

'These people, whoever they are . . .' Only partly attending, George was texting someone at some length.

'George mate, I'm not being funny, but why?' Lee asked. 'I know you and Wilko have got this thing about tunnels . . .'

'There's something there,' George said.

'Yes, but what? And who are "they"? Do you know?'

George looked up from his phone. 'No. But I know . . .'

'The powers that be have taken over,' Wilko said.

'Taken over what?'

'The baby's death,' he said. 'Brown and his team got as far as investigating a pub in south London and then suddenly that lot swoop in.'

'Who exactly?' Lee asked.

'Special Branch? Counter Terrorism? Or even spooks,' Wilko said. 'Dunno. But it's gone up the food chain.'

'So this pub . . .'

'I shouldn't be saying anything.'

'But you will,' Lee said. 'What is it?'

'Seems they've found the kid's father. Middle-aged white bloke called Macbeth.'

'Shakespearian,' George said.

They ignored him.

'So where's this pub come in?'

'It's his local,' Wilko said. 'Says he met the mother there. Had a bunk up with her, once, he says. No knowledge of the kid.'

'So what's this Macbeth like?' Lee asked.

'No idea.'

Lee wondered why he'd met up with these two. But he told them about what Gary Connor had said regarding Danielle Saint.

'I want to talk to her again,' Lee said.

'Really?' Wilko shook his head. 'Where's your evidence she knows anything?'

'Conversations with Mumtaz. She'd written her name down . . .'

'Proving what? Danielle Saint could say Mumtaz made it all up. You know that!'

'Yes, but why would she?'

'I don't know,' Wilko said. Then he looked at Father George.

'Oh, er, me, yes . . .'

'Well?'

'Although they've, in a sense, haunted me all my life, I've never been into any of these tunnels . . .'

'So you don't actually know whether they're there,' Lee said.

'Oh, I do!'

'How, if you've never been into any of them?'

Lee was becoming impatient, which Wilko could understand. He put a hand on Lee's wrist.

But it did nothing to calm him.

'I wish I'd never got involved in this!' Lee said. 'Chasing after some kid with a bit of blood on his face! Mumtaz all over that! Give her a lost child and . . . And now I'm lumbered with you two!'

And while Wilko may have taken offence, it was clear that George hadn't. Smiling, he said, 'Because I've seen an entrance to one of them.'

'Where?'

'The Temple.'

Lee groaned. 'George, that's . . .'

'I always knew there was something underneath our old building when I was a child,' he said. 'It frightened me and so I never truly investigated it – until today. My brother lives in our parents' old place and he gave me his

235

key to the basement. It took me a little while and I had to manhandle a tumble dryer but I found it.'

'An entrance?'

'I opened it and looked inside,' George said. His face became white and then he added, 'I know you're thinking that the Temple is very far from St Paul's, but . . .' Then he frowned. 'These entrances . . . Once you've seen one, you start to see others.'

There was a sound of water running again, this time louder than in the room where Mumtaz had been held.

They'd gone back to the door they'd seen on the way to the dead end, which led to a room that had proved to be empty and pitch black until John had managed to find the light switch. Still empty, the room sloped down to a central depression. John and Mumtaz walked towards it, looking over their shoulders at the open door behind them. When they arrived at the centre they saw that the depression contained what looked like a well – a deep, circular brick-built shaft which disappeared into water so dark at the bottom it looked like oil. The water lapped. There was a very dodgy-looking ladder on one side of the hole leading down into the watery depths.

Mumtaz looked at John. She said, 'In the past the river was much closer to the cathedral than it is now.'

'Was it?'

'Yes. And it's tidal,' she said, 'which means that maybe at certain times of the day this well is dry.'

He stared at her.

'The water must be coming in from the river,' she said.

'Otherwise why would it move like this? There has to be an opening down there somewhere.'

'You think?'

She shrugged. 'That's my hunch,' she said. 'I don't know. But following the logic that the shores of the Thames are exposed when the tide is low, it seems to me that this well has to lead, ultimately, to a way out.'

'So what do we do?' John asked.

'Well, we can carry on wandering these tunnels until we either find an exit or not, or we could wait here and see whether the water recedes.'

The boy had gone. It was too dangerous to talk to his father and so Arthur went to the pub. Weirdly for The Hob there was a group of unknown faces sitting by the windows. He couldn't understand them. Tourists.

He went up to the bar and called over to Bradley.

'Is Val in?' he asked once he'd caught the lad's eye.

'Yeah. Want me to get her for you?'

'Yeah.'

The boy left and Arthur reached across the bar to grab a pint glass, which he filled from one of the pumps. Some of the tourists stared, but he didn't care. He'd pay for his pint later, or not.

After a few minutes Bradley appeared with a woman of about sixty who beckoned to Arthur. He went over and she opened the bar.

'We'll go upstairs,' she said. 'Strangers in the house.'

Valerie Rudolph wasn't your typical pub landlady. She looked, and sounded, rather more like the sort of woman one might meet in the Royal Enclosure at Ascot. Tall, slim and groomed, Valerie's pale face showed some signs of Botox use. This manifested in a slightly expressionless countenance.

Arthur followed her up a set of narrow stairs to the flat above the pub. Again, this was a surprise to those who might have been expecting Edwardian stuffiness. By contrast Valerie's place, one of many Arthur recalled, was an education in Scandinavian minimalist chic. Poulsen lamps, Nordik soft furnishings, funky Bang & Olufsen speakers and absolutely no mess whatsoever.

Arthur sat down on one of the pristine chairs and came straight to the point.

'The boy's got out.'

Val folded herself into the chair opposite and said, 'How?'

He shook his head. 'I won't lie, I must've left the door open.'

'That was silly.'

Arthur raised an eyebrow. 'I'd call his dad normally but given the situation . . .'

'I know,' she said.

She was very calm. But then she always was, whatever was happening.

'How much does the boy know about the network?'

'Nothing,' Arthur said. 'When we took him to the Shrine he was blindfolded.'

'And yet somehow he managed to run away and get to your front door,' she said, again calmly. But her eyes, on fire, told a different story.

Arthur shook his head. He said, 'Colin was gonna kill him.'

'Because he threw up?'

'Nah, it's what he said before the Sacrifice,' Arthur said.

'Wasn't he sedated?'

'Course. But when Colin brought it in, laid it down, me and Bill from Hounslow had to hang onto him. Going on about what was we doing and why, and all them things I thought he knew.'

'Colin hadn't prepared him.'

'No.'

'And now he's on the radar of the police,' she said.

'I've heard Colin's missus is up the wall with it all,' Arthur said. 'Worried about her boy, now her husband . . .'

'She's Colin's responsibility,' Val said. 'I don't know why he's still with her anyway. She's not one of us.'

'Yeah, but she can be a problem to us if she don't get the boy back,' Arthur said. 'The plan was always to send him home once he'd come to his senses.'

'And if he didn't come to his senses?'

Arthur shrugged.

Val frowned. 'Do you think he can find his way out this time?'

'I dunno. Where we put him's nowhere near the Shrine.'

'Deeper?'

'Yeah.'

'As deep as that woman . . . ?'

'Not that deep,' Arthur said. 'That deep's reserved for bodies.'

* * *

239

It was cold. Lee Arnold pulled his overcoat tightly around his shoulders and lit a fag. They were on a street called Addle Hill, a turning off Carter Lane which led down to a road called Knightrider Street. Lee, who remembered enjoying a US TV show called *Knight Rider* back in the 1980s, was mildly amused behind his frustration. The series' talking car was almost as absurd as the sight of Father George minutely investigating manhole covers. There was, it seemed, only one mark which distinguished ordinary manhole covers from those which led down to Wilko and George's mythical tunnels. And although George had told them that once you saw these entrances you could spot others easily, he had clearly been exaggerating. Now crouched on the ground outside a modern-day 'gourmet' pie shop, George was looking at a manhole cover through a magnifying glass. You really couldn't make it up.

Even Wilko, who had been well on board with all this, sidled up to Lee and said, 'Good job it's dark or someone'd get him sectioned.'

Lee wondered how often other people had wondered whether George should be sectioned or not. His parishioners for instance.

Lee whispered to Wilko, 'I'm not humouring him for much longer. I'm getting into that house tonight whether you and him like it or not.'

Wilko's phone rang and he turned aside to answer it just as George moved on to another manhole cover. Was what they were doing just a reflection of how bizarre beliefs seemed to have gained traction in recent years? To Lee, who had never 'done' religion or alternative therapies and who had never harboured even an opinion regarding aliens from space, the tunnels were just another mad thing on that continuum. Or were they? Well of course they were! Just as he didn't believe for a second that 5G communications were in some Byzantine way connected to Microsoft magnate Bill Gates supposed desire to 'rule the world', he did not hold with these tunnels.

He stood, waiting in the darkness for either one lunatic to get off his phone or the other madman to stand up straight and stop looking at manhole covers.

They sat in silence, watching the water at the bottom of the well, fancying at times that it was receding. Mumtaz didn't know what to say. John was fragile. He'd seen and maybe even done things she couldn't bring her mind to imagine. And while she wasn't exactly happy to let him talk about such things in his own time, she managed to content herself that all she could do now was wait. For the water to recede, for John to speak . . .

It burst out of him.

'I always knew my old man was a bit of a knob, but I never imagined he was . . .' He shook his head. 'I thought he was like a lot of people, you know, sort of using words that were bad and made you cringe. Old people do it, laughing at old comedians who take the piss out of people for the way they look, the colour of their skin and that. Casual racism they call it. Don't get me wrong, I've never liked it but it was just sort of there. Mum don't like it either but like me, she just sort of let it go . . . I never thought about . . .'

'Where that might lead?' Mumtaz said.

'No,' he said, 'because that wasn't part of it, not really. No, this is my dad's family and the people they've always known. Cousins are in it, uncles . . .'

'Luddites?'

'I dunno when it started,' he said. 'But I do know it was before the Second World War. They supported Hitler.'

Neither of them said anything. The City of London had been almost bombed into the ground by the Nazis in World War II. There was an almost universally held belief that everyone in Britain had been opposed to Hitler and his fevered dreams of white supremacy. Mumtaz had learnt a little about the British Fascist Party headed by Oswald Mosley when she'd been at school, about the Battle of Cable Street which had happened in 1936 not far from where she'd been born. The fascists had been defeated by the people of the East End and had disappeared. That was the narrative. But of course they hadn't disappeared at all – in the sixties and seventies they'd become the National Front, then the BNP and now they seemed to exist amongst purveyors of conspiracy theories online and on right-wing media outlets. Events like the Holocaust were receding into the past and, to some at least, nationalism appeared to be on the rise once again.

'It's a religion,' John said. 'They, we, worship King Lud, the first British king they say. There's a skeleton in the Shrine they say is his. You have to swear to be a soldier for Albion on it. Then they blood you. I knew nothing

242

about any of it until Dad brought me here and gave me to Arthur.'

'Who is?'

'He's the Servant of Lud. His family go right back to them times. They've always lived here. There's always been Luddites. These tunnels were built by them. They say you can get a whole army down here and that's what they want to do.'

'Build an army?'

'Yeah.'

In spite of herself, Mumtaz laughed.

John said, 'Mad innit, I know. An army of fat old white blokes and fucking football mallets, but they mean it! I watched them kill a baby! I screamed and screamed, my dad punching me and telling me to be a man and . . .'

He sobbed. Mumtaz moved over to him and put an arm around his shoulders. He was just a kid. How could his own father involve him in such a thing?

'Who killed the baby, John?' she said.

He tucked himself into her side like an infant. Mumtaz felt both protective towards this boy and appalled. John's family were part of something she could barely comprehend. This was, surely, a terrorist organisation? If they were building an army . . . To do what?

John coughed as he began to bring his crying under control. Then he said, 'Arthur.'

'Arthur killed . . .'

'She screamed!' he said. 'I wanted to die. Then when she was still, me dad put his fingers in her blood and smeared it over my face. It was then that I ran.'

'To the front door of the house?'

'I dunno how I got there,' he said. 'I just legged it. I couldn't go back and trace my route if me life depended on it. I opened the door and there were the two lads. If I hadn't turned back to see if I was being followed, I would've got away. But I did look back and there was Arthur and me dad behind him and it hit me.'

'What did?'

'I'd have to dob in my old man to the police,' he said.

And then he began to cry again and she held him.

When Jordan arrived he was already wearing one of the white plastic coveralls the SOCOs wore when investigating a crime scene. Thin and disposable, he'd found them in a bin outside the dressing rooms.

The rush hour was coming to an end now and so not too many people stared at them as the three other men put the coveralls on over their clothes in the street. If questioned they would say they were 'flushers' or sewer maintenance workers.

Father George had found what he'd been looking for when Wilko was on the phone to Jordan. The mark that distinguished a 'real' manhole cover from a tunnel entrance was a tiny moulding of a menorah or seven-branched candlestick. A Jewish symbol, the menorah also represented the six branches of knowledge which look up to the central light, which was God.

'The Jews who chose to remain after the expulsion in the thirteenth century used these tunnels to hide from the Church,' Wilko told the others as he pulled on his SOCO

244

coveralls. 'I've picked up info about it for years. Then they . . . Well, who knows who's down there now?'

'Yes, but Wilko, as soon as that baby's body was found, you began talking about the tunnels . . .' Lee said.

'Because anything that happens round here could have a connection,' Wilko said. 'The tunnels exist. Who made them originally, we don't know, but they're here and in my experience, in the past, the coppers have either not known about them or ignored them. Now they might, *might* have something with your partner, Lee. Just don't go off on your esoteric schtick, George. And that's all I'll say about it.' Then he looked at Jordan. 'Can you lift up that cover for us old gits, son?'

Using the tip of his expandable police baton to hook the cover up, Jordan Whittington opened up a whole new subterranean world to his colleagues.

There was that pregnant girl again. Arthur turned away. He didn't want her coming over and asking about that woman. That was all done and dusted. They'd thrown her into one of the deepest rooms and she'd cracked her head and stopped breathing. Sometime when he could be arsed he'd go down there and shove her down the well. With luck she'd be dragged out into the river where she'd be picked up by some boat or other, ID'd by her DNA and deemed to have had an accident. End of.

And the girl wouldn't say anything. Arthur turned back and saw that she was looking at him. But she didn't say anything and she didn't come any closer. She was like a lot of them. She agreed but she wasn't prepared to do anything. She, in particular, also slept with the enemy. That would end badly but then that was her business. He knew what she really felt and, if necessary, he could use that against her.

She was lonely, poor thing, and out of her depth. But he didn't care. As Val often said, even those who follow are only human stepping stones.

Manson had told him nothing really. Alone in his office, DI Scott Brown brooded on how the case of the St Paul's dead baby had been ripped away from him. His suspect Colin Macbeth had been released and Brown's team had been dismantled.

All DI Manson had said was that Jordan Whittington had been 'made' by one of their operatives in that pub in Bermondsey, the one where Macbeth had said he 'might' have met the mother of the dead baby. What had happened to that woman? He couldn't believe that a mother would willingly give up her child. Was she dead too?

Now that Counter Terrorism had shut them down, would they ever know? All Manson had said was that they'd been undercover at The Jolly Sailor for months. He wouldn't say what kind of terrorist activity he and his team had observed in the pub, but Brown surmised it was of a far-right white nationalistic type. Or not. In the world of the great smoke and mirrors generator that was the Internet, those wishing to kill others for God or love or money hid in the strangest places. Every day the world seemed to move further and further towards the kind of crazy conspiracy theories espoused by old nutters like

Wilko. Fucking Nazis and Freemasons underneath every rock, according to him.

However, before Manson had left, he had taken the time to get Brown on his own for a moment. Quite unbidden he'd said to him, 'We will get whoever killed that baby in EC4.' And then he'd added, 'We may already have him in our sights.'

And while Brown felt that Manson may have just said that in order to mollify him, he couldn't quite make himself believe it.

Both lying on their stomachs, Mumtaz and John watched the last of the water recede and then looked at each other. One of them had to climb down that ladder if they were going to find out if there was a way out at the bottom. It was a no-brainer.

Mumtaz said, 'I've no idea what sort of state this ladder might be in at the bottom.'

'Looks dodgy up here,' John said.

'Which is why I'm going down.' Mumtaz stood.

'Ah, no, I think it's . . .'

She swung one leg over the parapet and put a foot on the first rung of the ladder. Metal, and she felt it vibrate as it took her weight. She looked at the screws that secured it to the brickwork and saw them move. But what choice was there?

John said, 'I think I should go . . .'

But he was clearly afraid and he was, at sixteen, just a child. A traumatised child in fear for his life. Mumtaz knew she would have done this for Shazia without a thought. She said, 'You hold on to the top of the ladder and steady it if necessary.' Then she smiled. 'We're going to get out of here, John.'

SEVENTEEN

The young lad switched his torch on and illuminated what was a very short, narrow tunnel. There was a rushing sound coming from somewhere which, considering the entrance to this tunnel had been less than a metre away from the manhole cover, probably meant they were close to sewerage. It would be raw too. Lee could feel his hair stand on end. And what was that smell?

George was in front of Lee, Wilko behind and Jordan heading up the posse. On one level what they were doing was farcical, while on another it was a reflection of how hard it could sometimes be for the police to gain entry to properties where an offence could possibly have taken place. Especially, it seemed, where a missing person was involved. History was littered with cases of properties either not searched or incompletely searched – where a victim was

249

eventually discovered, usually dead.

The smell of shit was getting stronger and Lee began to feel sick. Would he be doing this if Mumtaz was just an ordinary punter? Not a chance.

'Canon?'

Canon Palmer looked up from the book on his desk into the eyes of Enid Hardwick.

'Yes?' he said.

Without being invited, she sat down in the chair opposite his desk.

'About the tunnels . . .'

'They were all blocked up years ago, decades,' he said. 'Father George Feldman is a sincere and passionate priest but he lives in the past. No one here had or has any involvement in the dreadful murder of that child. As I told Father George and the police, there are no tunnels. We failed to shut the gates on the night in question, that is all.'

He was becoming angry. But she persisted.

'Canon,' she said, 'you and I both know people. You have worked with them, or rather . . .'

'The Church always works with the sick, the delusional . . .'

'I'm talking about the Reverend Harold,' she said.

The canon's office became quiet, save for the ticking of the carriage clock on his mantlepiece.

Eventually the canon said, 'It is important that young priests experience all kinds of situations. Some parishioners can be challenging . . .'

'The Reverend de Vere, in my opinion, is being rather

more influenced by – let's name names – Mr Hobbs – than he is managing to influence him,' Mrs Hardwick said. 'I am not saying that Mr Hobbs is in any way responsible for the death of that child. But I know you know of his toxic views, because I have heard a conversation between you and the Reverend de Vere.'

'You should not—'

'Canon, please don't tell me what I should and should not attend to! You and I both know that the Reverend de Vere was supposed to lock the precinct gates that night. You and I also know that you didn't say so to the police.'

'Locking up is a joint enterprise . . .'

'Which was assigned to Harold de Vere that night!' she said. 'By you!'

He looked down at the paperwork on his desk.

'The Reverend de Vere and myself have had several conversations about Mr Hobbs and his alleged activities,' he said. 'It was and is my belief that the Reverend de Vere was challenging Mr Hobbs's distorted opinions whilst at the same time giving his views respect.'

'The man's a nationalist nutter!' Mrs Hardwick said.

The time for cool heads and reasoned argument was over. She'd had a text from Father George, telling her he was going to attempt to get into those tunnels now blocked off from the great church.

'Canon, a child has died and a woman is missing,' Mrs Hardwick said. 'Father Edward has appeared. How much more evidence do you want? Get Harold de Vere in here now and call the police!'

* * *

The bottom of the well was slimy and wet and Mumtaz was glad it was too dark for her to be able to see anything in detail.

She could see the boy looking down into the shaft and called up. 'I'm going to look for where the water might be coming in. I'll have to feel my way.'

Neither of them had a phone or a torch and so in the absence of any other light source they were effectively blind. As she moved her hands slowly across the brickwork, Mumtaz wondered what they would do even if she did find an exit. It would probably mean they'd have to move through a tunnel in complete darkness, the threat of rising water levels a constant concern.

They could die – easily. And so when her fingertips did find a void in the brickwork, at first she said nothing. The edge of the hole was wide if not tall. They would have to duck down low to fit inside. They would also have to pass through the slime- and ooze-crusted sides of the tunnel. She ducked down to see whether she could discern any light at the end of it.

John said, 'Can you see anything?'

'Yeah, I . . .'

But there was no light. Not even a pinprick. When she stood up she said, 'There's a tunnel that I hope leads to the river, but I don't know. Come down and tell me what you want to do.'

Brown had gone home when the call came in. DS Melina Pinker took it. She said, 'I'm sorry but that case has been taken out of our hands.'

252

She heard the canon sigh. She had no idea what an ecclesiastical canon did, but she did know that he was by way of being a powerful figure in the cathedral.

He said, 'So who is now in charge of this investigation?'

Telling him that Counter Terrorism were now involved would probably cause alarm. She said, 'May I ask what aspect of the investigation this is concerning, sir?'

He sighed again and then said, 'It's a member of my staff . . .'

'Yes?'

There was a long pause and then she heard a woman's voice say, 'Oh for God's sake!'

'Hello?'

'Hello,' the woman said. 'What Canon Palmer is trying to tell you, is that a member of the ministry team here at the cathedral has come under malign influence and we think that this may be pertinent to your investigation.'

'What sort of malign influence?' Pinker asked.

Did they mean a ghost or . . . ?

'He has been having regular discussions with a man we believe is a far-right activist,' the woman said.

Pinker sat down. 'I see. Can you give me some more details, please?'

Father George stopped. Breathless, he turned to Lee and said, 'There's some sort of hatch ahead. Constable Whittington is attempting to open it.'

'OK.'

Wilko, wheezing behind Lee, said, 'Let's hope it leads somewhere bigger.'

Try as they might, none of the men could avoid the crushing feeling of claustrophobia being in such a narrow space evinced. Cramped and hot, it also reeked of human waste. Lee turned his head away from George's looming behind and stifled a cough. He had occasionally wondered how all the tunnels underneath the city fitted around each other. Sewers, Tube lines, cellars, foot tunnels. So far he felt none the wiser and now that they were stationary, he could feel panic beginning to build inside his chest. It was the same feeling that had assaulted him when he'd been in tanks. He'd fought in the first Iraq War during his service with the army. It was why, later, when he returned home, he'd become an alcoholic. Dying in a tin can where you barely had enough room to fart had been an everyday occurrence in Iraq. It had left its mark.

He could hear the young PC grunt as he attempted to either pull or push something up ahead. He tried to regulate his breathing but it wasn't easy, even with his face turned away from George's backside.

Wilko said, 'What's happening up there?'

Jordan Whittington grunted again and then said, 'Nearly got it!'

'Got what?'

Another grunt and outflow of breath was followed by a sharp scraping sound. Then they all heard Jordan speak again.

'Shit! It's enormous!'

'What is?' Wilko asked.

Lee was beyond speech now, his breathing exercises having turned into panting. However, there had been a change in the air around him. It felt slightly cooler.

Father George's spare behind began to shift, shuffling forwards. And in common with the phenomenon that happens to those wishing to urinate who suddenly lose control just as they are about to reach the toilet, Lee Arnold screamed as he crawled through a small hatch into a huge cavern-like space.

Standing up, he found himself next to PC Jordan and George, looking at a waterfall, which was grey.

'Oh, George, George, George!'

Barry Feldman put his head in his hands before removing the bottle of port he'd just opened from his kitchen counter and taking it into his living room. He'd always been against his brother getting involved with the Church. Not because he was Jewish but because, like their mother, Barry had always felt that George was easily seduced by 'esoterica'.

Veronica, their mother, had been a sucker for anything occult. Barry remembered her spiritualist phase well. Those winter afternoons when mad old bats purporting to be 'mediums' came to the flat while his father was prosecuting an alleged murderer, rapist or gun-toting thief. Then there'd been Kabbalah, when Veronica had spent a lot of time with a woman called Therese who had introduced her to the Jewish origins of what she had called 'western magik'. George could remember Therese, and Barry wondered how much of what had been said by her he had taken in. In Barry's opinion that was certainly when Veronica began to get her 'nerves', as his father had called his wife's increasingly fearful and sometimes bizarre behaviour in the mid-1960s.

George spent most of his time with his mother at that point, and Barry remembered their father speculating about how healthy that may or may not have been for the boy. He heard things down in the basement – as did his mother.

Had Veronica passed her fears about growing anti-Semitism in her East End home on to George? Had those old tunnels become barracks for far-right activists after World War II? Were those people or rather similar people still using the tunnels?

Barry put an end to this train of thought by telling himself to 'fuck off'. But it didn't stop his mind whirring. Before he'd left to go God knows where, George had phoned Barry to tell him he'd found the entrance to one of these tunnels in the basement underneath his flat. He'd been manic as hell and high as a kite and so Barry had put the phone down on him.

Later, he'd tried to phone George back, but the call had gone straight to voicemail, indicating that the device was probably off. This had left Barry feeling very uneasy. George in that state could have gone off anywhere in order to do just about anything. And what if there really was an entrance to a tunnel underneath his building?

Barry, although desperate for an evening slumped in front of the television, knew that he couldn't rest until he'd been down to the basement and looked for this bloody thing himself. Reluctantly he stood up and then strolled out of his flat.

* * *

George turned his head away from the pounding water cascade and said to Lee, 'Don't let it splash into your face!'

Wilko, who had just emerged from the hatch, said, 'Fuck me!'

The sound the water made as it fell down into an unseen void was considerable, and so they all had to shout to be heard.

Jordan said, 'It's sewerage, Wilko! Don't get it on you!'

'Christ!' Wilko said. 'A fucking river of shit.'

They were on a ledge opposite the cascade. Fortunately it was wide, which allowed Wilko to move past Lee and speak to George and Jordan. The young man was shaking now and Wilko felt guilty for involving him. Not that Jordan had protested when George had told him what was planned. Through first Wilko and then George, the young man had developed a fascination for subterranean London that was only ever going to be satisfied if he saw it for himself.

George said, 'This must be where the tunnel intersects with the sewer.'

Lee Arnold, now bringing up the rear, said, 'No shit, Sherlock!'

George flung him a sour look and then said, 'Look, this isn't going to be straightforward. Of course the tunnels are going to intersect with sewers, maybe even Tube lines.' He took something out of one of the pockets in the SOCO suit. 'We need, I think, to go north . . .'

He had a compass which he now peered at using the torch on his phone. Then he pointed in the direction the path seemed to be leading.

'We need to go straight ahead.'

Lee looked over the edge at the bottom of the waterfall. A river of shit, piss and unmentionable tatters of probably toilet paper, wipes and nappies. What was he doing? Even if these tunnels were as ancient and well used as Wilko reckoned, that didn't mean they were going to lead them to Mumtaz – which was the point. But then Wilko had always been a persuasive old bastard. What Lee should have done was go back to speak to Danielle Saint. Only Wilko had reckoned she might cry harassment. But so what if she did? Lee wasn't a copper any longer.

And yet he felt that he was walking on eggshells. Why had he allowed Mumtaz to follow an unpaid lead brought to her by a couple of teenagers? Why hadn't he marched straight into the house with the blue door and demanded to see her? He was even treading on eggshells with bloody Gary Connor! But then he, if indirectly, was involved. Danielle Saint was his stepmother's niece, people he had been informed were 'scumbags' and 'racists'. Were they? Or was that just Gary's bitterness at his stepbrother talking?

George took the lead from Jordan now and they began to move forwards.

She'd called Brown at home. He'd not been amused but Melina Pinker hadn't known what else to do. Canon Palmer and this Mrs Hardwick were on their way to the station with a priest called Harold de Vere who, apparently, had something to tell them about the death of the baby in the churchyard.

Brown had rocked up with that DI Manson in tow and now they were both in Brown's office with the people from the cathedral. It was hard to know what was going on. Melina had thought that their involvement with the baby's death had come to an end and maybe it had. Maybe Brown was simply going to pass whatever this was over to Manson.

The obbo at the pub in south London had been curtailed and so maybe the investigation into Colin Macbeth was at an end. But how could it be? DNA evidence had shown him to be the baby's father. Manson had to still have eyes on him, surely. Brown had told her very little but he had revealed that Manson and his team had been working on activities centred around the pub for some months.

But what kind of activities?

She had gone back to trying to concentrate on her paperwork when her phone rang again. This time it was the front desk.

'Gentleman down here says he needs to speak to someone about his missing brother,' the desk sergeant said.

Melina told him she'd come down right away.

The woman's body had gone. Arthur looked in every nook and cranny but all he found was what remained of her handbag. Once he'd sent that message from the woman to Lee Arnold, he'd smashed up her phone. But where was she?

Big Kev had thrown her down there. Arthur himself had heard the crack when her skull hit the floor. Kev had told him there was no pulse. None. And yet she was gone. Had she fallen down the well? He moved towards it and looked down over the side. She wasn't there. He hadn't expected her to be. Even if she had fallen down there, she'd just be pulled out into the river, eventually. One day a corpse would be found, but no one would be able to trace it back to him, or the house. The tunnels were, and remained, hidden. The cathedral had bricked up any entrances that had existed after the war.

Arthur himself couldn't remember much about the Blitz. Against advice, his family had stayed in London together with the landlord of the pub next door. Back then The Hobgoblin had been called The Bell and the landlord had been called Mr Salzedo. It was Mr Salzedo who had shown his father the tunnels and it had been that same gentleman his father had killed down there.

That, however, was the deep, deep story that was for the consumption of no one but Arthur.

John's thin body shook. There was absolutely no light in the tunnel that led from the well and ultimately, hopefully, to the river. They had neither phones nor torches and depending on how long it took them to traverse the tunnel, they might be drowned in a rising tide.

'I'm not going to make you go in there,' Mumtaz said. 'I can't. But I do think that it's the best hope we have at the moment. We know it leads to the river, we just don't know how far away that is. Do you have any idea about where we might be now in relation to the house?'

'No . . .'

'I don't have the faintest idea either,' she said.

'So we have to . . .'

'We don't have to,' Mumtaz said. 'But if we don't try this we may regret it. You said yourself these Luddites are crazy. Thinking about where I was and how I ended up there, I think I'm supposed to be dead already.' She put a hand on his arm. 'For what it's worth, I think I at least have to go.'

John looked at her. She was a strong person to have survived; she was also older than he was and had the same sort of confidence his mum had once had, before she'd lost control of his dad.

Colin hadn't been involved with the Luddites for that long. He hadn't joined the BNP until John was five. Some skanky relative he used to drink with down The Jolly Sailor had joined and had managed to persuade Colin to do so too. John's mum had told him that when it had started it had, for Colin, been more about the beer than the politics. But then there'd been some run-in with one of Colin's suppliers – an Indian – and things had never been the same. Then he'd joined the real nutters, the Luddites. John didn't know how he'd met them or where, but from then on his parents became strangers to each other.

John suddenly felt a searing need for his mother and put a hand up to his face to stop himself crying out. Then he put his arms around Mumtaz and said, 'Please don't leave me!'

'John, I won't . . .'

'Don't . . .'

They stood wrapped in one another in silence until, unable to bear the lack of resolution any longer, Mumtaz said, 'John, I have to go.'

He pulled away from her and looked into her eyes. She was right. She, if not he, had to go. They would kill her. However, the thought of being in those tunnels without her was like contemplating life without his mother and so he took a deep breath and then said, 'I'll come with you.'

'How old is your brother, Mr, er . . .'

'Fifty-eight,' Barry said. 'His name's George Feldman.'

Melina looked up. 'Father George Feldman?' she said.

'Yes. How do you know?' Barry put a hand up to his head. 'Christ, don't tell me he's been bending your ear about these sodding tunnels!'

'Mr Feldman,' she said, 'can we start from the beginning, please. Your brother, Father George . . .'

Barry had been down to the basement of his building. He'd found nothing, but then he hadn't expected to find anything. George was going the same way as their mother and he feared he could be anywhere in pursuit of his fixation. He told DS Pinker how George's state of mind had been deteriorating since the killing of the baby in Paul's Churchyard. She, probably quite rightly, looked at him in a way Barry interpreted as disbelief.

Eventually he said, 'I'm not mad you know. I know I sound as if I am. I am a QC. Hard to believe given what I'm talking to you about . . .'

'No, no,' Pinker said. 'Not at all actually. But I do

think that you should maybe speak to my boss and the people he is with.'

There was fur. And warmth and the sound of claws scratching against stone. A rat.

John shrieked in spite of himself and pulled his hand away. But not quickly enough. The pain wasn't that bad but he knew it had bitten him and he knew, even though he couldn't see anything, that it had drawn blood. Warmth ran down his fingers.

Mumtaz, ahead, said, 'What's the matter?'

'A rat,' John said.

'We have to be close to the sewers,' she said.

'It bit me,' he said.

'Did it break the skin?'

'I think so . . .'

She didn't say anything for a moment. A bite from a rat was always cause for concern, not least because of the danger of contracting rat-bite fever, a condition that could be fatal. Whether John knew about this, Mumtaz didn't know. But for the moment they both had to ignore it.

Eventually she said, 'Don't worry. We'll get it treated when we get out of here. But if we can move a bit more quickly that would be good. Be careful where you put your hands. Maybe move along with them on the ceiling.'

'OK.'

But Mumtaz's heart was in her throat. If John could get bitten once he could get bitten again – and so could she. Just by being where they were, unprotected by hazmat suits, minus the respirators worn by the flushers

263

who maintained the nearby sewers, one or both of them could contract Weil's disease, a disorder associated with contaminated water, or succumb to the high concentrations of methane and carbon dioxide gases that could build up underground. And there was not a chink of light to guide them. Moving, more quickly now, in absolute darkness was disorientating and terrifying.

Mumtaz had never felt that London was anything but her familiar, benign home, until now. It felt as if her city had suddenly turned and wished to make an end of her.

EIGHTEEN

DI Brown was the one on the left. The other man, on the right, was unnamed. But Barry knew this of old. Probably some counter-terrorism type, or a spook. If he was right, then all that man would do was listen. He wouldn't ask any questions, would not respond, and Barry would be kept, effectively, in the dark.

'Your brother went to the cathedral churchyard,' Brown said.

'I went with him,' Barry said.

'Why?'

'He asked me. We are very different men, DI Brown. My brother is a man of God, steeped in the esoteric. I am a cynical barrister steeped mainly in antique legislation and a deeply disillusioned opinion upon the alleged goodness of humanity. My brother is forever attempting to bring me around to his point of view, but to no avail. This occasion was no different. I think he wanted me to feel the "evil" he claimed was emanating from the cathedral. I couldn't. I can appreciate Wren's church as a work of art but on the "spiritual" plane I am lost.'

'So your brother felt "evil" and you didn't?'

'No. I admit I was fed up with the whole thing by that time and bade him farewell in the churchyard. He then went into the cathedral on his own. Tragically for St Paul's Cathedral, George is obsessed by the idea that it too, in common with the rest of the City, is honeycombed with subterranean tunnels. This is against all available evidence to the contrary and only conforms to the word of a woman who was out of her mind.'

'Who was?'

'Our mother,' he said. 'Poor old Veronica, mad as a box of frogs.'

He told them about George's childish fears about malign beings living underground, and about their mother's belief that centuries before what remained of British Jewry had hidden in tunnels underneath the City.

'It's all rot of course,' Barry concluded.

Brown looked at his colleague, who said, 'And what do you think about the tunnels, Mr Feldman?'

'Me? Nonsense,' Barry said. 'George had this notion that there was an entrance to said tunnels underneath my building, but there isn't. No such thing exists.'

'Are you sure?'

Barry shrugged. 'I've not long ago been down there and I found nothing,' he said. 'Felt a total fool to boot.

But George is not like me. In a way he is vulnerable, especially to the esoteric. I fear he may have done something stupid.'

'Like what?'

'I really don't know, but his phone rings out and he is not at home.' He leant towards them. 'To be honest I wonder whether he's found his way into a sewer in pursuit of this madness. George is, if nothing else, a dogged chap.'

He'd found her looking in through the front window of that awful pub, The Hobgoblin. As ever it was full of men, young and old, drinking, yelling and sometimes swearing at the TV which was set to some sports channel.

He said, 'What are you doing?'

Danielle visibly jumped before she turned to face him. Her belly was enormous. With her long blonde hair, her swollen ankles and that coat that no longer fitted her, she looked like a woman from a poor housing estate.

'Henry!' she said, when she saw him.

'I went home and you weren't there,' he said. 'So I rang but you didn't pick up. I've been looking for you. I was worried.'

'I'm alright,' she said. 'Just . . .'

'Just what?' he asked. 'The doctor has told you to rest. What are you doing?'

'I, er . . . I have to get out sometimes . . .'

'I accept that, but why are you hanging around this pub? It's an awful place! With any luck it'll be gone in a few years' time.'

'They've a right to be there, those men,' Danielle said. 'This is their place.'

'Their place?' Henry shook his head. 'God, what is this? Have you had some sort of working-class epiphany?'

'What?'

'Dani, tell me honestly, do you have anything to do with that woman who the police came round about?'

'No!'

He sat down on a bollard and looked up at her. He said, 'Look, I know that this . . . You and me . . . Well it's not ideal . . .'

'I told you, you didn't have to do this,' Danielle said. 'Having me living with you is your choice, Henry. We both know if it weren't for the baby . . .'

'You should've had an abortion,' he said.

'Yeah, but I wasn't gonna do that, was I?'

'No.'

Inside the pub there was a huge roar. Cheering.

Henry said, 'I don't know what you do. I go to work every day, I come home, make or buy some food and then you go to bed early. What do you do with yourself, Dani?'

She shrugged.

'I mean,' he continued, 'for all I know, you could have met this woman.'

'I didn't!'

'And . . . The old man who lives in that house . . .' He pointed at the house with the blue door, just as a large group of men ran out of the pub and knocked on the door. Seconds later someone opened it and they all piled in.

'Do you know what goes on there?' Henry asked Danielle.

'No!' Emphatic denial again, and this time she turned away from him too.

Henry did not believe her.

The intersection with the sewerage system was behind them now and the men were back inside a narrow, if mercifully tall tunnel this time. By the light of his phone torch Colin Wilkinson could see that above them was a high vaulted stone ceiling, supported by walls made from what appeared to be very old bricks.

To be vindicated in his belief in this place felt good. But however warm and fuzzy that might make him feel, Wilko was also aware of the fact that none of them knew where they were. They knew they were heading roughly in the right direction for Carter Court but, even if they did make it there, what were they going to find?

If only his 'feelings' about places like this came with instructions. Wilko didn't know what this was. A baby had been killed in a ritualistic fashion, evil had come to EC4 according to George, and Lee Arnold and his missus had been looking into the disappearance of a boy when she too had gone missing. He didn't know what it meant. All he did know was that it meant something – which at the present time was fucking useless information.

'John, are you alright?'

'Yeah . . .'

Mumtaz could hear he was struggling and her heart

went out to him. But she didn't dare stop, not now. She didn't know how long rat-bite fever took to come on, much less Weil's disease. Maybe one or other of these was already making the boy feel weak.

She heard him say, 'How long have we been in this tunnel?'

She said she didn't know, and she didn't. Enveloped in such overwhelming darkness, there was no frame of reference whereby time might be measured. And with the exception of John's rat, their tactile experience of the tunnel had been consistent. Above and to the sides were stone walls; beneath their knees and feet, it was damp and sludgy. With regard to smells, there was an overpowering scent of mustiness, of things made wet and then long neglected. The smell of sewerage had actually become less noticeable. But then maybe that was because they were used to it.

Once again Mumtaz tried to remember how she'd come to be in this situation. But try as she might, she couldn't remember anything about being in that house. One moment she'd been outside the blue door and the next she'd been in that room with the well in total darkness. Why had whoever had done this to her, acted in that fashion? If John was right about the Luddites, was it because she was Asian? Or was it just simply because she'd been asking questions? But then how could John be right? Surely if such an organisation existed, someone would know about it? But then maybe someone did and they weren't doing anything about it?

She hit her head. Mumtaz stopped. Had the tunnel come to an end? Oh, God no!

John said, 'What's the matter? Why've you stopped?'

To have reached a dead end after so long in the dark was unthinkable. It was also, Mumtaz felt, not really possible. Water had poured in through this tunnel to the well. It had to have an outlet somewhere. But then maybe it was small? Maybe too small to crawl through?

'Mumtaz!'

He sounded terrified. She said, 'It's OK, I'm just seeing where it goes . . .'

Up ahead there was just stone. It was the same on her left side. When she moved her hand to the right, at first it met a hard surface. But then as she began to move her hand around she discovered the existence of a hole. Judging its dimensions using only touch wasn't easy, but she eventually managed to deduce it was big enough for them to crawl through. Just. Even more cramped than the tunnel they had been in before, and she warned John things were about to get rougher.

'Can you manage it?' she said. 'Or do you want to go back?'

She heard him begin to cry.

'John . . .'

'We must go on,' he said through sobs. 'We must!'

And he was right. Mumtaz ducked down into the even smaller tunnel and began to shuffle her way along. When she'd managed to move away from the entrance she called John to encourage him forward. When he caught up with her, she could feel his body shaking.

But she only had a moment to give him a few words of encouragement before she suddenly felt that her hands were getting wet.

* * *

271

Scott Brown didn't know exactly where he'd got the idea that Manson was engaged in something that night. He'd said nothing and had come out to Bishopsgate as soon as Brown had called. Maybe Brown sensed the extra tension that always accompanied the eve of some big bust or high-profile take-down. But then maybe Manson was always like this. Maybe being in counter-terrorism made you hypervigilant, constantly on edge?

When they were alone, Brown said to Manson, 'What do you think?'

'From your point of view? Nothing,' he said.

'On what basis—'

'Because I'm telling you to do nothing,' Manson said.

There was a belief amongst some coppers, men and women along the lines of Wilko Wilkinson mainly, that all the Special Branch and counter-terror top brass were psychopaths. The thinking being that you had to be one to catch one. Manson's marble-like eyes gave some credence to this theory.

'So what do I do with the clerics, the QC?'

'You send them home,' Manson said. 'They have reported their concerns.'

'What about the young priest?'

The Reverend de Vere had described his relationship with a man called Arthur Hobbs, who lived close to the cathedral in Carter Court. While the reverend's original aim had been to try and disabuse Mr Hobbs of the deeply racist views he had espoused to him, it seemed that Harold de Vere had become too close to this elderly man. A change of heart had, it seemed, taken place at some point. And while the Reverend de Vere still didn't hold with Mr Hobbs's views, he had been both convinced and intrigued by the fact that Hobbs claimed to be part of an ancient movement committed to feudal values. As the youngest son of a baronet, there was an argument that the Reverend de Vere could be particularly sensitive to such a suggestion. That aside, whether or not de Vere had left the gates to the cathedral churchyard open deliberately on the night of the baby's death was still unknown. Canon Palmer had admitted that on that occasion de Vere had been the person who should have shut them. It seemed that everyone in the cathedral had anxieties about de Vere's frequent meetings with Hobbs. However, de Vere, who appeared genuinely distressed, held to the notion that he had forgotten. He'd had an appointment to meet his mother for dinner at Claridge's later that evening and in his rush to get away fell down on his duty to his employer. It happened.

Then there was crazy Father George's brother and the tunnels. Scott Brown had heard Wilko bang on about tunnels underneath London, but he'd never taken much notice. Now Barry Feldman was saying that his brother might have gone underground to look for them, and this had something to do with the cathedral. The young priest had spoken of tunnels too. Apparently Arthur Hobbs knew about them. His ancient society or whatever it was used them. What was true and what wasn't?

But Manson had been interested enough to bring himself over to Bishopsgate when he clearly had other things on his mind. Manson and his team had intervened when City Police had started staking out The Jolly Sailor pub, where they had been treading unwittingly on the toes of Counter Terrorism. They'd been staking out the pub because the father of the dead baby, Colin Macbeth, may have met the mother of the child at the venue. Macbeth, while denying DNA evidence of his paternity, was nevertheless not averse to one-night stands with women he picked up in pubs. Or so it seemed.

The Jolly Sailor was a low-level right-wing hang-out and now there was this intel from the priest about an ancient society dedicated to British feudalism. Scott Brown had anxieties about things like this. One thing he had in common with Father George was his belief that society was breaking down. Like the priest, Brown believed that part of the reason for this was misinformation spread via the Internet, specifically through social media outlets. Suddenly everyone had a voice – including those who shouldn't, ever. He also knew that within the ranks of his own officers, that perception was an unusual one. In addition Brown knew that one of the few people who shared this view was Wilko Wilkinson.

When Manson had gone, Brown tried to call Wilko but he wasn't picking up.

'It was never gonna work,' Danielle said as she folded her clothes into her suitcase.

Henry didn't know how to feel. When it had first happened he remembered thinking, *I've made my secretary pregnant. I am a living cliché.* And when she'd told him, he'd had to run away and think about what to do next. He'd gone to his parents' villa in Greece where he'd managed to convince himself he could live with her. Not marry her. That had never crossed his mind and, as they had journeyed into their experimental partnership, that notion had appealed less and less. He didn't love her, they had nothing in common and her sulky response to his friends upset him. But while his affection for her had receded, his love for their child had increased.

'I don't want you to do this,' Henry said.

'Well I want to,' she said.

Should he have just left her there outside that pub without comment? Maybe he should. Maybe she got some sort of comfort from being around people who resembled her own family. Not that his one experience of her father had left Henry with anything other than a positive feeling. Raymond Saint was a quiet, gentle man. Henry had felt quite sorry for him, a lone man in a house full of loud and opinionated women. He had rather liked Danielle's immediate family, even if some of her more distant relatives had given him the cold shoulder.

'Dani . . .'

'I can't be done with the snobbery,' Danielle said. 'Like there's people I should mix with and people I shouldn't.'

'What do you mean?'

'I mean I'm pissed off getting looked down at,' she said. 'That couple next door . . .'

'Zander and Pippa. What about them?'

'They don't even look at me!'

'You said you're fed up with people looking down at you, which is it?' he snapped.

'Oh, fuck off!' she said.

'Those people who hang around that pub . . .'

'They're the people who've always lived here!' she screamed. 'People always trying to push them out of places to make flats for people like your mates and their fucking hand-made, fucking thousands of pound bloody cooking pot kits from the rainforest! Then using them to cook bloody seaweed! I do not want my baby to eat weird food, I don't want a doula at the birth and I don't want you throwing my Auntie Pat out of Mum's house because she smokes!'

'But—'

'No!' she said. 'I can't stand it here any longer! If you want to do something useful then you can call me a cab.'

Henry lowered his head. This had all come on so quickly, he didn't really know what to think. Maybe if they had some time apart, it would do both of them some good. Clearly Danielle had been harbouring this resentment against him and his lifestyle for some time. He hadn't thought that he'd pushed his views and his friends at her – exactly. But then maybe she felt that he had?

Quite where what he said next came from, Henry didn't know. It just blurted out of him.

He said, 'So that woman the police were asking about yesterday? Did you speak to her or didn't you?'

Danielle stopped what she was doing.

John was quite a way behind her now. As soon as she'd felt water splashing around her hands and knees, Mumtaz had picked up her pace. There was no choice but to just keep going forwards now. If they stopped or tried to find their way back, they were dead. Now that the tide was rising, they were in competition with it. Either they outran the river or it killed them.

'John,' she called out as she scuttled forwards through what was now mud, 'can you swim?'

'Yeah,' he said. 'River's coming in now, isn't it?'

'Yes,' she said.

'Can you see any light or anything up ahead?'

'No I can't,' she said. 'Don't think about that, just keep going.'

But then as she lowered a hand to place it again in the rising slush, she suddenly realised there was nothing there – and she just dropped, like a stone.

NINETEEN

To begin with, Jordan just thought that what he was hearing was an echo of their own voices. But as they moved forwards, he began to think that what he was hearing was actual other voices. He stopped and told the others to be quiet.

While none of them could make out words, they all heard voices which seemed to be coming from their direction of travel.

Eventually George said, 'Who could that be?'

Lee, ever the pragmatist, said, 'Could be flushers. As we all saw, we're right near the sewers.'

'Or it could be them,' George said.

'What?'

'People from the house.'

'If you're right . . .'

'Well if I'm not right, then what are we doing down here!'

'To be quite honest with you, Father, I don't really know.'

George turned to look at Lee and said, 'Well, if you feel that way . . .'

'Ssshh!'

They all fell silent.

'I think it's getting closer,' Jordan said.

Wilko, whispering, said, 'Can you make anything out, boy?'

'Not if you keep wanging on,' Jordan said.

They all listened. At first all they heard was drips and then a man's voice said, 'Here. Footprints.'

She seemed to fall for ever. Through blackness and a vast drop in temperature. When she momentarily landed she felt first a deep, sludgy softness envelop her fingers and her knees. There was something hard underneath it which caused her body to bounce and she was once again airborne. Had she been able to, Mumtaz would have screamed, but no sound came out of her mouth and the next thing she knew she was underneath water.

Deep, and due to the fact that her body was continually buffeted by things she couldn't see in what was now a watery darkness, she fought to close her mouth as she imagined a vortex of raw sewerage aggregating around her. They'd been close to the sewers all along and now the tunnel she had so stoically trudged through with the boy had disgorged them into one. As she fought to hold what remained of her breath, Mumtaz willed herself to open her eyes, but she couldn't. If she was in a sewer then the water had to have a top surface! Except that it didn't. Maybe the water level, now that the tide was coming in, was up to the ceiling. But a gap of some sort was her only hope of survival! She pushed and fought and battled her way up.

When her head emerged from the water, she opened her eyes expecting to see or feel a roof above her head. But there was no roof. Panting and treading water to keep herself afloat, she looked up into the star-streaked, street-lamp-flooded sky over the River Thames. Laughing with relief she looked towards the shore, where she saw the figure of a screaming human being emerging to join her from a cascade of filth erupting from a pipe.

He didn't know what to think. Something was afoot which might or might not include his brother and Barry was anxious. He'd got the cab just outside the police station and was now heading for home. The DI with Brown had unnerved him. He'd seen people like him give witness statements behind screens used to protect them from retaliatory action by criminal gangs and terror organisations. Usually little better than the people they hunted, these robocops as he called them were a necessary but uncomfortable evil.

Evil made him think about his brother again and Barry frowned. George had always been odd. Not just when he'd been a child but all through his life. Involvement with the miners' strike in the eighties hadn't helped. Half or more of those who went up to Yorkshire to support the miners had been unhinged. Loony lefties. George had broken down after the Battle of Orgreave. After that was when God had intervened.

The cab was travelling along New Change, which skirted the eastern end of the cathedral, when Barry noticed that there were a lot of police vans around. Something was going on; he didn't know what but he reasoned it had nothing to do with his brother. He'd only just reported the bugger missing and it was hardly as if poor old George was 'anyone'. A half-mad priest with a penchant for ghosts was all he was. And yet the thought of life without George, annoying though he was, made Barry want to cry.

Henry was breathless after running all the way up four flights of stairs to the flat.

'No cabs,' he said to Danielle.

She was already packed, coat on, standing by the front door.

'There must be,' she said.

Henry shook his head. 'There's something going down round by the cathedral,' he said. 'Dunno what. Police everywhere.'

At first Danielle didn't believe him. She walked back into the flat and looked out one of the front windows into Carter Lane. Three officers wearing riot helmets and carrying guns were walking along the street.

Danielle turned back to Henry and said, 'What do they want?'

'I don't know,' he said. 'Maybe they're still looking for that woman you spoke to. Or maybe they've found her.'

'I don't know nothing about that woman, I told you,' Danielle said. 'Can't lay that on me.'

He shrugged. 'When you looked at her picture, you knew who she was,' he said.

'I'd seen her, yes, but . . .'

'You knew her,' he said. 'I knew it and so did the police.'

He walked towards her but she shrank away. 'So why didn't you say anything?' she asked. 'People like you, you're not supposed to break the law, are you.'

'People like me?' Henry shook his head. 'What's that? People like me as in a lawyer? People like me as in someone who is middle class? Or people like me as in a Jew?'

She said nothing.

'And you're silent,' Henry said. 'Fair enough. But if you think I didn't know about how you and the other girls in the office behaved when we were out, you're very much mistaken. Laughing at the "Jew-boy lawyers" . . .'

'I never!'

'You did,' he said. 'And to my shame that didn't make me fancy you any the less. And now you're pregnant with my child, while an Asian woman I think you know is missing, maybe even dead. I don't know why, I don't know anything. In spite of that and in the teeth of your desire to leave me, I will still protect you if I can.'

Danielle swayed slightly as if she was about to faint. Henry went to her and grabbed her arm.

'Come and sit down,' he said.

She let him take her through to the living room and

283

help her gently down onto the sofa. She felt tears fill her eyes.

'What is it?' he said. 'Tell me.'

Danielle wiped her face on the sleeve of her jumper and said, 'It was the old man, Arthur.'

'What?'

'Lives next door to the pub. We got talking,' she said.

'What about?'

'Same things my family have always talked about,' she said. 'Pakis taking our jobs . . .'

'You dad doesn't speak like that!'

'No, he doesn't,' she said. 'But all his family do. My granddad was in the National Front. Why Dad moved away from Bermondsey, to get away from all that. But then his sister Pat moved to Dagenham too and all his family started visiting. I was only little then and it was fun.'

'Fun?'

'We didn't have much,' she said. 'It felt good that it wasn't our fault.'

'What about your dad?'

'You've met him,' she said. 'He's a nice man. He just faded into the wallpaper. Even Mum took their side. And when I come here it all made even more sense, what they had said. Poor people being pushed out the way for immigrants and the rich. What do you think all this posh food and posh bikes mean to people like us? You shame us for not being concerned enough about the planet and that.'

'The Earth is dying, Dani, we have to do something.'

284

'I know! But we don't have the money to eat vegan stuff and we have to have cars to do our jobs and yet you make us feel like we're stupid and that being poor is our fault!'

'We don't!'

'You do! You just don't see it!' she said. 'The only person I've met here who I can relate to is Arthur. He understood. Said it was a fight, us against you. When that woman came poking around here with her posh voice, I told him because I reckoned she was one of them too.'

'What made you think that?' he said.

'She's a private detective,' she said.

'So?'

'So she'd come to scope out Arthur and his men,' she said. 'That's what he told me and I thought that was wrong.'

'His men?' Henry said. 'What does that mean?'

She looked across at him with eyes that were suddenly very cold. She said, 'There's going to be a war soon, Henry, and we have to be on the right side.'

Mumtaz was further away from the northern shore of the river than John was. She could see him laboriously clambering up the shingle that remained now that the tide was rising. She knew that if she didn't get to where he was soon, she would die. The waters of the Thames were ice-cold this time of year and her body already felt as if it might shiver itself to death.

Against the strong desire she had to just close her eyes and sink, Mumtaz made her body strike out for the shore and John's motionless body. Her limbs hurt so badly; as she made her first breaststroke she felt as if her arms in particular were being ripped away from her. But then she saw a figure approach John and yelled out, 'Help!'

The figure first pulled John away from the rising water and then flung itself into the Thames. The last thing Mumtaz remembered, until she too was laid on the shore, was a voice calling out to her, 'Hang on! I'm coming!'

Henry had never been a violent man, especially with woman, but now he wanted to punch her. How could Danielle, a woman he had wanted so very much, a woman he had made pregnant, believe such rubbish.

'A war?' he said. 'What kind of war?'

'Between people like me and people like you,' she said. 'The poor English people rallying around the Queen to protect her . . .'

'From what?' he said. 'A load of Green protesters carrying avocados? Or is it an international cabal of Jewish bankers maybe? Or is it just anyone who doesn't have the Union Flag up their arse?'

She looked down at the floor.

'This is all bullshit, Dani!'

She said, 'Something needs to change.'

'What?' he said. 'You think that by raising some farcical army you're going to wipe away all the poverty, persuade the rich to part with their largesse . . . ?'

'I don't know.'

He shook his head. 'So what did you tell this Arthur about Mumtaz Hakim?' he said.

'Just that she was a private investigator,' she said. 'Then she disappeared.'

'And you saw fit to lie to the police about that.'

'I didn't know what else to do,' she said. 'I didn't want Arthur to get into trouble.'

'Arthur, who wants to start a class war.'

'No!'

'No? Well I don't know what else you might call it!' he said. 'You know, Danielle, you are going to have to explain all this to the police. And if you think I am going to protect you then I can assure you, you are wrong.'

'Can you see anything?' Wilko whispered in Jordan's ear.

The young man was looking around a corner into a tunnel that was brightly lit at the far end. Figures moved around in the light: dark, tall, helmeted figures carrying sub-machine guns.

Jordan drew his head back to face Wilko and said, 'They seem to have some impressive hardware.'

Wilko took a peek himself and said, 'Fuck me!'

Unable to move forwards due to the appearance of these people, the four men were effectively trapped.

'Who the fuck are they?' Lee asked, knowing that he was unlikely to receive an answer. 'And where are we?'

Jordan moved away from the corner and said, 'We're going in the right direction. Logically we should be very near to where we need to be. But this network . . .'

'It's huge,' George said. 'I mean, if it goes west as far as the Temple . . .'

'With respect, Father,' Jordan said, 'we don't know that.'

'But what about the mark I found on the cover underneath my brother's building! It's the same as the one we found here!'

'Doesn't mean it's part of the same network,' Lee said.

George looked deflated. Lee, observing this, said, 'But then again it could be.'

They lapsed into silence. Only the voices of the men in the tunnel to their right broke the silence.

'So what do we do?' Wilko said as the lack of movement began to agitate his nerves.

Jordan said, 'We wait.'

Then he moved back to the corner and peeped into the tunnel again.

Then a voice in that tunnel shouted, 'Oi! You!'

The man, Mr Dean, had been wearing two coats and a body warmer. He took both coats off and wrapped one around John, while he draped the other across Mumtaz's shoulders.

John was barely conscious as Mr Dean and Mumtaz hauled him up from the shingle and onto the concrete barrier at the end of the Millennium Bridge. Fortunately he was skinny and light and Mr Dean was very strong, because Mumtaz was almost played out. It was only via a supreme effort of will that she managed to haul herself up onto the concrete barrier, where she lay, staring at the sky like a beached fish.

Now over the barrier, Mr Dean was rubbing John's hands and face while pulling the coat closely around his body. The boy groaned but didn't speak.

Seeing that Mumtaz had joined them, Mr Dean said,

'What on earth were the two of you doing?'

She pulled his coat tight up to her neck. 'It's a long story,' she said. 'What were you doing?'

John moaned again. Mr Dean said, 'That's it, mate, breathe.' Then he looked at Mumtaz. 'You probably didn't hear me . . .'

'I know you're Mr Dean,' she said.

He smiled. 'No, just Dean, love, no mister. I'm a mudlark,' he said. 'Left me bloody detector down on the shingle, silly sod. Serves me right carrying on when I should've been long gone. Always looking for the big find, see. Horde of Roman coins, I dunno. Anyway, good job I was where I was, or you two would've been dead.'

Mumtaz felt tears sting her eyes. 'I'm sorry about your detector.'

'Oh don't worry about that,' Dean said. He took a phone out of his pocket. 'Need to get an ambulance for you two.'

He dialled 999 while Mumtaz looked on. Then she said, 'Oh and call the police too, please.'

'Police?'

'Yes,' she said, 'someone just tried to kill us.'

'You're not flushers. Who are you?'

The men in the body armour carrying sub-machine guns were police.

Wilko went to unzip his SOCO suit, but the cop who had detained them stopped him. Another officer trained his gun on the little group. Wilko stood still and put his hands in the air.

'If you let me take this off, I can show you my warrant card,' he said.

The man directly in front of him looked at his colleague and said, 'Alright, show it. But you do anything dodgy and we'll just shoot you. Got it?'

'Got it.'

Wilko had joined the police straight from school. He'd been around coppers all his adult life. Only twice before had he come across coppers like these; once in 1992 when the IRA had bombed the Baltic Exchange, and in 2005 when Islamist militants set off bombs in the Tube and on a bus.

He passed his warrant card to the officer, who trained his torch on it and then said, 'Wilko.'

'Yeah.'

'Heard of you. What you doing down here?'

'Looking for a woman,' Wilko said.

'Funny place . . .'

'A missing person,' Wilko said. 'Mumtaz Hakim. What are you doing down here?'

The officer looked at his colleague, nodded, and then said, 'We're looking for an unknown number of men. Might be armed, might not be.'

'And who are—'

'And we're looking for Mrs Hakim too,' the officer said. 'Now you'd better come with us.'

TWENTY

Arthur saw Val looking up at the house as the police led her away. One vanload of blokes had already been sent on its way to the cop shop. Most of the other blokes had disappeared underground. Not Val though. She hated it down there. She got others to go down instead.

Arthur had known he'd be unable to keep up with the others when the police arrived and so he'd hidden himself up in the attic. They were coming for him, going through the house like a dose of salts. With luck they wouldn't find him, although really he knew that they would. He just didn't want to make it easy for them. And he'd tell them nothing even though he knew that Val would sing. She'd pull every string she had to and she'd get away with a slap on the wrist. They always did. And anyway she didn't believe. Not like Arthur, although . . .

He had time on his hands and so he thought about that. His dad had believed in a big way. He'd been with Mosley all through the thirties, a young man in a smart black shirt. But he'd still gone drinking at what some of the patriots called the 'Jews pub' on Carter Court. It had been his local. Arthur remembered the old landlord, Salzedo, although not clearly. Funny old stick, but he'd been genuinely sorry when he'd gone missing at the end of the war. Pub had stood empty for years then. Most of EC4 was either empty or in ruins back then. Except the house.

It wasn't until the fifties when Arthur was a teenager that his dad had shown him the tunnels. No Shrine back then, just tunnels. Then in the sixties Arthur's dad had died. Cancer. Went out of the world screaming in agony he had, but not before he'd told his son the truth. It was Salzedo who had shown him the tunnels. He'd liked Arthur's dad, poor bloody idiot. He'd told him the tunnels were where the Jews had hidden after they were thrown out of the country, in the fourteenth century. All that time! Literally living under the earth until they could come out and take over. Such a patient enemy was to be feared, his dad had told him. Down in the depths they'd rowed, his father and Salzedo. His dad told him he'd hit the old man with intent to kill him.

Young at the time and well versed in the 'cause', Arthur had admired his dad for that. Now? He turned away from it. Now, for the moment, it seemed it was all coming to an end. Who had dobbed them in, he wondered? The young priest? He couldn't think of anyone else. People who got too close tended to disappear, and those in the movement – well, their induction made sure they never blabbed.

John was taken straight through into an examination bay. He was conscious but was showing signs of delirium. Mumtaz, in a different treatment bay, had told staff about the rat bite John had sustained. Now wrapped in a space blanket, she was drinking some really foul hot chocolate from a plastic cup when two police officers entered the bay. She was more relieved to see them than she had been when she'd first seen the A & E doctor.

However, as soon as she began to speak, she realised that what she was saying was coming out too quickly and garbled. The female officer sat down beside her and took her hand.

She said, 'It's alright, Mrs Hakim, we know who you are, officers have been looking for you.'

'Yes, but you have to know about the house!' Mumtaz said. 'It's in EC4, Carter Court . . .'

'There are officers there right now,' the woman said.

'Now?' But how had they known? 'But . . .'

'I can't tell you anything else at this time,' she said. 'Don't know much about it myself. But that area is locked down at the moment. You can take it easy now. It's all in hand.'

'Oh . . .'

'Now, look, staff called us only because you insisted.'

She had insisted. She had screamed and shouted and hassled until she'd got her way. Now they were telling her to take it easy. But how could she? Those people had tried to kill her!

'Luddites!' she screamed. 'They're called Luddites and they're mad! They kill people!'

The male officer left the cubicle while his colleague attempted to reason with Mumtaz.

'Now, Mrs—'

'No, you don't understand!' Mumtaz said. 'They're murderers! Ask John! He watched them kill, they made him . . .'

And then she was crying and screaming nonsense and drowning in her own snot.

These six officers were not the only ones in the tunnels.

'There's three other teams of six, plus we've boots on the ground all over EC4,' a Sergeant Williams said.

They still hadn't said what branch of the service they came from but Wilko, Jordan and Lee reasoned they were probably Counter Terrorism. The heavy armour, the way they spoke, the way that one of them was talking about bomb identification and disposal, pointed in that direction.

Sergeant Williams continued, 'You say you got in from an entrance on Addle Hill. How'd you know it was there?'

'There's a mark,' George said. 'How did you get in?'

'Through the house. What's this mark?'

'Well, it's er, it's only small, you can hardly see it . . .'

'Sarge!'

One of the other men called Williams over.

Looking at the four men he'd intercepted, Williams said, 'You lot wait here and not a sound.'

He went over to his colleague who was looking at a small computer screen.

Lee whispered, 'They must've been watching this place.'

'Clearly,' George said.

'They're not going to tell us anything,' Wilko said. 'This lot don't.'

'What lot?' Jordan asked.

'One of the lots who do what they please,' Wilko said. 'The ones who are allowed to do that.'

'There's no point speculating who they are,' Lee said. 'Christ's sake!'

Williams returned and said, 'Situation is there's a group of men down here we need to shut down. We believe they know these tunnels far better than we do and so they can probably leave and return when they want to. If you know anything you think we need to know, now's the time.'

They told him about a possible entrance in the Inns of Court, about how the tunnels, at points, intersected with the sewer system and about the small menorah stamped onto the entrances to tunnels. Williams didn't know what a menorah was. George had started to explain when they all heard a noise that sounded very much like a cry of pain.

'Hello, Arthur.'

They'd found him, as he'd known they would. Maybe Val had told them? Now he was in an interview room somewhere with a man who'd just told him he was being detained under prevention of terrorism legislation. He supposed that made sense to them, even if it made no sense at all to him.

'We've been watching you,' the man said. 'Very interesting.'

Arthur was going to stick to his guns. He said nothing.

'And Lady Valerie,' the man continued. 'Her family have been on the radar for years, but you must know that. Given your age I imagine you knew her father, Lord Rudolph. Been reading up about him in the last few months. You know he knew everyone in London in the sixties, a proper Swinging London type, he was. Swanning around Carnaby Street, went to Eel Pie Island with all the other hip young things, saw the Stones, Bowie. All free love, folklore and joss sticks. He even bought a pub in the City where he used to entertain his society friends. Famous for celebrity spotting The Hobgoblin was, back in the day. But then you know that. And then there was the other side to Lord Rudolph, wasn't there?'

His Lordship had spent much of his time off his nut on drugs, as Arthur recalled. Handsome and engaging, he'd quickly got to know his neighbours, principally Arthur's dad. He'd got in the habit of having a drink with old Percy at lunchtimes. He didn't live at the pub but he spent most of his days and evenings there, when he had nothing better to do. They talked about folklore and history and Rudolph had been strangely in tune with the old man's political beliefs, which had come as a surprise. One late afternoon after an ad hoc lock-in with His Lordship, Percy had shown him the tunnels. The aristocrat had been very impressed. He'd said, according to Perce, that 'you could get an army down there'.

'Lord Rudolph,' the man said, 'knew Mosley's wife.

You know, the leader of the British Fascists? Diana Mitford and her husband were regular visitors to the Rudolphs' villa in France during the fifties and sixties. What fun that must've been, eh? Touching little anecdotes about Hitler and Mussolini . . .'

Lord Rudolph tired of the pub after Perce died. It stood empty for years until Rudolph's daughter began using it as a 'pad' in the late seventies. Different, like her father, but she was much more controlled. She didn't use drugs or even drink that much, but she did share her father's politics. And she eventually remembered what he'd once told her about the tunnels. It was Val who had sought Arthur out and not the other way around. It was really Val who came up with the idea of Lud. But it was Arthur who had believed.

They were just blokes, stumbling about and twisting their ankles. Who the hell they were, Lee didn't know. Some of them were laughing and he could smell beer. And yet these coppers had come down tooled up for a firefight.

The cop team, minus two, had hidden in the tunnel from which Lee and the others had emerged, and then confronted the men. Unable to go back because of the two officers who had closed off their exit, they had capitulated immediately. There were about twelve in all – young, old, in-between. Voices Lee noticed were either dead posh or dead not.

The robocops told them that they were being arrested under prevention of terrorism legislation, which seemed strange. But none of this was bringing him any closer to

Mumtaz. As they began to move out along with the cops and their prisoners, he asked Williams, 'Any news about Mrs Hakim?'

Williams shook his head. 'We're going back to the house now,' he said. 'Maybe we'll find out then.'

He was trying to be calm, but it wasn't easy – and yet if these men had anything to do with Mumtaz's disappearance, he was finding that hard to take in any way seriously. They were so ordinary, almost pathetic – some even looked as if they might be homeless – as they shuffled along between the ranks of the officers. And yet if they were so ordinary, what were they doing in these tunnels?

'Fitzy? Is that you?'

Jordan, who was up ahead, was talking to one of the cops. Heavily armed like the rest of them, the man looked at Jordan who repeated, 'Fitzy?'

But the man just pushed past him without answering. When Lee caught up with the young man he said, 'What was that about?'

'I swear that bloke's a man I saw when I went undercover in a pub in south London,' Jordan said. 'Called himself Fitzy. A homeless alcoholic.'

'But not really.'

'No. Working for this lot. He must've tipped his bosses off when I rolled up at the pub pretending to be a rough sleeper.'

Lee frowned. 'Why were you doing that?'

'That baby in the churchyard,' Jordan said. 'We found the father. Claimed not to know anything about the kid but

298

reluctantly admitted to a one-night stand with a black girl he picked up in this pub called The Jolly Sailor in Bermondsey. I was scoping the place out, see if I could come up with a name for the girl. It was after that DI Brown took us off the case, said he was obliged to hand it over to others who already had an interest.'

They weren't common, Arthur Hobbs's type, but Manson had come across a few in his long police career. The pathetic little old man act didn't cut any ice with him. If the intel he and his team had gathered about Hobbs over the last few months was correct, then the old man was lethal. And in spite of the information he was receiving from his guys in the tunnels, about how ordinary and in fact biddable Hobbs's so-called 'army' was proving to be, somehow Manson had taken his eye off the ball when it came to Macbeth's baby. He should have ripped Carter Court apart when intel about a baby had come in, but he hadn't. Had he been too afraid to investigate what lay beneath the house with the blue door? If that had been the case, was it because of the stories they all told about how vast the tunnels were, how people had got trapped inside them and died, how when the tide was high, some of them flooded? If he had been influenced by such stories then he was a fucking mug, even if the one about flooded tunnels was true.

Manson put his fag out on the pavement and then went back in to continue his chat with Arthur Hobbs.

Sitting down, he said, 'So Arthur, the name Mumtaz Hakim mean anything to you?'

299

'No.'

'Sure?'

'Yeah.'

Manson sat back in his chair. He was going to enjoy this.

'Because you see, Arthur, I've just been told about a woman, called Mumtaz Hakim, who was found on the northern shore of the Thames at St Paul's.'

'Nothing to do with me,' Arthur said.

'Mmm.' Manson crossed his arms. 'She claims to have entered your house two days ago and then remembers nothing until she woke up in a room containing a well some time later.'

'So?'

'So? So, who put her there Arthur, and why?'

'Weren't me.'

'Oh she's not claiming it was,' Manson said. 'Mrs Hakim genuinely doesn't know what happened to her when she entered your house. On the other hand, however, the young man she was with when she was found on the shore, does know you and will, it seems, testify against you in connection to the murder of a newborn baby.'

This time Hobbs said nothing. Nor did he, in Manson's view, react.

'Terrible business,' Manson continued. 'Found in St Paul's Churchyard. I'm sure you heard about it. Oh, but then of course you knew if, as our witness states, you did it.' He shook his head. 'God, Arthur, you've come a long way from those skinhead-heavy National Front rallies of the 1970s, haven't you? You and Lady Val all dolled up like The Sweet amongst all the Skins on Brick Lane, hurling cobbles at grocers. Whose idea was Lud? Hers or yours? I think it must've been hers, but then I could be wrong. People tend to think the upper classes are more educated than us don't they? But it's not always the case, is it?'

Arthur said, 'I wanna brief.'

'Course you do and you can have one, it's your right,' Manson said. 'But this isn't going away, Arthur. In fact for us this is just the endgame of a really long and complex operation, and so we've a lot to talk about. Haven't even got to the arms yet, have we?' He stood up. 'Let's get you that brief shall we? Know anyone do you?'

'These tunnels go on for ever,' George said. 'And there are rooms. People used to hide down here.'

Sergeant Williams cast him a sour look. 'Rooms, yes,' he said, 'but the tunnels don't go on for ever, only in the minds of these nutters. We've learnt a lot about this place in the last six months.'

'Have you?'

'Do you know how many terrorist threats we take down every year?' Williams said.

'No . . .'

'No you don't, because a lot of what we do just happens around you,' he said. 'This is a constant battle, mate, and it's getting worse.'

'So who are these—'

'Sssh!'

They all stopped. George saw Jordan at the head of

the group and watched as Williams moved towards him. There was a door to their left which the young man was pointing at. He whispered to Williams and then stood aside.

George said to Wilko, 'What's going on?'

'Dunno. Think there might be someone behind that door.'

Two of Williams' colleagues stood behind him, moving the rest of the cohort back into the tunnel. The remaining police officers covered the men they'd apprehended earlier and George heard one of them hiss, 'Make any sort of sound and you're fucking dead.'

George felt Lee Arnold at his back and looked to him for some sort of confidence or consolation, but the man's face was static. Of course, he'd been a policeman and knew what was going on. Or not.

George saw Sergeant Williams turn the knob and then push the door open with his foot.

'Police!'

What looked like a vast tongue of flame emerged from the open door together with a sound so loud, George thought that his eardrums would burst. Williams, directly in front of whatever this was, first ricocheted back and up and then collapsed onto the colleagues behind him, screaming.

Valerie Rudolph's solicitor came from one of the most prestigious firms in London. This wasn't surprising. She had money and she'd used the same outfit when she'd had run-ins with the law in the past. DI Manson looked at the woman and her Savile Row-suited solicitor as they disappeared into a side room for their initial confab. Arthur Hobbs would get a duty brief.

Manson had come across Lady Val a few times back in the late seventies when he'd been a constable. Rich and entitled, she'd identified with the largely skinhead National Front back then. She'd surrounded herself with disaffected youths and middle-aged malcontents like Arthur Hobbs. Her main address was still in Knightsbridge but she also had The Hobgoblin, which was where she'd launched her 'activism'. Manson had thought she'd given all that up years ago, until they'd started to pick up rumours about possible fascist activity around a pub in south London. The Jolly Sailor in Bermondsey had always been a bit of a destination for far-right nutters, but this had been more than that. Recruiting had been going on. At first they'd only managed to identify a local family, the Saints, but then one day Val had rocked up and then things had snowballed. Then they'd looked into The Hobgoblin, rediscovered Arthur Hobbs and heard whispers about secret societies and arms.

When the brief came out of the little room Manson had given them with Val, the solicitor said, 'You know I'm going to have to insist that you release my client don't you, DI Manson?'

'Of course,' Manson smiled. 'And you know that she's been arrested under anti-terror legislation and so I can't do that. But I know you had to try.'

Both the solicitor and Manson smiled, the latter fully aware that in spite of everything Lady Val would eventually walk away unscathed. Because if those in the aristocratic establishment didn't protect her, those she had almost certainly hoodwinked, would.

TWENTY-ONE

The officer who had been standing to the left of Williams when his body was almost cut to shreds by sub-machine-gun fire was the man Jordan had called 'Fitzy'. The officer behind Williams was dead. The team, though shocked, regrouped quickly, while the men they had detained cheered.

Someone yelled, 'Shut the fuck up!'

Silence fell. Fitzy moved away from the line of fire and instructed his remaining men to keep the detainees covered. Then he whispered to Jordan and Wilko, 'You had firearms training?'

They said they hadn't, but Lee had been in the army and so Fitzy handed him an automatic pistol. Smoke billowed out of the room the shooter with the sub-machine gun was still inside, as well as from the dead bodies in the tunnel.

Fitzy squatted down to the side of the open door and said, 'You can't get away, mate . . .'

He didn't know that. For all he knew that sodding room could have another exit.

No one answered him. Had he slipped out via another door? Fitzy looked to his colleagues for any sign they knew what might be happening, but none was forthcoming. Then Lee Arnold cleared his throat. Realising he could maybe see a little inside, Fitzy mouthed, 'What?'

Lee mouthed back, 'Don't look, he's in there.'

Fitzy, clinging tightly to his own weapon, said, 'Who are you?'

Father George, aghast, whispered to Wilko, 'What's he doing? He's just killed two men!'

'Yeah, and pointing that out at the off is really going to help when you're trying to negotiate with a nutjob or a fanatic,' Wilko whispered back. 'If he can, he's got to draw him out so there's no more loss of life. Watch and learn.'

She was sedated and so Mumtaz had no idea when they moved her away from A & E and put her up on a side ward somewhere in the hospital. But when a nurse came in to check on her it was still dark. Mumtaz asked the nurse to pour her some water because her throat was dry and then she said, 'Is John alright? The boy I was brought in with?'

'I don't know,' the nurse said.

'Can you please find out?'

She was very young and looked a little uncertain of herself, but eventually she said that she would see what she could do. When she'd gone, Mumtaz, her head somewhat clearer now, began to think about Shazia – and Lee. She'd just disappeared and they would have no idea where she was. They'd be worried. But her phone was long gone and she was attached to a drip so she couldn't move around. Then she thought about her parents and began to panic. There was a button she could use to call a nurse somewhere . . .

'Mate, you can't go anywhere,' Fitzy yelled from his hiding place beside the door. 'The way that sub went off, I can tell you don't know what you're doing. Put it down and come out with your hands up.'

There was no reply.

'You and I both know we can't all be down here for ever—'

'The tunnels stretch for miles,' a voice interrupted.

'Mate, they go a long way, I'll grant you,' Fitzy said, 'but we know about them now. We have for months. You've been conned, pal. There's no such old religion as Lud, never was. There's gonna be no revolution.'

'You don't know nothing, mate!' a voice echoed through the tunnels.

'I know there are others,' Fitzy said. 'I've got some of 'em here.'

'Nah.'

'You come out and have a look.'

Jordan looked around at the restless men they had detained and began to feel jittery. Fitzy was beginning to sound a bit like Wilko and these men were sobering up.

307

Suddenly one of them spoke. 'You hang on in there, Colin!'

One of the coppers smashed him around the side of his face with his weapon and he fell to the floor. There was absolute silence then until Fitzy said, 'Put the gun down, Colin.'

'Never.'

'I told you, your revolution's over.'

'You think?' the man said. 'You'd be surprised who's on our side. I don't mean people in the movement, I mean people you wouldn't even dream about.'

'You think?' Fitzy said. 'You think we don't know there are people like you everywhere?'

The man said nothing for a few minutes and then he blurted, 'Because of them we'll all be alright and you know it!'

Under his breath, Fitzy said, 'Fucking hell.'

The man laughed and then Fitzy said, 'I don't know what they've told you, but it's only by giving yourself up now, you stand a chance. You've shot two police officers, my colleagues—'

'Shut up!'

He was becoming agitated. Lee could see him casting about inside that room, hauling that gun, that he didn't know how to use, like a sack of spuds. He looked at Fitzy and mouthed, 'He's getting shaky.'

Fitzy nodded and then he said, 'At least I want you to put the gun down. Do that and we can talk about this.'

But there was no reply, just the muffled sound of him talking to himself. Lee saw him run a hand through his hair and then punch himself on the side of the face.

Then he screamed.

Val did her 'no comment' routine and Manson wrapped the whole thing up for the night. He was knackered after the exertions of earlier in the evening and, even if the operation wasn't over, he knew he needed a moment to himself.

He went outside and lit a cigarette. Even if the whole fucking thing fell apart, at least the Hakim woman was safe and the Macbeth boy. The first thing the kid had said once he'd come round in the hospital was that 'Arthur killed the baby'. Maybe he thought he might die and needed to get that off his chest?

According to the hospital the kid was doing OK, although whether he'd agree to eventually testify against his own father was unknown. Besides, how much or how little Colin Macbeth was involved in murder was still a mystery. So far twenty-nine men had been arrested, but very few arms had been recovered. The intel he'd originally received from Interpol, and which had kicked the whole operation off, had been principally about weapons. Specifically weapons arriving in containers of bicycles which were manufactured in Belarus.

The police had intercepted the consignment and discovered that the arms had been very cleverly disguised as bicycle components. They had allowed them to reach their intended destination which had been a bike shop in Norwich. It hadn't been a huge place, but then the bikes had been taken on to a local manor house owned by one of Lady Valerie's oldest friends. A team of officers had been despatched to a tiny village just outside Diss the previous afternoon. Manson had no doubt that some very powerful people would try to get Val and her mate, The Honourable Caroline, off – and maybe, given the current climate in the country, they would succeed. But it wasn't a certainty because this time Val's creatures had actually killed.

Manson muttered to himself, 'Fucking Luddites.'

He laughed because it was the most ridiculous terror cell he'd ever come across. Then his phone rang and the laughter stopped.

Colin's screaming seemed to go on for ever but Lee Arnold, his eyes darting between both the man in the room and the officer called Fitzy, held his nerve. He knew that Fitzy was aware he had eyes on Colin and that he would signal to him should he need to. If the situation deteriorated.

From his vantage point, which was not that good, Lee could see that Colin was now sitting on the floor, crying, his body folded over the sub-machine gun. Would it be safe to go in on him while he was in such a state? Probably not. Fitzy was, at least in part, relying on him to monitor Colin's state of mind.

Lee wondered whether the metallic smell of fresh blood had got through to Colin yet? It was very strong now and he began to notice that glutinous lumps of dead flesh were detaching from the ceiling of the tunnel. Some of the men under detention were retching now and Lee briefly looked over at Father George, who was crossing himself and murmuring a prayer.

How was this going to end?

Shazia was crying so much that Krishnan had to take the phone from her. When she'd first heard Mumtaz's voice, she'd screamed.

'Amma! Oh my God, where are you?'

Mumtaz had tried to tell her in as logical a fashion as she could, but all she'd succeeded in doing was making the girl cry. They were, in part, tears of relief, but also the mention of the word 'hospital' had panicked her.

'Which hospital?' she'd asked. 'I'm coming! What happened? Where have you been? Are you injured? Are you sick?'

Mumtaz had tried to calm her down, but then she'd sobbed so hard she'd had to pass the phone to her boyfriend.

Krishnan, much more calmly, said, 'Mumtaz, are you alright?'

'I'm fine,' she said. 'I'm off my head on sedatives, but I'm fine.'

'Good. Now do you want us to ring anyone? Your parents? Lee?'

Less emotionally involved, Krishnan was concentrating on practicalities.

Mumtaz looked up at the nurse who had lent her a phone and smiled. She hadn't wanted to use it to make multiple calls.

She said to Krishnan, 'If you could let my parents know

I'm OK that would be great. I don't know how much they knew. I'll leave it to you. I've tried Lee once myself but he's not picking up.'

'OK. I'll try him too,' Krishnan said. 'I'm not going to ask you the whys and wherefores.'

'Thank you!'

'Just tell me the name of the hospital you're in and we'll be over.'

'Oh don't come now,' Mumtaz said. 'I need to sleep if I can. I'm in St Thomas'.'

'Good.'

'Thanks so much, Krish, and do give my girl a hug from me,' she said.

'Of course. See you soon, Mumtaz.'

He ended the call and Mumtaz gave the phone back to the nurse. 'Thank you.'

The nurse smiled and said, 'Now you try to get some rest, yes? Everything is alright now.'

Mumtaz slid down between the bed sheets.

'My daughter's boyfriend is such a nice young man,' she said. 'I do hope they stay together. Shazia, my daughter, is not an easy girl.'

And then almost immediately she fell asleep.

One of his officers, called DS Loft, led DI Manson through the house and down into the tunnels. Now wearing a Kevlar vest and a helmet, he asked the officer, 'Who's in charge?'

He'd been told that Williams and an officer called Kay were both dead.

'Fitzallan, sir.'

'Right.'

'Perp's got a sub-machine gun,' Loft said. 'He's in one of those rooms they have down here.'

'How did it happen?' Manson asked.

'Far as I can tell, a noise was heard coming from the room. Williams announced his presence, opened the door and the bloke opened fire.'

'Williams was standing directly in front of the door?' Manson asked. 'Christ! You'd think he'd know better than that!'

He was both terrified about what he would find when they got to the scene, and furious with Williams and Kay for dying needlessly. That said, as they walked down into the earth through tunnels of varying heights, widths and states of illumination, Manson did begin to feel some of the dread he knew accompanied working in enclosed spaces. In tunnel systems, however ruthlessly one might clear them of hostile actors, there was always the fear that death could lurk around the next corner, in the next room. Williams and his team had been down for longer than any of the others and so there was also the issue of fatigue to take into account. Fatigue and uncertainty.

Williams and his team had reportedly detained twelve Luddites. Christ, even the name made Manson blush! That modern, supposedly educated people could engage in something so delusional was beyond him. In addition, there were four other people the team had met somewhere in the tunnels. Who they were and why they'd been down there, Manson hadn't been told. For the moment he worked on the assumption these were probably terrorists too – if one could call Val Rudolph's motley crew terrorists . . .

Manson had personally led the first team into the tunnels. This was after the pub had been cleared and in pursuit of all those who had run from the pub and underground. Some had even gone to Hobbs's house next door and entered via that. A few had got snarled up at the entrances, while others had been pursued down tunnels that sometimes led to dead ends. A lot of the men, who were almost all middle-aged, simply ran out of steam and gave themselves up. But if it was true that the man with the gun now was actually Macbeth, then he wouldn't go easily. Not only was he connected to hardcore fascist families by blood, but he was also the father of the dead baby, the 'sacrifice'. Also, if Hobbs had got hold of that baby then Macbeth must have taken it, willingly or by force, from its mother. And where was she? Who was she?

As they descended still further, Manson began to feel hot. There was also a familiar smell in the dank air, of blood. No arms had been discovered until this incident. Manson had a good idea about how much hardware had been smuggled into the tunnels and it was a lot more than just one sub. Retrieving and then disabling said weapons before they got onto the streets was one of the main aims of the operation. But where were they?

Colin was silent. He was also out of Lee Arnold's eyeline. Lee didn't know who he was. During the course of this whole affair, he'd concentrated almost exclusively on Mumtaz. Who these people hanging out in the tunnels

314

were, he didn't know, like he didn't know why the police were involved. Colin had killed two police officers and so he was going away for ever. Had Mumtaz's two little lads really stumbled into some sort of sinister plot when they'd met that boy on Arthur Hobbs's doorstep?

Even as he said it in his head, Lee felt as if he were skirting around the edges of one of Wilko's more fantastical historical daydreams. And yet here he was, in a mythical underground tunnel, listening to the sound of a man holding a sub-machine and whimpering to himself.

Fitzy caught Lee's eye and indicated that he was going to speak again. Lee nodded.

'Here, Colin,' he said, 'there is one way you can make this better for yourself, you know.'

Lee couldn't see how that could be, but . . .

Although Colin didn't respond, Fitzy continued, 'Show us where the arms are, mate. We know you've got them, we'll find them eventually. But if you co-operate now—'

'Fuck off!'

'Only trying to help . . .'

'Go and do some proper work, you bastard!' Colin said. 'Go down to Dover and pull all those fucking migrants out of their hiding places in our lorries and throw them into the sea! Persecute us don't ya! Patriots!'

And there, Lee thought, it was – raw, furious nationalism. Every country had it; try as they might, no one could entirely kill it because it was based on victimhood, which was at least as powerful a political tool as religion.

'All we want to do is save this country and keep it pure,' Colin continued.

315

'We can talk about all this when you're out of there,' Fitzy said.

'No we can't because you won't!' Colin responded. 'You won't listen, you never do! People like you!'

Fitzy said nothing, partly because two more officers had arrived. One was slim and tall and probably quite young, while the other, the more senior officer, was a middle-aged man in a Kevlar vest and helmet. Both stood beside the far edge of the door, out of sight. The older man motioned to Fitzy who nodded.

'Colin?' he said.

There was a pause and then Colin said, 'Who's that?'

'My name's DI Manson,' he said.

'Never heard of you.'

'Don't suppose you have,' Manson said. 'I know about you though. I've been watching you and your lot for quite some time.'

Colin became quiet again.

Manson continued, 'So don't try and hit me with all the "cause" stuff. Let's get to the nitty-gritty, shall we?'

Not a word.

'So look, it's like this,' Manson said. 'You tell me where the woman is, the mother, and the arms, and maybe you can salvage something from this.'

Lee held his breath. This DI Manson was not pussyfooting around. He began to feel his heart beat faster.

'The mother first,' Manson continued. 'Where is she, Colin? What did you do to her? You kill her so you could take the baby?'

'No!'

'We know Arthur killed your child you know, Colin,' Manson said.

'No you don't, because it ain't true!'

'No? So what have you all been doing prancing about down here with masks and knives and mumbo jumbo, then?' Manson said. 'Lud demands sacrifice, doesn't he? Oh I know all about your little made-up religion. Be surprised what some of the alkies down The Jolly Sailor come out with when you buy them a drink. *Shouldn't use alkies* is I think, the moral of this story. Unreliable.'

Yet again, Colin became silent.

Manson said, 'You've a son, John.'

'No I don't!'

'You do.'

'He's dead!' His voice was full of tears. 'He wasn't up to it, he . . .'

The sobbing overwhelmed him and Manson signalled to Fitzy, who put his head around the doorpost. Lee knew of old what was about to happen next and he held his breath.

They could hold him for up to fourteen days without charging him. This was because the police had arrested Arthur under prevention of terrorism legislation. Terrorism! He was a patriot! If they only knew it, they'd thank him for what he'd tried to do. Brexit and all that was just window-dressing; what Britain really needed was a full-on return to a purely British way of life. People didn't know what a visionary Val was. Like her father, she'd seen the opportunities as soon as she'd walked the tunnels.

At the time, Arthur hadn't known much about Lud. Val had taught him and it had made him feel justified. He'd always had views on Englishness and now there was a religion that worshipped that! Had he always known it was a fraud? Maybe, but it didn't matter. It was the cause that mattered, getting back to English basics! Besides, he was only countering their lies. That was why his dad had killed Mr Salzedo, because he'd lied.

Why did people almost always put their hands up to their faces when they cried? Was it embarrassment? Was it symbolically not wanting to see what was happening to make you cry? Lee Arnold didn't know. He didn't even really see what went on between Fitzy and Colin in that room. All he did know was that the officer kicked the man's sub-machine gun out into the tunnel and pushed his own weapon against Colin's head. The officer with Manson picked up the weapon and disabled it while his boss went in. Lee heard him say, 'Down on the ground! Hands behind your back!'

Then he formally arrested him. The men they had detained earlier muttered, but they were soon joined by yet more police officers and Lee let out a long, shaky breath. Now all he had to do was find Mumtaz.

Then, quite unaccountably, he began to cry.

TWENTY-TWO

Nobody woke her. She just simply became aware of noise and movement around her. One of the walls of her side room had a window and Mumtaz could see nurses and ancillary staff moving about. Outside the sky was grey but it was well after sunrise. Still attached to a drip, she pressed her buzzer as she knew she would need help visiting the lavatory.

After the nurse took her to the toilet and helped her back in bed, she asked, 'The boy I came in with, how is he?'

The nurse didn't know but said she'd go and ask. When she came back she was smiling.

'John Macbeth is up on the ward now,' she said. 'He's still pretty groggy, but he's doing fine.'

'Can I see him?' Mumtaz asked.

'You both need to see the doctor first,' the nurse said.

She could understand the logic of that.

'And your daughter's here,' the nurse continued.

'Shazia!' Mumtaz was halfway out of bed before the nurse hauled her back in again.

'Your daughter is going to have to wait until the doctor has been,' she said. 'She knows this and is sitting quietly down in the cafe with a book.'

'Oh . . .' Mumtaz suddenly felt deflated again as well as very tired.

'You're popular,' the nurse said as she tucked blankets around her.

'Am I?'

'Yes. You've got two police officers waiting to see you too.'

Mumtaz frowned. 'I told them all I know last night, didn't I?'

'I dunno,' the nurse said. 'But they're waiting for you.'

And Lee?

'Anyone else?' she asked.

'No,' the nurse said.

Then she left, leaving Mumtaz feeling suddenly scared.

'So you're a PI,' Manson said as a statement of fact.

'Yeah.'

'So what were you doing . . . ?'

'Underground?' Lee shook his head. 'I wish I knew,' he said. 'Desperation . . .'

'Desperation?'

'My business partner went missing.'

320

He knew that Mumtaz was safe now. All he wanted to do was see her even though he knew he had to do this first.

'You were with two of our officers, PC Whittington and Sergeant Wilkinson.'

'Yeah. And George Feldman.'

'Father George,' Manson said. 'We know him.'

'Do you?'

Manson smiled. 'I feel I don't have to tell you that you ignore nutters at your peril.'

Lee shook his head. 'Sometimes.'

Manson shrugged. 'So tell me how Mrs Hakim came to be in EC4. Not your manor is it?'

'No . . .'

He told him about the two boys and their money-making scheme and about the young man they'd encountered who was bloodied and, they felt, needed help.

'Why didn't the kids come to us?' Manson asked.

It was a fucking good question and one that Lee had asked Mumtaz repeatedly. She'd cited the precarious position a police investigation would represent for the kids, particularly Habib. But then Lee himself hadn't taken it seriously. He'd let her take the boys' case because he thought it was 'nothing' and because he loved her. It was unprofessional and he knew it. He also knew that he had a duty to tell Manson just that.

'Look, I got you into this . . .'

'I was as fascinated as you were,' Jordan said.

321

Wilko wanted to bear all the responsibility for what had happened, but Jordan wasn't having it.

'Anyway,' he continued, 'you weren't wrong. Look at what we found down there! It was real, Wilko . . .'

'And it was in hand,' the older man said. 'We should have trusted—'

'What?' George cut in. 'Trust what, Wilko? You know how things are going in this country right now as well as I do. There's no stability, the Internet has sent people mad . . .'

'Has it? Has it really?'

George shook his head.

Wilko put a hand on Jordan's shoulder. 'I retire in less than a year,' he said.

'So what?'

'If it hadn't been for me, you wouldn't have been down there.'

'Well I can't see how anyone can get into any sort of trouble for helping to unmask criminals,' George said.

They'd been put into an interview room somewhere in the bowels of Scotland Yard, but no one had been sent to question them. They'd been given some pathetic plastic cups of tea, but so far that was it.

Wilko said, 'Men died, George, our officers—'

'We didn't kill them!'

'No, but maybe things would've worked out differently if we hadn't been there.'

It was only conjecture but all three of them knew it was possible. Then George said, 'Might've been worse without us.'

'Might've been, yeah,' Wilko said.

Then they all lapsed back into silence.

'Can I see her?' Lee asked Manson as the latter stood to let him out of his office. They were talking about Mumtaz. In the spirit of full disclosure, Lee had told Manson everything, including the fact that he was in love with her.

'Once we get the green light from her doctor, she'll come here,' Manson replied. 'I've got to get as much information as I can from her so we can charge these bastards. Probably best you go home.'

'I'd rather wait.'

Manson shrugged. 'Up to you, but it's not gonna be quick.'

'I know.'

Manson opened his office door.

'And I've got a full interview schedule,' he said.

A woman, probably somewhere in late middle age, walked past them down the corridor outside Manson's office. She was cuffed to a female uniformed officer. She was wearing, Lee noticed, a lot of very impressive jewellery. Manson locked eyes with her for a moment. Lee wondered who she was but didn't ask. What was the point? At this stage in the investigation the police were saying very little. It was a scenario that was familiar to him.

Once the woman had passed, Lee asked Manson whether Mumtaz's family had been told she was in hospital. He said, 'Yes. But you're not to discuss this with them.'

Lee knew that. 'Sure. I'm not certain I know much myself . . .'

'All you need to know, you do,' Manson said. 'Mrs Hakim is safe and so is the lad we found her with.'

'The boy those kids saw with blood on his face,' Lee murmured.

'We think so, yes. But I have to interview them both,' Manson said. 'You've been a copper, you know how it is. Priorities.'

Back down in the tunnels, those had been locating arms and finding the woman who had given birth to the murdered baby. The shooter, Macbeth, hadn't been keen to give intel on either of those subjects. Lee knew he had kept his mind off the subject of the child deliberately. It seemed the police thought he and/or Arthur Hobbs had murdered it. He'd seen a lot of awful things in his life, especially when he'd served in Iraq, but this . . . At least in Iraq, the poor bastards who sold their kids for the price of a meal did so reluctantly; they did it because they were dying. In Britain it made no sense. It especially made no sense for what, it seemed, might be some weird ideological reason.

'I'd go and get some rest,' Manson continued. 'I'm gonna need to speak to you again but for now, I'd go home. I'll let you know when you can see Mrs Hakim.'

He was right of course, and so Lee left Scotland Yard and made his way to the Tube. Before he boarded a train he picked up a copy of the *Metro* free paper. The front page was full of the security operation in St Paul's, but there was nothing about tunnels or about what kind of security alert it had been. It made Lee feel conflicted. A lot of far-right activity had been uncovered over the years, but it rarely caused the mass panic that accompanied Islamist operations. He had struggled with the idea that maybe this was deliberate. The idea that 'our own' didn't do such things persisted in spite of events like the murder of MP Jo Cox by a far-right activist back in 2016. And even though he wasn't in possession of all the facts about who had done what and precisely why in EC4 the previous night, he'd picked up enough to realise that what the police had been dealing with was home-grown and lethal.

The Reverend Harold de Vere had come in alone and of his own volition. According to him, the police operation around the cathedral had been the talk of everyone living locally. There had even been rumours about deaths . . .

'Mr Hobbs had asked to see me,' he told DI Brown. Although the investigation was now based at Scotland Yard, de Vere had come to Bishopsgate because it was where he'd been interviewed the first time. He also, he told himself, felt as if he could trust Brown.

'Asked when?' Brown said.

'Earlier in the afternoon,' de Vere said. 'He sent me a text. I replied that I was busy. He said he only needed a few minutes and suggested we meet as I was locking up later that evening.'

'So that's what you did?'

'Yes. He was waiting for me by the churchyard gate . . .'

'Which one?'

'The southern gate on St Paul's Churchyard road,' he

said. 'I asked Arthur to come inside. He said he didn't want to talk for very long and so I saw no harm in it. I took him to one of the benches . . .'

'Which one?'

'There are many benches in the churchyard. I took him to one of those near to the statue of John Donne. We've talked there before.'

'And did you lock the gate before you sat down?' Brown asked.

De Vere lowered his head. 'No.'

'Why not?'

'Because that would mean that I'd have to lock up and then unlock and lock up again to let Mr Hobbs out.'

'Could you see the gate from where you were sitting?'

'Yes,' he said. 'And . . . Someone did come in. I was about to turn him away . . .'

'Him?'

'It was a friend of Arthur's. I knew the northern gate was still open and so I let him pass.'

'Did you see him leave?'

'No, I was in conversation with Arthur by that time.'

'What about?'

He looked away for a moment as if embarrassed, then he said, 'It was a theological question.' He sighed. 'Unlike the Roman Catholic Church, the Anglican communion doesn't ban the practice of abortion. That doesn't mean that all Anglicans approve, far from it. Mr Hobbs is one of those and so . . . I am too.'

'And so Hobbs, an elderly man, needed to speak to you urgently about abortion?' Brown asked. 'Why?'

'Why? We have spoken of it before. It troubles him spiritually . . .'

'He's a man . . .'

'I cannot and will not betray the trust of a man who came to me in confidence,' the reverend said. 'Suffice to say he has his reasons.'

'OK, so how long did you talk for?'

'About ten minutes,' he said. 'I managed, inasmuch as I could, to allay his immediate fears and then he left.'

'But you didn't lock up?'

'No.'

'Why not?'

He sighed. 'All I can think is that I was still cogitating upon my discussion with Arthur,' he said. 'Abortion is a vexed issue for Christians . . .'

'So you don't know whether the man you'd let in to the churchyard had left or not?'

'I had other things . . . No,' he said. 'I didn't.'

Brown leant back in his chair and said, 'And so what was last night about then, Harry? When you came in here and told us that you completely forgot to lock that or any other gate up?'

'I did!'

'But you didn't tell us about Hobbs, did you? Didn't tell us about his mate either? What his name—'

'Colin something . . .'

'Colin Macbeth?'

Agitated, the priest shook his head. 'I don't know!'

'Well I hope you don't, in a way,' Brown said. 'Because if the team at Scotland Yard have to waste their time

327

prising it out of you, you ain't gonna endear yourself to anyone.'

Lady Val and her brief did the old 'no comment' boogie yet again and so DI Manson turned his attention to Colin Macbeth. Charged with the murder of two police officers, the pressure was now on Macbeth to assist the investigation. This as well as exhibiting some kind of remorse could help to convince the judge who would eventually sentence him not to hand down a full-life sentence. Or not.

'So Colin,' Manson said as he sat down opposite the man, 'where were we?'

Neither Macbeth nor his brief said a word. Manson, this time, was accompanied by another counter-terrorism detective called Joe Cooper. Unknown to Macbeth and his lawyer, Cooper was an expert on far-right conspiracy theories. Almost everything Manson knew about the Luddite ideology had come from Cooper.

'Arms,' Manson said. 'Yes, we were talking about arms, weren't we, Colin?'

'No comment.'

No commenting was fine, for the moment. Manson smiled.

'But then we don't need to discuss that do we, Colin?' he said. 'Because I've found those now. I've found them and I've found thirty-one men of different ages, levels of fitness, but a bit racially . . . Whatever the opposite of diverse is. I gather this is your army. And I have to say, very well armed for such a small number, so well done on that.'

Ballistic experts were working on the origins of the weapons. Early signs seemed to point towards Eastern Europe.

'So, I want to go back to the baby,' Manson continued. 'Now, just to let you know, DI Cooper here knows a thing or two about organisations like the Luddites, and so don't try to pull the wool over his eyes.'

Macbeth looked at his brief who shook his head.

'So where's the mother, Colin?' Manson asked.

Macbeth said nothing.

'Because if she is alive and you aren't telling us where she is, there could be consequences,' Manson continued. 'She could come forward for instance. Or maybe she's out there somewhere being terrorised by people like you. We know she's a black woman. We know she's recently given birth. We want to help her and if you help us, that will play all the better for you. And if she's dead then we will find her, so don't try to get some residual kicks from the knowledge that you know where she is while I don't. Because I will find her. You have my word on that.'

What would be interesting was when this man's son was brought in. Would he shop his dad? There were good indications that he would but, taking nothing for granted, Manson proceeded with caution.

'Tell me about the Luddites,' he said.

And then he saw a glimmer of something in Macbeth's eyes. He wanted to talk about this because he was proud of it.

*   *   *

Mumtaz held John's hand in the back of the car. Neither of them felt well, but the boy was also scared in spite of the fact that his mum was waiting for him at Scotland Yard. She was going to be his 'appropriate adult' and so would be sitting in with him during his interrogation.

He laid his head on Mumtaz's shoulder and said, 'We've been through such a lot together. I'd be dead if it wasn't for you.'

'You would have got out in time,' Mumtaz said.

'They wanted me dead,' John said. 'My dad . . .'

He began to cry. Mumtaz put her arms around him. What could she say? It seemed his father had, if not wanted him dead, been entirely careless about John's safety and his feelings. From what he'd told her the man had wanted to implicate the boy in murder, wanted him to accept his own twisted ideology. It raised questions about John's mother and where she fitted into all this. John was convinced she was innocent but how could she be? Even if her sins were only those of omission, why hadn't she moved to protect her child, to control her husband?

She'd been so happy to see Shazia. They'd both cried in each other's arms for at least ten minutes. The girl had made her promise she would never go 'off-grid' again, although how she'd actually fulfil such a promise given what she did for a living, Mumtaz didn't know. All she did know was that somehow that was a promise she couldn't break.

Shazia had told her that Lee had been out of his mind with worry. She still didn't know where he was but she had no doubt that he was working, somehow, on her behalf. She'd said, 'He loves you so much. I was almost as afraid for him as I was for you.'

Mumtaz knew that was true. Just the fact that he'd allowed her to go off on this wild mission to find Habib and Loz's 'bleeding boy' was testament to that. But had it been right? In his desire to give her everything she wanted, had he in fact given her too much?

She cradled the boy in her arms and said, 'I can't make anything better for you myself, John. But I'm sure that your mum will do her best to help you get through this.'

He squeezed her tightly and said, 'Promise me we'll always be friends, Mumtaz. I can't make what my dad did right . . .'

'You don't have to,' she said. 'If anything good has come out of this, it is that we have met. If anyone saved anyone else's life, then you saved mine and I will tell the police that.'

'Of course they didn't just leave!' George said. 'They were thrown out! 1290, the Edict of Expulsion enacted by Edward I. All Jews were thrown out of England because – long story short – some stupid people believed they drank the blood of Christian infants!'

'And they—'

'Of course they fucking didn't!' the priest roared. 'God give me strength! How can you people be so ignorant!'

Father George, and later, Wilko and Jordan were not being interviewed by Manson but by one of his deputies, DS Howard. If or until information to the contrary came

331

to light, the three men were assumed to be unconnected to the organisation known as the Luddites.

Howard, a woman in her forties, had proved herself a tough and uncompromising interrogator in the past – but having a furious priest sitting in front of her was testing both her abilities and her credulity.

'It was Oliver Cromwell who allowed Jews back in,' George continued. '1656. He needed money for his Puritan revolution and so he thought, "Ah, Jews!" Pure self-interest, but that was the point at which Jews could freely live in the country again.'

'Father George,' Howard said, 'this is interesting, but the tunnels?'

'The tunnels were where they hid . . .'

She looked down at her notes. 'From 1290 to 1656?'

'No! Of course not!' he said. 'I don't know when they were built – ask an archaeologist! But at some time an underground network of tunnels and rooms developed to allow the Jews who chose to remain or couldn't get out to pursue their religious practices in peace and security, away from the prying eyes of the Church. And yes I know that it's strange that I, a Jew, choose to live my life as a Christian priest but that's my business!'

He'd talked of ghosts prior to this. Firstly about the ghost of a priest who, he claimed, had first alerted him to the notion that all was not well in the cathedral, and secondly about the ghosts of the hidden Jews he claimed to have heard in the tunnels. Apparently his mother had heard them too. This was all really way above Howard's pay grade, but she was stuck with it.

'So how did you know that people were using the tunnels now?' Howard asked.

He sighed, seeming to calm himself. He said, 'Wilko, that's Sergeant Wilkinson of the City of London Police, and I have been talking about these tunnels for years.'

'Did you ever enter them until yesterday?'

'No. For myself, I think I didn't allow myself to look until . . . Until this evil thing happened.'

'The killing of the child?'

'Yes.'

Howard frowned. 'Forgive me, Father George, but why did the death of this child make you think about the tunnels? I mean as far as I can see, they had been a good thing in the past.'

'Yes, they gave sanctuary to Jews. But the network is vast, as I am sure you know, and over the centuries parts of the system have been used to jail so-called heretics, so-called witches and those opposed to whoever had power at the time. They also allowed ministers of the Church to conduct business in secret. Like most old things, Detective Sergeant, the tunnels have served many purposes, both good and bad.'

'I'm sorry, I still don't—'

'The way the child died was instructive,' George said. 'A ritual killing. Five stab wounds . . .'

'How do you know that?' she asked and then realised that she knew and said, 'Wilkinson called you.'

He took a deep breath and then he said, 'Before you consider disciplining Sergeant Wilkinson, know that he drew me in as a consultant. He knew there was something ritualistic about that killing and so he sought advice. I know that DI Brown was less than happy. But we are where we are now because Wilko shared intelligence with me. And yes, he and I got others involved, but only those we knew we could trust. A serving police constable and an ex-officer who is now a PI.'

'Lee Arnold had skin in the game in the shape of his partner.'

'Lee and Mrs Hakim had been looking into the case of a boy they feared might be in danger, and they were right,' George said. 'We helped one another. It may have been unorthodox but we helped you too.'

'You could have torpedoed our investigation.'

'We could have done, but we didn't. As far as I can see, DS Howard, we, albeit unwittingly, facilitated your operation. And yes, I know it might not have worked out well, but if you look at it from our perspective, you were doing nothing. Mr Arnold wanted to have you bring in a woman he suspected knew more about Mumtaz Hakim's disappearance than she was saying, but the police held back. I mean now we know why, but yesterday we didn't. We did what we thought was right, DS Howard.'

They'd brought him breakfast, but he hadn't been able to eat it. What was going to happen to him? And his men? What would Val tell the police? And how would this play with the public? Hushed up, he had no doubt. If people knew what they'd been trying to do they'd want some of that, he was sure. It had taken decades for the time to be right, for England to rise again.

Of course Lud had just been the vehicle. But that hadn't mattered. The aim had always been full independence. Not the wishy-washy version the government were trying to do. Lud predated Brexit by many moons and had inspired folks more than anything he'd come across before. If only Mosley had deployed him. How different would history have been . . .

DI Manson nodded.

'Any idea who it might be?'

'None, guv,' DS Reichs told him. 'But it's been down there a long time.'

Reichs had interrupted Manson's interrogation of Macbeth to tell him the search teams in the EC4 tunnels had found a skeleton in one of the many rooms that lined the network.

'Where was it found?' Manson asked.

'In the room they call the Shrine, sir,' Reichs said. 'Not seen it myself, but I've been told it's old.'

'Could be nothing to do with the Luddites then.'

'Possible, yeah.'

Manson breathed out and then said, 'Do you know whether Macbeth's boy's here yet?'

'He is, guv, yeah. With his mother and Mrs Hakim.'

'Good,' Manson said. Then he tipped his head towards the interview room he'd just left. 'I'll tell chummy, see what he has to say.'

'What are you expecting, guv?' Reichs asked.

'I don't rightly know,' Manson said. 'He claims the boy holds no interest for him.'

'His own son?'

'He, or Hobbs, killed Macbeth's own newborn baby,' Manson said. 'Make no mistake Reichs, these people are indoctrinated in an ideology that is completely without humanity. Some would say brainwashed.'

'Christ!'

'Don't think he's got too much to do with this lot,' Manson said.

TWENTY-THREE

His phone rang, just as Lee Arnold was putting his head down for a kip. It was Gary Connor.

Getting straight to the point, as was his custom, Gary said, 'Mate, I'm hearing things about Colin Macbeth, that he's been arrested.'

Lee said, 'Couldn't possibly comment, Gary.'

'Which means he has!' Gary responded.

Lee was glad that Gary had picked up on that. Deep down he was an alright bloke and Lee hated to think that he might receive negative push-back for something a distant relative of his brother's stepmother might have done.

'Fucking scumbags the Saints and the Macbeths,' Gary continued. 'Not gonna ask you why he's been arrested, but I can imagine. And I tell you what, mate, if Fallon wants to stay with Dillon after this then he's fucking welcome to her. I'll have Harrison though, I'll have my boy. I won't let him be brought up by them bastards!'

As he put the phone down, Lee wondered why Gary had phoned him in particular. Did Gary somehow know that Lee had been involved? But then thinking about it just made his head hurt. The East End grapevine was as mysterious as it was extensive and he had no doubt that, somewhere along the line, Gary Connor had infiltrated the police.

Lee flopped himself back on his sofa again and tried to ignore the fact that Chronus was squawking at something outside the window. As soon as he'd got home, Lee had called Shazia, who had told him that she'd seen Mumtaz, who had told her to tell Lee he was not to worry about her. She was fine apparently. But even on the edge of some much-needed sleep, Lee's thoughts were still on Mumtaz and, when he did finally wake up again, he had no doubt his thoughts would still be on her.

The boy was so pale he was almost translucent. His mother, a dark-haired woman in her forties, looked as if she was at the end of her tether. With no make-up, her eyes looked black from lack of sleep, her face lined with the strain she had been put under by the men in her life.

Manson had only had a few minutes to speak to her before he opened John's interrogation. But just that small exposure had revealed her as a woman who had suffered greatly and who was hell-bent on getting as far away from her husband as she could.

The approach Manson took with the boy was just to let him talk. Physically John still had some minor problems with his breathing and he was clearly exhausted, but in spite of that his story just rolled.

'My dad was always a racist,' he said.

Manson had asked him to go back to the beginning of what he knew about his father and his membership of the Luddites.

'But he was sort of almost like a comedy one, you know . . .'

'Alf Garnett, I used to call him,' his mother Jill put in, citing the famous character from an old BBC sitcom called *Till Death Us Do Part*. 'Not that he was funny . . .'

'I don't know when he got in with the Luddites,' John said. 'I knew he'd been to BNP stuff in the past with my uncles and cousins, but he never talked about it much. He knew Mum would go mad if she found out, but I only knew that after he took me to Arthur's house that first time.'

'When was that?' Manson asked.

He shrugged. 'About six months ago. Dad told me he was going to introduce me to some great people who would make us rich. I thought he was talking out of his arse, but I agreed to go because I didn't want to upset him. Dad's always been a bit of a loser which makes him upset, and when he gets upset he can get violent. He had a garage once but he screwed up his tax and had to sell it. He gave Mum a black eye.'

Jill Macbeth put a hand over her mouth and briefly shook her head. Every copper going had seen this look a million times before. It was that of a woman who couldn't believe she'd lived through that, who only now had the space to process her pain – and her guilt. Manson saw her place a hand on her son's arm and then kiss his hair.

'I know he used to be sorry when he took it out on Mum, but I'm not sure he is now,' John continued. 'They don't like women, the Luddites. Women are just for sex.'

'So there are no female Luddites?' Manson asked.

'There's the woman who runs the pub, The Hobgoblin,' John said. 'Posh woman. But I don't know that for sure. I saw her with Arthur a couple of times. But so when Dad took me to Arthur's I didn't like it. A load of old men talking about how much they hated black people and Asians and the French. I didn't say anything because I didn't want to upset Dad. But when he asked me to go the next time, I said I didn't want to and that's when things got bad.'

'Bad in what way, John?'

He shook his head. 'He said if I didn't go he'd do something.'

'Do what?'

'Dunno, not really. But I thought he might take it out on Mum. So I went. It was messed up.'

'In what way?'

'It's a religion, although I don't think it's a real one,' John said. 'I've never heard of Lud. Some old English king. They all dress up to look like monks and Arthur gets them to drink blood. They tried to make me do it, but it tasted like shit. I spat it out.'

'Human blood?'

'I never asked,' he said. 'Probably. The next time I went they killed that baby.'

'Who did?'

'Arthur.'

'Are you sure about that, John?'

'Yes. How can I forget it?' he said and then he began to cry.

The police arrived just as Danielle was about to call a taxi. She didn't know who had shopped her, and found that she really didn't care. Henry had gone to work after telling her he didn't expect to see her when he got home. He'd cried. Not for her, but for the baby.

All night long she'd watched the police pound the streets of EC4 from the spare bedroom window. Decorated to be the baby's nursery, it only contained a cot and so when she did finally go to sleep it had been on the floor. When she'd woken up, Henry had told her to go. She'd asked him if he knew what all the police activity had been about and he'd just said, 'Terrorism.'

She'd switched on the TV after he left. All the news programmes seemed to be telling people was that a 'terrorist threat' had been neutralised in central London. They didn't say what sort of threat and so she'd looked on social media. Twitter and Facebook were alive with conspiracy theories about Islamist terror cells and how 'we' could no longer tolerate 'these people' in our country. Was it possible Arthur and his men weren't the target of the police operation? Was an Islamist terror cell also present in EC4?

She knew deep down inside that it wasn't. As Henry had said, she wasn't a fool. She'd hated that woman with her slim figure and her posh voice. Arthur had told her they were everywhere and they were. They needed to be stopped. And yet . . . People like that woman were often the same people who stood up for women like her. There was a reason she'd been attracted to Henry that went beyond his good looks. There was a reason she found men like Arthur and his people unattractive. But it was confusing. On the few occasions she'd listened to her father she knew that he didn't blame anyone for the inequality in society. He just blamed 'the system', which she had never sought to investigate because her old man had been such a lone voice.

There were three officers at her door, two men and a woman. They told her she was being arrested under counter-terrorism legislation. Again her father's image came to mind. He was going to be devastated.

'Dad used the knife to smear blood on my face,' John said.

'But it was Hobbs who killed the child?' Manson asked.

'Yes. Dad didn't. He watched but he didn't kill her.'

'What did you do when your dad smeared you with blood?'

'I ran,' John said. 'I had to get out of there.'

'Out of where?'

'They call it the Shrine. It's just a room where they have these ceremonies. The baby was a sacrifice to Lud. It was mad. I couldn't be there! They're all mad! It was like being in a horror movie . . .'

His mother put her arms around him and said, 'I should have—'

'Mum, you couldn't have done anything!' he said. 'He's gone mad! He wanted me to die because I disappointed him! What do you think he would have done to you?'

The room became silent and then Manson said, 'John, do you have any idea about who the child was or where she came from?'

'No.' He shook his head. 'Nothing.'

'Do you know how many people were in the Shrine with you when this happened?'

He thought for a moment and then said, 'Not really. Maybe about twenty? I don't know.'

'And did you recognise any of them?'

'I'd seen some of them before, but I don't know their names.'

'Could you recognise any of them, do you think?'

'Maybe . . .'

'So when you ran,' Manson continued, 'where did you run?'

'Down the tunnels,' he said. 'I didn't know where I was going. I just knew I had to get out and tell somebody. I threw up somewhere. I could hear them behind me! Then I was at the front door and there were these two boys. They just stood there and looked at me like they'd seen a ghost or something.'

'So why didn't you leave?'

The boy was silent for a moment and then he said, 'Because when I looked behind me, I could see Arthur and I knew that Dad was behind him.'

'Even so . . .'

'I don't know! I was so frightened! I don't know what I thought then! Maybe I thought they'd kill those kids? I don't know, I just shut the door.'

'What happened then?'

He shook his head again. 'I went back with them,' he said. 'To the Shrine.'

'Did you see . . . ?'

'Dad took it away then. I don't know where he went. Arthur put me in a room and locked me in.'

'Did you see your dad later?'

'He came and explained how he was disappointed in me, yeah,' John said. 'He told me that I was going to have to stay with Arthur until I came to my senses.'

'Colin told me John was with him,' Jill Macbeth said.

'And did you know where they'd gone?' Manson asked.

'Me and Colin split up a few weeks ago and all I knew was that he had a flat in Dagenham. It hadn't been easy to get him out, but I didn't want John to not see his dad. He still had a key to the house. I shouldn't have been so trusting.'

'I told Dad I could never be like him and the others. He lost his shit and shouted at me. He said soon everyone was going to be like him and anyone who wasn't was going to die.'

Manson said, 'Your dad said that people would die?'

'Yeah. Anyone not into the Lud thing I supposed.' He put his head down. 'I know Dad's family have always been dodgy, but not like this. Far as I could tell, none of

344

my uncles were down there. Nobody I know. Did Dad just lose his mind or . . . ?'

'My old dad knew about the tunnels, although he never said he'd been down,' Wilko told DS Howard. 'The old man knew a lot of things. He was a proper old-fashioned Londoner.'

'Did your dad ever tell you what they were used for?' Howard asked.

'Lots of things. Mainly to do with the cathedral, he reckoned. In Queen Mary's reign the Inquisition had cells down there. Some tunnels were used so clerics could get from the choir school to the church without having to walk through all the shit up in the streets. Dad was convinced that the tunnels were part of the Mithras Temple complex found at Mansion House in the fifties.'

'That the Roman thing?'

'Yeah,' he said. 'Mithras was a Persian god of war that Roman soldiers used to worship. Heavy on blood sacrifice. Me and George have talked about that a lot over the years.'

'Father George Feldman.'

'Yeah.'

'The exorcist.'

'Yup. And yes, I know . . .'

'Talking to DS Pinker over at Bishopsgate this morning and she tells me Father George reckoned he spoke to a priest at the cathedral who thought the place had become "evil". According to DS Pinker, she later discovered from cathedral staff that this priest was actually a ghost

345

called Father Edward who turns up, they think, when the cathedral is under threat.'

'Yeah, well . . .'

'Sergeant Wilkinson, I work in counter-terrorism,' Howard said. 'Ghosts are the least of my worries and in fact, I find I'm more inclined to believe in them than I am in much of the so-called intel that comes my way. Now tell me about King Lud . . .'

His dad had talked about Lud. Old King Lud the first, the past and future English king who had first seen off and then been defeated by the Romans, and who had come back as King Arthur and who would one day rise again. It was said that Lud demanded blood in the form of the Roman god Mithras when Albion was finally conquered by the Legions in 43 AD. Lud hadn't actually ever been away, waiting in his temple down underneath the streets of London, looking for those who believed in him to come and revive the old religion again. Her Ladyship had been a mine of information about Lud. She knew everything. The police kept on asking him about it, but she was the expert, even though Colin didn't say that, of course.

Lady Val was the one who knew everything and so it was important to protect her. Anyway they, the police, seemed to be more interested in the baby. He'd had a soft spot for Angie. There'd been a couple of black girls went down The Jolly Sailor but Colin had only fancied Angie. When he first started buying her drinks, he hadn't known she was a smackhead. He'd found that out when they'd had sex in the beer garden. He'd been besotted and very guilty. How could he fancy one of them? How could he have got one of them pregnant?

She'd wanted to get rid of it and Colin had told her he could arrange that. He'd spoken to Arthur who had told him he'd like to help in some way. He hadn't judged him. Weeks had passed then, and Angie had begun to get agitated. Then Arthur had got back to him. He'd said that there was money for junk if Angie agreed to have the baby and then let him take it off her. He hadn't lied to Colin, he'd told him they'd done this before. Lud liked it. But Angie hadn't been told. She'd never asked.

Of course, it had been born small and fractious. She'd had it, as Arthur had told her she must, at home and then given it to Colin. He'd handed over five grand on the condition she keep her mouth shut. She'd told him she was going abroad. Whether she had or not, he didn't know. All Colin Macbeth did know was that he wasn't going to tell the Old Bill any of that.

'I know you don't want to give me the names of the two boys who alerted you to John Macbeth's whereabouts, but you also know I have to have them,' Manson said to Mumtaz.

'Yes,' she said. 'But I don't want them to get into trouble.'

Manson sighed. 'They were selling an unlicensed pain control product.'

'I know, but they were trying to help people. That cream has been in short supply.'

'And yet by your own admission they were also trying

347

to make money to procure an abortion for Lawrence's girlfriend.'

'Yes, yes, but I suspect the boys were duped,' she said.

'Irrelevant.'

'Yes, but . . . Oh,' she threw her arms in the air, 'but look what came out of that! They indirectly enabled you—'

'We had been monitoring Hobbs and co for months,' he said.

She wanted to ask him why, in that case, he hadn't gone in to save John himself, but she knew that was pointless. He wasn't going to tell her anything about his operation. She was there simply to give an account of what had happened to her.

Nevertheless she said, 'They're good lads, DI Manson. They could've just kept quiet about what they'd witnessed but they had genuine concerns for John, which were borne out.'

'Pity you didn't come to us then, Mrs Hakim,' he said.

'I've told you why not.'

'And I've told you that I will have to temporarily revoke your licence.'

He had. So far it seemed this was not also going to apply to Lee, but it was a bitter blow to Mumtaz.

'I know,' she said. 'And I understand that. I would probably have done the same in your position.'

'But you will also get your day in court,' he said.

'I can't recall whether Hobbs himself actually tried to kill me or not,' she said. 'I have no memory of what happened when I entered that house. Someone threw me into that room and, I think, they left me for dead. I certainly wasn't fed and no one came to check on me.'

'Why did you go into Hobbs's house? You weren't invited.'

'OK,' she said. 'First of all, I must state that I believed the two boys when they came to me for help. I had no doubt in my mind they saw a frightened boy with blood on his face at that address. We all knew about the death of the baby in the churchyard by that time, and so bad things were happening in that vicinity.'

'Did you meet with Sergeant Wilkinson of the City Police at any point?'

'Yes I did,' Mumtaz said. 'He is an old colleague of my employer Mr Arnold. We were joined later by Constable Whittington.'

'What did you talk about?' Manson asked.

'About the tragedy in the graveyard.'

Manson shifted uncomfortably in his chair and then said, 'Would it be correct to say that Sergeant Wilkinson had a, um, a rather mystical take on the subject?'

Mumtaz had to think carefully. She didn't want to make Wilko out to be a total fruit cake, because he wasn't.

'He thought the manner of the child's death was significant.'

'Did he tell you what the manner of that death was?'

'No,' she said. 'Sergeant Wilkinson is basically an amateur London historian and so he relates some modern phenomena to things that happened in the past.'

'Like what?'

'Like the tunnels that you and I both "found",' she said. 'Of course, I've been in hospital and so I don't know . . . Well I do. If what John told me about these Luddites is correct, it would seem that they killed that poor child in a ritualistic manner. Sergeant Wilkinson believes, as I understand it, that such things we thought were lost in the past are being manipulated by some people now for ideological reasons. But in answer to your original question, DI Manson, I'm not entirely sure why I went into Hobbs's house. I have so little memory of that time. The doctor at the hospital said I'd received a significant blow to the head which could be problematic re memory for a while. All I can tell you is that at that time I feared my cover as a historical researcher may have been blown.'

'Why?'

'I met a woman called Danielle Saint,' she said. 'A woman in the last few weeks of her pregnancy. I met her one day in Carter Court and we began to converse. I know she knows Arthur Hobbs because she and I met with him one day in the Hobgoblin pub. It was shortly after that Danielle rightly identified me as a private detective.'

'Did you deny it?'

'No. She is obviously no fool but I didn't tell her what I was really doing. I think I probably made something up about a marital case. I can't remember the details now.'

'Officers interviewed Danielle Saint and her partner when you went missing,' Manson said. 'Mr Arnold found a note about her on your desk. Both Ms Saint and Mr Blizzard denied knowing anyone matching your description.'

'To be fair I never did meet Mr Blizzard. But Danielle and I spoke for considerable amounts of time.'

'She is being questioned formally this time,' Manson said.

She nodded.

He said, 'Tell me about the tunnels. How did you get out?'

Mumtaz suddenly felt she was almost back inside that narrow, stinking place and she said, 'John and I just kept moving. I don't know how we got out. I need to stop now.'

TWENTY-FOUR

This copper didn't state his name, not even for the benefit of the tape, much less for Arthur's sake.

Without preamble, the man said, 'Talk me through blood sacrifice.'

Arthur's brief told him to 'no comment' it and so he did.

But the copper, if indeed he was a copper, took it in his stride and just sat down. He folded his arms. And then he said nothing.

'Lud's a myth,' Wilko said. 'Whether he ever existed or not isn't known. Supposed to have defeated the Romans the first time they tried to invade the country. Said to be buried somewhere between St Paul's and the north bank of the Thames.'

'Where the tunnels are?' DS Howard asked.

'Yeah.'

'So were you aware of Lud becoming a right-wing rallying point?'

'Not really. I've known about the theoretical existence of the tunnels all my life. My dad used to talk about them.'

'In what way?'

'Me dad was an old Londoner,' Wilko said. 'He was full of London stories. Tunnels ran from the cathedral to the old choir school. They was used as ways whereby priests might get about without being seen or having to get wet. Later I heard stories about Jews living down there after they were expelled from Britain. After the war me dad claimed to have seen some of the tunnels exposed after the bombing. But they was all covered up and any entrances that might have survived in the cathedral were bricked over. My dad was a funny old git. He was one of the British soldiers who liberated Belsen Concentration Camp and so he had some strong views about nationalism, fascism. He reckoned the only way to stop things like that was to expose everything to the light.'

'What do you mean?'

'I mean facing the fact that old myths can be manipulated,' he said. 'Things like King Arthur, Lud. Dad had seen that in Nazi Germany with Hitler and his Wagnerian myths of a once-great nation of pure Aryans. We have to keep an eye on that sort of thing if we don't want a repeat performance.'

'So when did you connect that to the tunnels?'

Wilko sighed. 'I s'pose I could say I had an inkling many years ago, but in reality it was only when the baby

354

died, when I found out the manner of her death. Me and George Feldman, we'd talked about it in the past . . . Years ago the bloke who was then the landlord of the Hobgoblin pub had disappeared. He was never found and . . . I know George is a weird old bleeder, but he does know things . . .'

'What things?'

'Like me dad,' Wilko said. 'Call them occult forces if you like. The unseen ideas and folk memories some people manipulate in order to gain control. It's real. It's happening now and if the powers that be have any sense, they will expose it in all its gory detail now.'

The silence persisted and Arthur began to feel cold. Eventually, his brief, a Mr Chandler, said, 'I think that my client and myself need to know who you are.'

The copper smirked.

'Sir . . .'

'Your client needs only to answer my questions,' the man said. 'Arthur, blood sacrifice?'

Mr Chandler shook his head.

'Because we know that's what it was,' the man continued. 'We also know that it was part of your plot to overthrow the state. A pathetic plot, to be enacted by fat, middle-aged men, but a plot nevertheless. And so like Guy Fawkes, Arthur, you will be charged with high treason. You will be happy to know that this no longer carries a sentence of death – that was abolished for this offence in 1998 – but you will go to prison for the rest of your life, as will your co-conspirators. And because this is going to be a complex investigation, costing the state you claim to love millions, you could be on remand for a very long time before you even come to trial. So, with this in mind, I hope you can see that whatever way you can help us before all that happens, will make things go easier for you. I mean, Lady Valerie for instance . . .'

'She owns the pub next door,' Arthur said. 'That's all I know about her.'

'Really? So the pictures we have of you and her at right-wing rallies are purely coincidental?'

'Yeah.'

'Arthur, we have been observing you for many years now,' he said. 'We've seen you through your skinhead phase, evolve into your BNP persona and then we've seen you consort with those who run the country. It was when that happened we started looking more deeply at you and your activities. That was when it became apparent to us that where you lived might be significant. Men with certain reputations coming and going from your house to the Hobgoblin pub . . .'

'Dunno what you're talking about.'

'No? Then maybe you can, instead, tell me something about the disappearance of a man called Hymen Salzedo,' he said. 'To remind you, he was the landlord of The Hobgoblin prior to its dereliction and before the tenancy of Lady Rudolph. The tunnels run underneath the pub and can be accessed from it. I wonder whether Mr Salzedo, a Jewish man, knew this.'

'I dunno.'

'You're old enough to remember him.'

'Yeah. I do but never had nothing to do with him.'

'Because you are anti-Semitic?'

'No!'

'Mmm.' He put his chin in his hands and then he said, 'You're going to be charged with high treason, Arthur. This is your last chance to tell us why we shouldn't do that.'

'Because I love my country,' Arthur said.

The man stood up. 'No, you don't,' he said. 'You love something that never existed.'

And then he left.

Lee Arnold willingly drove into the heart of central London very rarely. But when, later that evening, Mumtaz called to say that Scotland Yard had finished with her for the day, he jumped in his car and sucked up the congestion charge.

As soon as they were alone in the car, which he'd parked around the back of the Yard, they held each other wordlessly for a long time. And when he did finally disengage from her to start the ignition, still neither of them spoke. The only thing they did until they got back to his flat was hold hands on top of the old car's gearstick. An unremarked and unspoken act of connection and love as they drove through the dark streets of London, illuminated by coloured lights from party boats on the Thames and the strange, other-worldly glow coming from the tops of the high-rise buildings of Canary Wharf.

But once back in Lee's Forest Gate flat, all that changed. Firstly, surprised and amazed to see Mumtaz after such a long time, Lee's mynah bird, Chronus, squawked, whistled and sang her a slightly miffed greeting which was only brought to an end by Lee covering up his cage for the night. Then Lee and Mumtaz drank tea and then they talked.

As he held one of her hands, Lee said to Mumtaz, 'I still can't get my head around why you thought that Lawrence and Habib's story about the bloodied boy was so important.'

'I didn't necessarily think it was important,' Mumtaz said. 'To be honest I was in no way expecting what happened to happen. What I do know is that studious Bengali boys like Habib do not put the good opinion of them that their fathers may have, at risk. Those boys were deeply concerned.'

'Did you tell the coppers about them?'

'I had to,' she said. 'God knows what the pharmacist Farooqi will say to Habib! But this is national security.'

Lee had put up on his laptop some of the news stories about the EC4 police raid for her to see. There had been no mention of the pub, The Hobgoblin, or any connection to the cathedral or even a whisper about any tunnels. A terror plot had been uncovered – what kind of plot was not specified – and a number of people had been arrested.

'I don't know, but from what I saw down in the tunnels, I reckon it's probably thirty to forty people,' Lee said.

They were sitting on the floor. She snuggled into his side and he put his arm around her. 'What were they like?'

'Ordinary. Frightened.'

She shook her head. 'And Colin Macbeth?'

'Ah, he was different,' Lee said. 'He was frightened but he wasn't ordinary. He killed two police officers.'

'How?'

'They were stockpiling arms down there for the glorious revolution.'

'Poor John,' she said.

'The kid?'

'Yes. He reckoned his father was willing to sacrifice him to this ideology. How do people get to be like that?'

'All too easily.' He kissed the side of her face. 'I don't understand it any more than you do. But it seems to me that people are all too willing to believe any old shite these days. Maybe it's the Internet? Or maybe it's . . . Maybe these things go in cycles.'

'Things like nationalism?'

'Yeah.'

'So it's like the 1930s again?' she said. 'I've heard people say that.'

He shrugged. 'I dunno, but I don't like it.'

Huddled in front of Lee's gas fire, they were warm and cosy and Mumtaz felt safe. But were they? Lee didn't know any more. He thought they'd been safe but what had happened in EC4 had shaken him. Not so much the incident itself, but the thinking behind it. For years he'd watched as forces he couldn't understand gained traction. He'd dismissed such narratives as rubbish and yet when he thought about the reasons why he'd left the police, he knew that part of that decision had come about because he couldn't stand the way an increasing number of his colleagues treated members of minority communities.

359

And at a senior level any concern was just words. Quickly forgotten.

After a pause, Mumtaz said, 'You know that without John Macbeth I would never have got out of those tunnels.'

'Did he know the way out?'

'No,' she said. 'But until he found me I was entirely alone in the dark, sitting on the edge of a well. Arthur meant to kill me. He thought I was dead. When John arrived we sought a way out together. We shared ideas and he told me a lot about his father and the Luddites. It's not the young people who think like this you know, Lee, it's the older generation. How could his father put that boy in harm's way? You know, John saw Arthur kill that baby . . .'

She began to cry and he circled her with his arms.

'Ssshh. He's safe now.'

'But what will he dream about?' Mumtaz said. 'That? His awful father, blooding his face . . .'

She put her head on his shoulder and he stroked her hair.

'John's safe now.'

'Physically yes,' she said as she wiped her eyes. 'But the psychological damage, what about that? I know he's got his mum now, but that also begs questions about how and why she couldn't protect him from his father. I mean, if she met another man, would she turn a blind eye . . . ?'

'Ssshh.' He put a finger up to her lips. 'We don't know whether she did turn a blind eye. Not yet. We don't know how this thing's going to play out ultimately and you, I think, probably need some kip.'

She freely admitted that she needed sleep badly, and so he took her to his room and put her to bed.

Now fully awake himself, Lee walked back into his living room and sat down again. Alone with just his own mind for company, he pondered upon what had happened over the past days. He'd not wanted Mumtaz to get involved with those two boys from Spitalfields and yet what would have happened had she not done so? It had become clear that Counter Terrorism were already alive to Arthur Hobbs and his organisation. But that then begged the question: why hadn't they saved the baby? If their intelligence was so good, why hadn't they picked that up? Or had they chosen for some reason, maybe tactical, not to intervene at that point? He'd been a copper. He knew that was possible and it made him shudder. He also knew that this could all just disappear into the background once the initial shock of the incident had passed.

It was late, nearly midnight, by the time Jordan Whittington arrived home. He'd hoped that maybe his grandfather would still be up, because he felt the need to talk. And Bert Whittington was still up. What was more, he'd been to the chippy and so Jordan had rock and chips waiting for him in the oven. Even through his exhaustion, it tasted wonderful.

The old man knew his grandson had been detained on police business of some sort and suspected it had something to do with the activity that had happened in EC4. But he waited until Jordan had eaten before he asked him about it.

Jordan said, 'You know I can't talk about work, Granddad.'

'Who am I gonna tell?' the old man said. 'Mina down the chippy?'

It was a fair point. The old man saw few people these days and most of his friends were dead. More significantly, he wanted to see Jordan do well and so he wouldn't jeopardise that in any way.

Jordan told him: about the plot they had uncovered, about the men they had taken into custody, about the tunnels.

'Wilko always knew they were there,' he said. 'And Father George.'

'Dunno about the priest, but makes sense with regard to Wilkinson,' Bert said.

'What do you mean? You don't know him?' Jordan said.

Bert laughed. 'No, you're right,' he said. 'But I did know his old man. He was one of the soldiers liberated Belsen.'

'Yes, I know. How do you know? You've always boasted you kept well clear of coppers – apart from me.'

'Him and me used to drink down The Blind Beggar.'

Jordan rolled his eyes. The Blind Beggar was the pub where notorious East End gangsters the Kray brothers had used to drink too. He'd grown up hearing Kray stories – everyone, or so it had seemed, had known the twins.

'You can mock,' the old man said, 'but Perce Wilkinson and me both knew the value of keeping our enemies close; still do in my case. Perce, in his cups, would say stuff and that included about the tunnels.'

'So you didn't think he was a fruit cake, then?'

Bert shook his head. 'My old gran took me down there when I was a nipper. Showed me where her dad had been born.'

'What? You mean . . .'

'Oh they wasn't Jews,' Bert said. 'But the Jews helped them.'

'"They" being?'

'Your ancestors,' Bert said. 'Criminals to a man. Not in the way we'd know criminals now of course. More people down on their luck. Them as had to nick things to survive.'

Jordan said, 'So why haven't you told me this before?'

'You're a copper,' Bert said. 'And your dad was a criminal. Didn't want you getting the idea all of us was.'

'Do lots of people know about the tunnels?'

'Not now,' Bert said. 'Why?'

'So if the police wanted to sort of cover them up . . .'

'Oh they probably will. Who cares?' he said. 'The bad people are in custody and so the thing's over. Until the next time.'

'What do you mean?' Jordan asked.

'I mean that them people you arrested might be a lunatic fringe today. A bunch of silly old geezers who want the world to go back in time. But tomorrow, who knows? It's why we have to be vigilant, all the time, boy. I hope they're going to throw the book at them.'

'Me too,' Jordan said.

And then both men became silent as the fear they both felt rolled over them like a wave.

TWENTY-FIVE

12th January 2020

Lee Arnold hadn't been brought up to be a churchgoer. But after reading the news online on Sunday 12th January, he'd decided to go to High Mass at St Mary Magdalene's Church in Epping. Right on the edge of the forest, the church was picturesque in a semi-derelict way, filled with statues, bells and incense; it was the kind of theatrical setting he knew suited Father George Feldman.

Unaccustomed to the form of High Mass, Lee didn't know when to kneel, what to say or indeed anything. Although he did attend to George's sermon, which was less about God and more about how his small congregation should look after one another and be good neighbours. Had George maybe tailored his sermon to the news? Or were the tunnels and the Luddites and the death of that child still fresh in his mind? Lee knew they were in his head, all the time.

Lee queued up behind George's aged parishioners to thank 'Father' for his sermon. It wasn't until he was almost at the head of the queue that he noticed someone was behind him.

Wilko.

'I think I need to go home.'

Shazia Hakim looked up from her book. 'Amma? Why?'

Mumtaz sighed. 'It's been so lovely being here with you and Krishnan, and we had the best Christmas, but . . .'

'But what?'

Shazia straightened out her long limbs, got off the sofa and walked over to Mumtaz, who was standing looking out of the living room window.

'But I need to sort my life out,' Mumtaz said.

Three days after she'd been interviewed by Counter Terrorism for the last time, Mumtaz had come to stay with Shazia and Krishnan at their flat in Rotherhithe. And although Lee and her parents had visited there, and even shared Christmas with the young people, Mumtaz had spent a lot of her time alone. What she'd been through in the tunnels had changed her. Although she'd always been aware of a level of prejudice at work in British society, she had never even dreamt of anything like the Luddites. How could such hatred exist? How could anyone believe the lies those people told? How could they have done the vile things they did? And why now did she feel so terribly unsafe?

The two boys, Loz and Habib, had been required to answer questions by the police. And of course their respective parents had been devastated when the truth about the boys' activities – both fiscal and, in Loz's case, sexual – had come to light. Luckily the girl Loz had wanted to impress hadn't been pregnant after all, and Mumtaz had been told by her father that the police had praised the boys for seeking help when they had seen John Macbeth with blood on his face. But both of them were still far from being off the hook with either their parents or the law. All the men, and apparently one woman, had been charged with sedition and Arthur Hobbs with murder. Now on remand, the defendants would face trial in the summer – which was when Mumtaz, Lee, John Macbeth, Loz and Habib would have to give evidence. Just the thought of it made her feel sick.

Shazia said, 'Do you want to go back to work?'

Mumtaz hadn't worked since her ordeal, even though Lee had almost immediately returned to run the agency. Besides, she'd had her licence revoked. But then working was, in a way, Lee's therapy. All she seemed to want to do was nothing. Most of the time she didn't even think about what she'd been through, but she knew it was there in the background, haunting her every moment.

'Not really,' Mumtaz said. 'But I can't let Lee carry on paying me for no reason.'

'He doesn't mind. He loves you.'

'I know,' she said.

Sensing there was a 'but' coming, Shazia prompted, 'But?'

Mumtaz smiled. 'Have you seen the news story about a virus in China?'

'Yes. Why?'

'I don't know. I read it and then I felt I needed to go home.'

'It's not here, Amma,' Shazia said.

Mumtaz turned to look at her. 'You think that being British will save us?' she said. 'Didn't save us from those nutcases in the tunnels under EC4, did it?'

Shazia put her arms around Mumtaz and hugged her tight.

'Racists are everywhere,' Shazia said. 'We know that.'

'Yes, but to be at that level . . .' Mumtaz shook her head.

'Amma, Lee will take care of you.'

'My white saviour,' Mumtaz sighed.

'He loves you,' Shazia reiterated. 'People can think that if they want. Krish is my Hindu saviour—'

'People don't say that!'

'How do you know?' Shazia said. 'I know his dad and his brother joined us for Christmas, but did you see his mum? No. They're Brahmins. His mum doesn't want her eldest son to be with a Muslim. I'm not good enough for him. But I say, "Fuck her," and I mean it. What Krish and I have is good and people can put whatever interpretation on that they like. I don't care and neither, if you love Lee, should you.'

Mumtaz didn't answer. Not because she couldn't, but because she didn't know what to say. She knew she did love Lee, on some level, but not in the way that he loved her. Maybe she'd been too damaged by her late husband to ever be able to trust a man, any man, ever again?

George's house was as shambolic as he was. When the three men arrived, they found the priest's brother, Barry, supping sherry in front of a log fire surrounded by snoozing cats and the remnants of used Christmas crackers. George didn't have a TV but music from a small CD player filled the room with joyful Vivaldi and the whole scene was warm and comfortable, especially after the priest gave Wilko a beer and Lee a mug of hot, strong tea. When they'd all settled themselves down in battered, fur-covered chairs, George said, 'My brother knows everything I know so you can talk freely about recent events.'

'How do you know we want to?' Wilko asked.

'Why come to High Mass if you didn't have an ulterior motive?' George said. 'Neither of you believe.'

'Nor me,' Barry said. 'And even if I did, nothing would induce me to swap this fire for the chilly delights of St Mary Magdalene's. Bloody church is drowning in money and you're required to do your thing to the sound of mice chewing the woodwork.'

'Yes, well . . .'

'They're going to fill the old tunnels in,' Wilko said.

'Who are?'

'Dunno. City of London I imagine.'

'If they had any sense they'd turn them into a tourist attraction,' Barry said.

'As what?' Lee asked. 'Come and see where a bunch of nutters plotted to overthrow the state?'

369

'It wasn't a serious attempt, was it?' Barry asked.

'No?' Wilko shook his head. 'A newborn child lost her life, Your Honour. And that skeleton that was found down there was a MisPer from the sixties. Hymen Salzedo. Hobbs could've killed him too. Far as I know, it's only the foot soldiers who are talking now. Not Hobbs, Macbeth or Her Ladyship. Anyway, she'll walk.'

George said, 'You think so?'

'The land of the rich is a different country,' Wilko said.

'Yes, but this was, is, a plot against the state,' George said. 'Treason.'

Wilko shrugged. Lee had only seen Wilko once since the events in the tunnels. He'd told him he was going to retire in March.

Barry lifted his glass up to the thin January light and looked into his deep-red port. 'But what is treason, exactly?' he said.

'Endangering queen and country,' his brother replied. 'Working on behalf of a foreign power.'

'Yes, but Hobbs and co weren't working for a foreign power, were they.'

'The arms recovered were traced back to Russia,' Wilko said.

'And so?'

'And so we all know Russia's still the enemy,' Wilko said.

'Ah, but do we?' Barry smiled. 'I imagine that although the arms may well be of Russian manufacture, proving they came to the UK with the tacit approval of Mr Putin and co is quite another matter.'

'Mate, we all know about attacks on the West . . .' Wilko began.

'Ah, but do we?' Barry said.

His brother butted in. 'Barry, you're being obtuse,' he said.

'And you listen to too many left-wing conspiracy theories.'

'I was right about the tunnels,' George said. 'And about the presence of evil. That poor young priest, Harry de Vere, was completely taken in by Hobbs and his evil right-wing conspiracy theories. I know the judiciary is littered with old farts who care little for diversity, but I thought you were better than that, Barry.'

Lee saw the twinkle in Barry's eye even if George didn't. Barry smiled at him and said, 'Lee knows.'

'He's joshing you, George,' Lee said. 'And I get it. Barry's a rational bloke and he's a brief so he has to look at things in the round.'

'What I'm saying, oh brother of mine,' Barry said, 'is that much as I hope and even possibly pray that Lady Rudolph and her deluded followers go to prison for the rest of their useless lives, this is in no way a done deal.'

'Because the country is on the brink . . .'

Barry shook his head. 'What you have to understand about what happened in EC4 is that what happened did so across multiple spheres of influence encompassing politics, identity, belief, even folklore. The lives of those involved will be investigated minutely in the years to come. But I suspect that what will be found will be alarmingly ordinary.'

'What do you mean?'

'I mean that anyone can do terrible things and anyone can believe utter tosh, given the right incentives. They may be monetary or just that feeling one gets when one's opinions and beliefs are heard. I think we Brits believe that things like this can't happen here, but they do. In fact I suspect they may now happen with increasing regularity. And no, George, I have not suddenly become a raging leftie. I am simply an old lawyer who is also a pragmatist. When old dead gods, like Lud, like the mythical Aryans the Nazis invoked, come out of their holes, people need to look out.'

The men became quiet again for a while. Lee asked whether he and Wilko could smoke and were told that they could. Barry joined them and lit up a very large cigar.

Lee said, 'That makes sense to me. The woman who lied about meeting Mumtaz . . .'

'Yeah,' Wilko said, 'Arthur Hobbs saw something in her and he said all the things she wanted to hear. I mean, I have to be honest lads, the middle-class hipster brigade are decimating the old working-class communities and they're being high-handed about it. It's not enough they own all the property, they have to change the shops and the local amenities too. Gets my blood up, I'll tell you. But I'm not going to sacrifice my firstborn to an ancient god over it.'

'That little girl was Macbeth's own flesh and blood,' Lee said. 'And we still don't know what happened to the mother.'

'In my experience,' Wilko said, 'we won't unless she comes forward herself. Macbeth knows he's going down for ever and so if he knows something, he'll keep it to himself. Him and Hobbs are fucking psychos and that's what psychos do.'

'What do you mean?' George asked.

'There's power in keeping secrets,' Wilko said. 'You know something other people don't and there's nothing they can do about it. Dr Harold Shipman, the serial killer, kept his motivation for killing his patients unto death.'

Lee shook his head. 'This is gonna be a shitstorm when it comes to trial.'

'July,' Barry said. 'Provided of course this Chinese disease doesn't kill us all off first.'

'You think it'll come here?' Wilko asked.

Barry shrugged. 'Anything is possible,' he said. 'If tunnels once used by ancient Britons to worship their gods, turned into prison cells by the Inquisition, then into homes for Jews in hiding can morph into the focus for an, albeit shabby, nationalist army, most things have to be at least probable.'

'But what of Mrs Hakim?' George asked. 'How is she after her ordeal?'

'Not back at work yet,' Lee said. 'It's fine. The agency's running on casuals. It's a quiet time of the year.' Then he sighed. 'But it's shaken her.'

'It would do.'

Lee smiled. George meant well but he didn't know the half. Ever since Mumtaz had left his flat to go and stay with Shazia and Krishnan, she had become unreachable. Not physically. At Christmas they'd all had fun together at the flat in Rotherhithe, but part of Mumtaz had been missing. Now when they saw each other, it was as if she was playing the part of a woman who was doing her best to keep him happy. He didn't like that. The darker side of her life, the place where the damage done to her by her husband was kept, was now very far away. Her deepest joys and bloodiest fears, things she had shared with him readily before EC4, had now been closed off, shut down and she was no longer Mumtaz again. That at least was how he perceived it.

When he finally left George's place and went home, Lee called Mumtaz and tried to speak to her about the way that he felt. But all she would say was that she had left Shazia's flat and was now back home with her parents for the foreseeable future.

'I'm giving up the flat,' she said, referring to her small apartment in Forest Gate. 'So if you want me to resign, I can.'

'No,' he said. 'Like I told you from the off, you come back when you feel ready . . .'

'You need to replace me,' she said.

Replace her? In what sense? She was so cold it made Lee feel slightly sick.

'Mumtaz . . .'

'I don't know what I want to do, Lee,' she said. 'All I know right now is that I want to go home.'

'Yes, but can I come—'

'No!' She sounded genuinely alarmed. 'No,' she said more gently. 'Lee, I have genuinely loved you. My life would be nowhere without you . . .'

'And so—'

374

'Hear me out!' she said. 'Please!'

He became quiet.

She said, 'I know that if it wasn't for you looking for me, I would have lost hope in those tunnels. I know you did that out of love, and I have to tell you that not a moment went by without my thinking about you . . .'

There was a 'but' . . .

'But this country and this city is not the same place it was when we first met,' she said. 'When we first became a couple, I was only worried about what other Asian people would think. Now I worry about white people too. I worry about you. What do these crazy people make of a white man with an Asian woman? How do we know they won't one day come for you—'

'Mumtaz . . .'

'No!' She began to cry.

'I'm coming round,' he said.

'No!' This time she screamed. 'No, you must stay away! Please! Please promise me you will stay away? Please!'

She'd lost her nerve and there was nothing he could do. The terrible, painful lack of belief in herself that he had witnessed when she had come for her interview all those years ago, had come back. She felt worthy of nothing and no one and his soul ached for her. But he knew from experience there was nothing he could do. Not yet. When he finally put the phone down after she ended the call, Lee Arnold burst into tears. Had he been more demonstrative in his love for her, more vulnerable, would things be different now? He doubted it. But he blamed himself anyway.

They were and had always been, in some ways, so alike.

EPILOGUE

A woman called Angela Moreno died from COVID-19 at St Thomas' Hospital, London on 12th April 2020 – the same day the Prime Minister of the UK was discharged from medical care after having beaten the coronavirus. Angela, a black woman from Bermondsey, south London, died alone and unregarded, just another dead junkie, while the nation cheered their leader as he returned home to Number 10 Downing Street.

In Hanbury Street, Spitalfields, a father and his daughter waited for news about the old man's wife. Admitted to the Royal London Hospital with Covid three nights before, Baharat Huq's wife, his child Mumtaz Hakim's mother, had been placed on a ventilator. Neither of them knew whether she would make it. Like the rest of the UK, Baharat and Mumtaz were unsure as to whether it was even possible for an elderly woman in poor health to survive.

And the not being able to be with her, due to Covid lockdown restrictions, was eating them both alive. More often than not, Baharat would just simply cry. Mumtaz cooked food endlessly, food neither of them ate. Then she threw it away.

Now in the depths of despair, waiting for an update from the hospital they both knew wouldn't come until the evening, Mumtaz went to her bedroom and called an old friend.

'I thought you might not pick up when you saw it was me,' Mumtaz told Lee Arnold.

She heard him laugh. 'Never!'

It made her cry and, when she finally managed to tell him about her mother, she heard a sob behind his voice too.

'I hope she makes it, Mumtaz, I really do,' he said. 'She's a lovely lady.'

'She liked you.'

She had. When Mumtaz had told her mother she had split with Lee, the old woman had been distraught. *Why,* she had asked her daughter, *would you turn your back on love?*

And she'd had a point, which was why Mumtaz was on the phone to Lee now. Although in truth simply discovering that he was still alive and well was almost enough. Almost . . .

He'd asked about Shazia and Krishnan, who were dealing with lockdown as young people in couples tended to do – by watching box sets and having a lot of sex. Lee had laughed. But then he'd asked about her and Mumtaz had told him that, much as she loved her parents, she was as lonely as the grave. She told him what her mother had said when she had dumped him. And in typical Lee fashion he had offered to break lockdown and drive over to Spitalfields right that minute.

But she'd told him not to. In spite of the terrible fear she kept to herself of dying alone and unregarded, like Angela Moreno, a woman of whom she was not aware, she knew that he shouldn't come. It was wrong. Instead she said, 'When this is over, if you still want to see me . . .' And then she cried again. 'Oh Lee, every day without you has been . . .'

She cried so much she could no longer speak and so he spoke instead. He said, 'I've no work, no money, I live with an abusive mynah bird and I'm over fifty. I have nothing going for me, Mumtaz.' Her sobs were louder now, bitter and regretful.

'But if you will still have me, I'll be there for you. I never wasn't there for you, because whatever other people might think,' he continued, 'I love you and I am the one that's right, Mumtaz, not them. You and me, we're right and if what's happening now means we have to start our lives and our work over again, then so be it. As long as I'm with you, I can do anything.'

BARBARA NADEL was born and brought up in the East End of London. She has a degree in psychology and, prior to becoming a full-time author, she worked in psychiatric institutions and in the community with people experiencing mental health problems. She is also the author of the award-winning Inspector Ikmen series. She lives in Essex.

@BarbaraNadel